A Slice of Magic

The Magic Pie Shop Book 1

A. G. Mayes

A division of HarperCollins Publishers
www.harpercollins.co.uk

Harper*Impulse* an imprint of
HarperCollins*Publishers*
The News Building
1 London Bridge Street
London SE1 9GF

www.harpercollins.co.uk

This paperback edition 2019

First published in Great Britain in ebook format by
HarperCollins*Publishers* 2019

A catalogue record for this book
is available from the British Library

ISBN: 978-0-00-831913-7

Typeset in Birka by Palimpsest Book Production Ltd,
Falkirk, Stirlingshire

Printed and bound in Great Britain by CPI Group (UK) Ltd,
Croydon CR0 4YY

To Rosemary for making the magic pie.
To my family, who taught me to see the
magic in the world.
And to my husband who jumped into the seat next
to me on the emotional roller coaster of writing this
book, threw his hands up in the air and said,
"You can do this!"

Chapter 1

Day 1 — Wednesday, November 2nd

This whole crazy thing started with a voicemail.

Last night I was face down on the sofa in my basement studio apartment. I let the phone fall away from my ear as I listened to yet another long-winded voicemail from my mother complaining about her difficult clients. I let out a sigh of relief into the pillow as her message ended. When the next message began I sat up straight on the sofa as I heard a voice I hadn't heard in a very long time.

'Susanna, I know I left suddenly, but I need you.' Aunt Erma sounded anxious. Tears welled up in my eyes. 'Things are going on here. I can't really explain it all right now, but I need your help at my pie shop. It's asking a lot after everything.' She paused to take a deep shaky breath. 'I'll email you the details in case you decide to come.' Another pause. 'Please come.'

I sat frozen for a minute and then put down the phone. Just like when she left so long ago, I had many unanswered questions. I tried to call the number she had called from, but the phone just rang and rang.

I checked my email and found directions to a small town a couple of hours north. I hadn't known she lived so close. The email ended with her repeated plea of, 'Please come.'

I couldn't sleep that night. My mind was uncovering the memories of Aunt Erma that I'd kept buried for so long. Her face was a little fuzzy, but her laugh came back crystal clear. I remembered the way she made a whole room sparkle when she walked in.

My mother had gotten rid of all the photographs of Aunt Erma after she left. I'd salvaged one before they all disappeared. I still had it in a box in the back of my closet. I kept it hidden so my mother wouldn't see it when she came over. I hadn't looked at it in years because it brought up too many questions and too much pain.

I climbed out of bed around three in the morning to find it. My tiny apartment had a surprisingly large closet. More than once I'd considered converting it into a workshop. But the lack of windows and my occasional bout of claustrophobia kept me from following through. I pulled boxes out of the back corner of the closet until I found the one labeled "Random Crap."

I lifted the lid and dug through the things I just couldn't let go of. There were the cassette tapes I used to listen to while dancing around the living room, a Christmas tree ornament shaped like a pie, and several of my favorite t-shirts that were stained or torn. Then I found it. The smooth purple frame with the picture of my parents, Aunt Erma, and I crowded around my fifth birthday cake. I felt breathless under the weight of the memory. We all looked so happy. I stared into her sparkling eyes. If anyone could get me to make an impulsive decision, it was Aunt Erma.

The next day began as one of those crisp November mornings where the sun feels warm and the breeze feels cold. A perfect day for a new adventure.

I threw my suitcase in the trunk of my car next to the ever-present tool bag that had belonged to my father. The red canvas was faded, and it had his initials embroidered on the front pocket. I ran my finger along the stitching then cringed a little when I thought about my call to Hal, my boss at Hal's Handyman Services. I had been relieved when I got his voicemail. I left a rambling message about needing a week off for a family emergency even as I wondered if a week would be enough time.

According to my GPS, the drive would take two hours and twelve minutes. I slid across the front seat into the driver's seat of my little red car and prayed it would be able to make the journey. A week after I bought my car from a friend of a friend, the driver's side door stopped opening from the outside. A few days after that, the muffler started falling off – it was long gone now – and the car started shaking every time I hit the brakes. I promised myself that would be the last time I bought anything just because it was red.

I was grateful for the distraction the car provided. It was

easier than wondering how I could help at a pie shop. My baking resume was short. It included a few batches of flat cookies and one failed attempt to make scones for my friend's baby shower that left the mother-to-be with a chipped front tooth.

I wanted answers to the questions that lingered from my childhood – the ones my mother refused to discuss. That's how I ended up here in my car with a packed suitcase and a printed copy of the directions in case my old GPS failed me.

I imagined being in the kitchen with Aunt Erma again. Now that I was an adult, I pictured us joking and talking about life, but still eating lots of chocolate.

I stretched the two hours and twelve minutes into an even three hours by stopping three times for coffee and car snacks. By the time I passed a large wooden sign with sparkly gold letters that welcomed me to the small town of Hocus Hills, I had gone through two lattes, one mocha, a bag of chips and half a box of donuts.

The breeze rustled through the trees, and the leaves were so bright red, yellow, and orange that they practically glowed. The streets were lined with small shops with colorful awnings. I passed a large grass filled town square with a bright blue gazebo in the middle. The sidewalks were wide leaving lots of room for people to walk, and on this sunny November day, there were plenty of people out strolling around. A few heads turned my way. I wasn't sure if it was because of my loud muffler-less car or because I was new in town. I was so amped up on sugar and caffeine that when I pulled up to park in front of the pie shop, I was in the middle of a beautiful, or at least loud, sing-along with my *Annie* soundtrack.

There was a tap at my car window and I let out a blood-curdling scream in the middle of 'The Sun Will Come Out Tomorrow.' I turned to see a startled woman with big brown eyes and graying brown hair pulled back into a low pony-tail, peering in at me. She wore a long, bright blue sweater dress and a white sparkly flower pin. Embarrassed, I slid across the seat so I could open the car door and get out. Maybe she hadn't heard anything, I thought hopefully.

'So sorry I startled you,' she spoke in a musical voice. 'Are you Erma's niece?' Wow, word got around fast in a small town.

'Yes, I'm Susanna.' I stuck out my hand.

She reached out and shook it enthusiastically with both of hers. Her hands were warm and soft while I'm pretty sure mine were still covered in a thin layer of powdered sugar.

'I'm Flora. I own the bookstore across the street. Oh my, you look a lot like Erma,' she noted, looking at my curly hair and big blue eyes. 'Your aunt had to leave for a few days, but she said you would have no trouble handling things while she was away.' My mouth fell open. She ignored my shock and reached into her sweater pocket. 'She left this note for you explaining things. I'm sure you'll be fine but let me know if you have any questions. I'll pop by later to check on you.' She shoved a purple sparkly envelope and a set of keys towards me. My eyes widened as the words, 'Mmm, pie,' came from my hand. 'Oh, that's just Erma's keychain,' she said, pointing to the pie-shaped keychain I was holding. 'She has so many fun things like that. Let me know if you need anything.'

'Um, thanks,' was all I managed to get out before she was off.

She paused and turned back, calling down the street. 'Oh, and I just love *Annie* too.' Well good, I thought; at least I was making memorable first impressions.

It was one of those fight or flight moments. I hadn't seen Aunt Erma for years. What did I really owe her? I looked from the pie shop with its twinkling lights lining the window back to my car with the half-eaten box of donuts. I sighed as my sense of family duty got the best of me and went to unlock the front door.

A little bell tinkled as I stepped inside, and I inhaled deeply. The place smelled like buttery pie crust and cinnamon. The bright yellow walls gave the illusion the lights were on even though they weren't. My eyes wandered around the room, and I traced my finger along the chipped edge of one of the purple wooden chairs. I noticed that a leg on one of the bright red tables had broken near the bottom, and the table was now supported by a couple of old encyclopedias. There were two overstuffed red chairs tucked into the corner by the window next to a small bookshelf. The wood floors were stained a dark walnut color, and they creaked under my feet. There were several framed pictures on the wall of people crowded around the red tables eating slices of pie. Intermixed with those pictures were posters of various kinds of pie. One had a large piece of blueberry and the words, 'A touch of magic in every slice,' scrawled in purple letters. Another had a picture of pumpkin pie piled high with whipped cream and, 'Pick up a pie and no matter where you are, you'll be home,' written in a cheerful red.

I stepped between the cash register and the display case to get back to the kitchen. The floor changed from wood to golden brown square tiles. The walls were the same bright yellow as the front. I walked past a sink and a dishwasher and then around a large kitchen island with a weathered wooden bottom and a stainless-steel top. All the cupboards that lined the walls were painted teal. There were two large refrigerators and two large freezers along the side wall. Across from those were four large ovens. I paused in front of what must have been a mixer. It was bright red and as tall as me.

I wandered around the room for a minute, occasionally grabbing random utensils off the hooks on the walls and studying them. I tried to figure out what they might be used for. I was pretty sure at least a few of them were torture devices.

As I reached the small desk in the back corner, I remembered the note in my hand. There was a lump at the bottom of the envelope and I pulled out a small bottle full of sparkly white glitter attached to a chain. I set it on the desk and pulled out the piece of paper. I unfolded the page and saw her familiar curly handwriting.

Dear Susanna,

Thank you for coming to help me. I'm sorry to leave you like this, and I'm sorry I left you all those years ago. When I get back, I'll explain everything. I'm sure you'll do a great job keeping the pie shop running. I'll be gone for a few days. A week at the most. There are enough pies for today in the fridge, but starting tomorrow you'll have to make your own. Wear the necklace while I'm gone, it might come in handy. If you have any problems, Flora, Lena, or Mr Barnes can help you.

Love and Sparkles,

Aunt Erma

P.S. Please take care of my Mitzy for me.

I stared at the note. What the heck was a Mitzy?

There were two purple doors at the back of the kitchen. I opened one and peered out into a little alley. Behind the other one was a staircase. I heard the pitter patter of little feet and a small brown ball of fluff came flying at me.

'Ah!' I jumped back in surprise. The fur ball shot around me in circles before coming to rest at my feet, perfectly still except the wagging tail. Big brown eyes gazed up expectantly. *Oh no*, I thought as I saw the name 'Mitzy' written in rhinestones across the glittery red collar.

I took a step back, and the dog calmly stood, took a step forward, and sat down again. I checked the paper in my hand, hoping to find more thorough instructions, but there was nothing else. Between the ages of four and eight, I asked for a puppy every year for my birthday. Every year my parents bought me a stuffed animal dog and presented it as though they were fulfilling my every wish.

Since then I had learned to recognize dogs for what they were – dirty, smelly, and unpredictable. Great.

I could pinpoint the exact moment when my feelings about dogs changed. I was thirteen and I was over at my friend Lily's house. She had a twin brother, Ed, and I was totally in love with him. I was at their birthday party, and I had lost an earring. I was on my hands and knees looking for it under the sofa while everyone else was in the kitchen getting pizza. Ed came to help me find it. He told me he liked my side ponytail. At that moment, I knew we were going to kiss. As I leaned forward and closed my eyes, ready to take this next big step in my romantic life, I was greeted not by the warm soft lips I was expecting, but by the large wet tongue of their black Lab who had appeared out of nowhere to participate in this monumental occasion. Needless to say, a romance with Ed didn't blossom from that day, but my aversion to dogs did.

I shuddered. I could still remember exactly how that dog's tongue felt in my mouth.

As though she could sense I was at a loss, Mitzy walked over to the back door and looked meaningfully over her shoulder. I found a leash hanging on a hook nearby and clipped it on her collar. She led me around to the front of the shop where there was a patch of grass. While she did her business, I took the opportunity to look around and take in my new surroundings.

The pie shop was just off the main street. On one side

was a florist called Petunia's Petals. The windows were packed with various brightly colored bouquets. On the other side was a vacant building. Remnants of clear tape clung to the front windows, and I could see the outline of the letters over the door that read, 'Vinnie's Video Galaxy.' Flora was watching me through the window of her bookstore just across the street. She waved when she noticed I was looking back at her. I felt a little tug on the leash and realized Mitzy was directing me back towards the door.

'Excuse me.' I heard a voice behind me. I turned and saw a round man with thinning brown hair and a dark green cardigan hurrying towards me. He stopped by my side and pushed his gold-rimmed glasses further up on his nose. 'You seem to have forgotten to pick up after your dog.'

'What?'

'You need to pick up after your dog,' he repeated.

'Pick up what?' I asked.

He pointed to the pile in the grass. Mitzy assumed we were admiring her handiwork and wagged her tail proudly at us.

'Ew, no,' I said horrified.

'It's the law,' he said almost joyfully. 'I'm Sheriff Buddy.'

I glanced around uncertainly. 'I'm Susanna. How do I...' I trailed off. Was this some kind of new girl hazing? He pulled a plastic bag out of his pocket. I'm guessing he always kept a stash on him in case opportunities like this arose. He demonstrated putting it over his hand and mimed picking up the pile before pulling it off his hand and giving it to me.

Disgusted, I put the plastic bag over my hand and picked up Mitzy's mess under his watchful eye. With a satisfied nod, he was off.

'Nice to meet you,' he called over his shoulder.

'You too,' I said, not really meaning it.

I disposed of Mitzy's mess before heading upstairs to Aunt Erma's apartment. There was a door at the top of the stairs that stood open. Had it been left open or could Mitzy open doors?

The apartment was colorful and cozy, just like Aunt Erma's house had been when I was a kid. She used to have a secret room in her house that only she and I were allowed to go into. It was filled with toys and games and books. We would pile blankets and pillows on the floor and spend hours in there. In retrospect it was probably just a walk-in closet, but at the time I thought it was the most fabulous place in the whole world.

The door opened into the living room where there was a soft red sofa in front of a small television. The sofa had a blue and green quilt draped over the back. Fairy lights lined the bookshelves on the wall. One of the shelves was full of toys. I recognized some of the toys from the secret room. There was a new addition, a doll with blue hair, wings, and a wand. When I picked her up she said, 'Can you feel the magic?' in a sing song voice. Hmm, a little creepy. I set her down facing the back of the shelf.

I walked through the living room to the kitchen. It was small. There wasn't even an oven, only a toaster oven on the counter. A small wooden table with two chairs was pushed into the corner. There was a bedroom just through the kitchen and a bathroom off of that. The bathroom had decals of frogs and monkeys on the walls. Mitzy followed me for about ten seconds before deciding I was boring and settling down to sleep in the middle of the queen-sized bed.

I was on my way back to the door when a framed drawing hanging on the wall caught my eye. As I looked closer, a lump formed in the back of my throat. It was a picture I had drawn for her when I was eight. It was me and Aunt Erma standing in the middle of a giant blueberry pie. Or at least that's what it was supposed to be. I squinted at the mess of jagged marker lines. I had presented it to her on her birthday, and she had fawned over it in the way only a loving aunt could, but a few months later she left and I never saw her again. I shook my head a little and turned to go back downstairs.

I opened one fridge door. It was packed full of butter, cream, apples, cherries, and blueberries. When I opened the door of the other fridge, I found shelves full of pies. I pulled them out, sixteen in total. Each pie had a yellow sticky note on top that said what kind it was and gave baking directions. I preheated three of the wall ovens at different temperatures to bake the four apple, four blueberry, and four cherry pies. There were four mocha cream pies that didn't require baking.

Once I put all the pies in the ovens to bake, delicious smells filled the whole shop. My mouth watered. I checked the timers every few minutes, the excitement building. I was going to get to eat Aunt Erma's pies again. I felt guilty for wishing that no customers would come today so I could eat all of them myself.

I dragged myself away from watching the pies bake to look for a recipe book so I could start planning for tomorrow. I started with the desk. The top drawer had jars full of pens, pencils, scissors, paper clips, rubber bands, and twist ties. The next drawer down had a stack of paper. I pulled the whole stack out and flipped through it, but every page was blank except for one that was in the middle. That piece of paper had a list of names on it. Maybe a guestlist for a party. I tossed it back on top of the pile, and then opened the bottom drawer. It had file folders with the top tabs labeled 'receipts' and 'bank statements.' None of them were labeled 'recipes.' I grabbed a sheet of paper that was crammed at the back of the drawer and hoped it would have a recipe or two printed on it. I unfolded it. It was a map. Hocus Hills was circled on the map, and Aunt Erma had drawn little stars with dates next to the names of surrounding communities. The dates were all within the last few months. Knowing Aunt Erma, she was probably keeping track of some butterfly migration patterns. I put it back in the bottom drawer and moved on to the rest of the kitchen. I opened up every single cupboard, but there was nothing – not even a recipe card.

Just like when I was a kid, I closed my eyes and wished Aunt Erma would come back. I was just getting ready to go upstairs and check the apartment for recipes when the timer beeped, letting me know it was time to take the first set of pies out. After a frantic search, I found oven mitts in a drawer to the left of the ovens. The mitts had cow faces on them and mooed every time I grabbed a pie.

Once all the pies were cooled and cut, I lined them up in the display case and wrote the different flavors on the chalkboard out front. I took one slice from each kind of pie and stashed them in the kitchen. If I was going to bake tomorrow, I had to have something to study I reasoned.

I flipped the sign from closed to open and unlocked the door just after noon. According to the sign in the front window, I should have opened at 11 o'clock, but I hadn't anticipated doing this on my own, and baking the pies had taken awhile.

My heart was pounding and I couldn't decide if I wanted someone to walk through the door or if I wanted it to stay safely empty in here. I was suddenly aware that the only sound in the shop was my breathing, so I found a CD player behind the counter and hit play. Show tunes filled the air. I slowly swayed and was just about to burst into the main chorus of 'Singin' in the Rain' when I noticed some people were approaching the door. I quickly turned the music down as the group walked inside.

The first one through the door was a man in a red fedora who wore a royal blue shirt with a red vest and dark brown pants. His slightly overgrown white hair stuck out the sides under his hat and dark thick rimmed glasses sat on his face. He looked like Spider-man's grandfather.

Next through the door was Flora, and right behind her

was a pleasantly plump woman with her white hair pulled into a bun on the top of her head. Her bright blue eyes sparkled, and she had a face that looked like it spent a lot of time smiling. She was wearing a lime green sweater with jeans and carried a very large yellow purse.

'Hello, Susanna,' Flora greeted me in her soft sing-song voice. 'I want to introduce you to Lena and Mr Barnes.' She gestured towards her two companions.

'Nice to meet you.' I was relieved that Flora was going to be one of my first customers. She seemed so sweet, like one of those people who would tell you what a wonderful job you were doing even if you were totally messing everything up.

'I am not formal,' the gentleman said, 'but I go by Mr Barnes because my first name is just too embarrassing. I don't think my parents wanted to have children.' He gave me a wink and took off his fedora.

'We don't even know what it is,' Flora said.

'We're the Morning Pie Crew. We'll probably always be your first customers of the day,' Lena chimed in, heaving her large purse onto its own chair. 'We've been trying to come up with a cleverer name, but nothing has stuck. Sometimes Henry joins us, but he had to work today.'

I had no idea who Henry was, but I just nodded and smiled.

'We need our daily pie fix,' Flora said, eyeing the case.

'I always tell people they should start their days with some cleansing breaths and a piece of pie,' Mr Barnes chimed in.

'And a little gossip,' Lena added.

'What can I get for you?' I asked.

After some hemming and hawing, I served up two mocha creams, one blueberry, and three coffees.

'You should probably make that four coffees, sweetheart,' Mr Barnes said to me.

'Why's that?'

'You have to join us, of course,' Lena said, patting the chair next to her, 'Grab yourself a piece of pie too. I recommend the blueberry.'

This seemed like an offer I couldn't refuse, and I filled a coffee cup and heaped a plate with one of the larger pieces of blueberry pie. I felt a little weird sitting down for a break already, but I was the boss so who was going to stop me?

'Lena and I live in apartments over our shops, and Mr Barnes lives in a house at the edge of town,' Flora said.

'So about three blocks away,' Mr Barnes said with a chuckle.

I learned that Lena owned the hardware store, and Mr Barnes owned the yoga studio on the other side of town. According to him, I could use a little meditation in my life.

'Come in for a free class,' he offered.

My mouth said, 'Of course,' but my mind said, 'heck no.'

I took a bite of my pie and sighed with pleasure as the flavors hit my tongue. The sweet crumbly topping mixed with the slightly tart juice of the blueberries created the perfect combination. I was still savoring when Lena launched in with the questioning.

'Why haven't we seen you around here before? Erma

talks about you but hasn't told us why you don't keep in touch. Was there some sort of falling out? Why haven't you tried to reach her before?' she asked.

'Lena,' Flora gently swatted her arm. 'Don't be rude.'

'I am not being rude, I am just trying to get to know the girl,' Lena said defensively. 'Fine,' she said, responding to Flora's very scary stern librarian face. 'What do you do for a living?'

'Are you a baker like your aunt, dear?' Flora asked.

'Not exactly,' I said, 'I work for a handyman company back home. My baking is usually limited to take and bake cookies.'

All of their eyes widened a little, and they plastered nervous smiles on their faces.

'I'm sure you'll do great,' Mr Barnes said after a slightly awkward pause.

Chapter 2

Day 1 — Wednesday

Word must have spread through town because I didn't get to sit for too long. People started pouring through the door. I noticed they weren't as concerned with ordering a piece of pie as they were with asking me questions. Where are you from? How long are you here? What did you do back home? Are you in a relationship? How long was your last relationship? Why do you think you aren't in a relationship? What kind of experience do you have with making pies? What is your favorite pie? Will you be able to make pie just like Erma does? Where is Erma? When will she be back? It made the questioning by the Morning Pie Crew seem tame. I tried to deflect their questions by giving short answers or awkwardly changing the topic to the weather.

It didn't take many people to fill the pie shop. They squished inside standing shoulder to shoulder and spilled outside onto the sidewalk. Somewhere in the blur of scooping pie and questions, I noticed the pie tins were getting empty. I glanced at the clock. It was only 1.30 p.m. I felt a trickle of sweat run down my back as I served the last piece of pie to a middle-aged man who wore a jersey with a picture of a cat holding a bat. He was asking me if I played softball and inviting me to join his team the Killer Kittens but all I could think was, how could this happen? What was I supposed to serve for the next four and a half hours? I thought a little guiltily about the pieces of pie I had stashed in the fridge. Not quite guilty enough to put them out though.

My hand shook a little as I wrote 'Out of Pie' on a piece of notebook paper and taped it to the front of the display case, cringing at the thought of people storming out in a fit of rage. Nobody stormed out. People just ordered coffee instead. Then they used the time when I was serving their coffee to ask me if I'd ever traveled out of the country, if my hair was naturally curly, and if I wanted children.

'OK, all you nosy Nellies.' Flora appeared in the middle of the crowd. Her quiet voice commanded attention. 'Leave this poor girl alone. She's got plenty to worry about without you all giving her the third degree.'

The crowd grumbled a little and began to shuffle out the door. I began to breathe a little easier once it was just me and Flora. She rolled her eyes at me.

'Sorry, they mean well, but usually people just pass through town. We don't have outsiders who come to stay like this,' she said. 'People have to come to stare. It's like you're the only clown at the carnival, and they expect you to do tricks for them.' She shook her head. 'If they start gathering again, you just holler for me, honey. You're doing great here.'

I thanked her and she was gone. It was a relief to have quiet in the shop again.

I found a 'Back in 10 minutes' sign on a shelf by the front door. I hung it in front of the open sign and locked the door before running upstairs to check on Mitzy. She was curled up on my jacket. Hadn't I left that hanging in the closet? I shooed her off it, and she moaned as she headed towards the door to be taken outside. I reluctantly found the plastic bags next to the dog leash. I detested the thought of picking up after her, but I was too much of a rule follower to risk defying the sheriff.

Once we were out on the patch of grass, I stood still, closed my eyes, and took a deep breath. I tried to pretend I hadn't seen Flora from her perch in the window of her bookshop.

'You can run a pie shop,' I repeated in my head over and over until I almost believed it.

I held my breath while I picked up after Mitzy. How many times could a dog go in one day? I threw it away and jumped back a little when a cat appeared from behind the dumpster. It had long shiny silver fur and huge bright blue eyes. Mitzy began to hop around like a little jumping bean, barking like crazy.

'Shh, Mitzy,' I scolded. 'Go on, cat.' I tried to shoo it away so I could get Mitzy inside. The cat listened about as well as Mitzy did and sat blocking the door, calmly blinking up at us.

'You need to move,' I said. I spoke slowly and loudly as though that would make the cat understand. Great, day one and I was talking to a cat.

'Meow,' it said back, but it didn't budge.

Finally, I grabbed the still barking Mitzy and carried her inside. I had to slide through the door because the cat tried to follow us in. I set Mitzy down once we were safely inside and she gazed up at me, her tail wagging proudly.

Back upstairs, I made sure all my possessions were out of reach before going back to the pie shop. It was still early, so, very reluctantly, I put my secret pieces of pie in the display case. Well, all except the piece of mocha cream. I needed something to get me through the day.

Just after three, a woman in a tailored black business suit came in. She looked taken aback when she saw me.

'Hi, what can I get for you today?' I asked with a smile.

'Where's Erma?' She glanced around suspiciously.

'She had to go on a business trip, but she left some delicious pies. It's been busy today, but there're still a couple pieces left.' I waved my arm across the bakery case.

She continued to eye me skeptically. 'And who are you?'

'I'm Erma's niece, Susanna,' I said with a big smile. She continued to stare at me. 'And you are...'

'Violet Flowerfield. When will Erma be back?'

'I'm not sure.' The smile on my face felt a little more forced now, but she didn't seem to notice. 'Is there anything I can help you with?'

'I'm here for an inspection,' she replied curtly.

Oy, a health inspector on top of everything else today?

Based on the deep furrow in her brow, she was not happy about her last inspection. I didn't know how that could be possible since the place had been so clean when I arrived. I was eager to help in any way that I could, including charming this grouchy health inspector so she'd get off Aunt Erma's back.

'Come on. I'll show you the kitchen.' I led her by the arm around the wall to the kitchen. The woman started to protest, but I was determined to help, so I gritted my teeth and gripped her arm a little tighter. 'See, everything is spotlessly clean.' I let go of her so I could present the kitchen with a flourish of my arms. 'Don't you have a clipboard or something so you can write all this down?' I noticed her hands were empty, but a briefcase hung over her shoulder.

She surveyed the kitchen for a minute, and suddenly I saw it through her eyes. A trail of crumbs led to the piles of pie smeared plates that I'd stacked by the dishwasher. The island was a rainbow of assorted colored mugs, several of which were still partially full of cold coffee. In my haste to keep up with the earlier rush, I had spilled coffee grounds all over the counter and floor by the coffee pot. How did it get so bad back here without me realizing it?

With her eyebrow cocked, she turned back to me. 'I need to speak with Erma,' she said.

'I wash my hands regularly,' I said, holding them out for her to see.

'This is really something I need to speak with Erma about,' she said, straightening out her blazer.

Wow, she was really One Note Nancy. I slowly exhaled

23

my frustration. 'I'm wearing my hat!' I pointed to the purple baseball cap on my head that had Erma's Pie Shop stitched across it in gold, in one last ditch effort to persuade this woman to pass us.

She gazed at my head for a moment before meeting my eyes. 'When can I see Erma?'

'I'm sure she'll be back in the next few days,' I said, hoping my words were true. 'I can let her know you stopped by.'

'Fine.' She turned to leave.

'Does she have your number?' I called as she headed out the door.

'She knows how to get a hold of me,' she said without turning around.

I started stacking dishes in the dishwasher. I looked at the huge mountain of crusty dishes and stopped. Why was I here? My car was out front. I could leave this all right now and who would even know? Aunt Erma wasn't here. She hadn't even bothered to call today. She hadn't left a forwarding number. What reason did I have to stay?

I thought about my job back home. The hours were long, and my boss was a big burly guy with just two emotions, angry and annoyed. Despite that, I knew I was really good at my job. I'd had a knack for fixing things ever since I was a kid and my talking doll stopped talking. I had ripped her open at the seams – which originally concerned my parents because they thought I was a serial killer in the making – and I carefully took the box from her torso out and reconnected some wires. The doll began to talk again,

24

and I duct-taped her closed. That was not manufacturer recommended, by the way.

Even though I'd just left home, I longed for the familiarity of my tiny studio apartment with the thin walls where the ever-present sound of cars rushing down the highway reminded me that I wasn't alone. There was no dog who might lick me in the mouth while I was sleeping. I had the number of the best pizza place on speed dial in my phone. Was there even a pizzeria in this town? My pillow was lumpy in all the right places. Why didn't I remember to bring my pillow? The pillow was the final straw. I was going home. If I left right now, I could be home before the pizza place closed. I went upstairs and grabbed my bag. I began to throw the few things I'd unpacked back inside. Mitzy watched me from her perch on the arm of the sofa.

'The shop will be better off without me. I don't even know why she called,' I justified to Mitzy. 'C'mon. I'll take you to Flora's,' I said, hoping Flora wouldn't mind the intrusion. Was it my imagination or did she just shake her head no? I sighed; I was in no mood to deal with a reluctant dog.

'Come,' I said a little more forcefully. Mitzy popped to her feet and went over to the bookshelf. She pawed at a book with a blank purple spine. 'Don't do that,' I said. She made eye contact with me and pawed at it again.

'Obedience school, that's what you need,' I told her as I grabbed the book off the shelf. The cover was embossed with a gold flower. I opened it up, and the pages were filled with pictures of me throughout the years. Me as a baby sitting on the floor with a bowl in my lap all covered in flour. Me at about three years old wearing a bright yellow dress proudly holding up a pie. Me in that same dress smeared in dark blueish purple juice as I cried at the over-turned pie tin on the floor. Me on Aunt Erma's lap as she read me a book. There were even pictures from after she'd left. Me awkwardly trying to pin a corsage on a boy before a school dance. Me and my mom at my college graduation. How had she gotten these pictures?

Before I could even give myself permission to cry, the tears began to fall. I felt the sharp loss of the family I'd once had. We had been so happy – my parents, Aunt Erma, and me. I had a chance to reconnect with Aunt Erma. Maybe we couldn't get those lost years back, but we didn't have to lose any more.

When the tears stopped, I sighed and unpacked my bag.

Chapter 3

Day 2 — Thursday, November 3rd

I woke up before my alarm. A rarity for me. Even though I had been exhausted, it took me a while to fall asleep. It was just too quiet. In my apartment back home I could hear cars driving on the highway all night. Here, nights were quiet aside from Mitzy's snoring. I eventually turned the television on for a little background noise. I had slept on the red sofa in the living room. The thought of sleeping in Aunt Erma's bed made me uncomfortable. I knew she wouldn't mind, but it felt like an invasion of privacy.

I stood up and stretched. My stomach knotted when I thought about baking pies by myself. Mitzy cracked open an eye when I got up, but since she wasn't nervous about anything, she decided to stay curled up on her perch on the back of the sofa.

As doubts over my abilities crept into my mind, I packed my bag again. If things went badly today, I wanted to be able to leave quickly. Then, I showered, got dressed, pulled my mess of curls back in a ponytail, and went downstairs with my coffee. I dreaded facing the mess in the kitchen.

I stopped in my tracks the minute I entered. The place was spotless. All of yesterday's dishes were clean and put away. The floor had been mopped. The kitchen actually seemed to sparkle.

What was going on here? I'd never been the victim of a break-in, but I was pretty sure most criminals didn't clean up. I debated about what I should do. Call the sheriff? And tell him what? That my kitchen was inexplicably clean? That would probably give him a good laugh. There had to be a good explanation for all of this, even if I didn't know what it was yet.

Mitzy brought me out of my head with a bark from upstairs, reminding me that dogs have to go outside in the morning even if they are reluctant to get up.

Once Mitzy was back upstairs and curled up on the couch (it looked like she had her day planned), I went back to the kitchen to once again look for pie recipes.

I opened cupboard doors and dug through the papers on the desk in the back corner hoping I'd missed something yesterday. But after another thorough search, I was still empty-handed.

I sighed and went upstairs to get my laptop. Mitzy had managed to pull down my pillow from the spot I had carefully tucked it and was now sprawled across it.

'Hey,' I said indignantly as I pulled the pillow out from under her and tried to brush off any dog essence. She looked surprised and confused. 'Don't lay on my pillow,' I scolded, and I swear she narrowed her eyes at me.

I put my pillow on top of the high bookshelf. Then I saw the necklace Aunt Erma had left for me. I had left it next to her less-than-helpful note. I examined the sparkly bottle at the end of the chain, and then slipped it on over my head. It wasn't really my style, but I tucked it under my shirt. It made me feel slightly more connected to Aunt Erma. I grabbed my laptop and headed downstairs.

As I began searching online for pie recipes, I thought about all the hours I had spent in Aunt Erma's kitchen growing up. I closed my eyes for a minute and tried to dig way back in my memory to see if I could recall anything Aunt Erma had taught me when I was a kid. It was amazing. I could remember the exact pattern of her star covered apron, every word to the songs we used to make up and sing, and the number of gnomes on the wallpaper border in her kitchen, but I could not for the life of me remember anything concrete about the actual baking.

I think the butter in the crust was supposed to be chilled. Or was it supposed to be melted? Or was I supposed to use shortening in the crust? I distinctly remember Aunt Erma telling me that one was better than the other, but which one? I let my head bang down against the computer keyboard for a minute before taking a deep breath and scrolling through the recipes. I found a couple that looked doable.

I lined up all the ingredients from the two recipes I had picked out and cracked open the back door to let in some cool air. Today was going to be a choice of two kinds of pie: apple or blueberry. I would make six of each pie and hope that the day didn't get too busy or I might have to shut down early. If these went really well, I might get crazy and add a third, like French silk. I loved French silk, but that recipe looked complicated.

I was very young when I started helping Aunt Erma in the kitchen. I remember her tying me to chairs with towels so I wouldn't fall off as I stood at the counter to help her. Mostly I helped by playing in the flour. My parents didn't let me make a mess in the kitchen like Aunt Erma did. She would pour a cup of flour onto the counter in front of me just so I could squish it between my fingers or spread it around and draw in it. She would sing and tell me stories that would leave me breathless with their magic. Keeping a child like me quiet took a special gift. I always thought it was funny when she would talk to the pies, singing little rhymes as she sprinkled the spices on top. She would wink at me and say, 'Now they can work their magic,' as she slid them into the oven.

I loved those days in Aunt Erma's kitchen. They were full of pure joy and deliciousness. Aunt Erma made sure we had a pre-baking snack, usually cheese and crackers and some kind of fruit. 'We have to make sure we have energy to complete this grand task of ours,' she would say as we stood by the corner of her kitchen counter. We would pause after making the crust for another snack, which was usually a few pieces of chocolate eaten while we stood in the middle of the kitchen surveying our work-in-progress.

She would ask me about my day and patiently listen to my long-jumbled stories about something that had happened on the playground or a dream I'd had the night before. She never interrupted me or told me I wasn't making any sense. She just let me talk.

Then there was the post-baking snack – a big slice of the fresh pie, which we usually enjoyed as we sat with our legs outstretched on the light green carpet in her living room. She never worried about me spilling pie, though I did more than once. Somehow, she always got the stains out of the carpet.

I stared at the ingredients and drank my coffee. Did I have time to eat some cheese and crackers? I looked at the clock and realized I had to focus. Maybe if I concentrated all my energy, it would somehow magically turn into finished pies. Unfortunately, the power of my mind seemed to be failing me, so I set to work. I added all the ingredients for the crust to the industrial mixer. It was a little daunting to flip the switch to the on position because even though it had a protective guard around the bowl, I was still afraid somehow I would fall in and get mixed to death. I carefully read and re-read the recipe to make sure I wasn't missing anything. I felt my confidence build as I looked at the giant ball of dough that actually seemed to resemble the pictures of pie crust I had found online. I covered the counter with a layer of flour and plopped the ball of dough in the middle so I could divide it into smaller chunks. Out of the blue, I sneezed right on the pie crust. A cloud of flour surrounded me.

I jumped when I heard a snort behind me. I turned and saw a tall man standing in the doorway. He was a good-looking guy who was probably in his early thirties with wavy dark brown hair, brown eyes, and thick eyebrows. His lips were pursed together as though he was fighting to suppress laughter.

He cleared his throat trying to compose himself. I attempted to brush the flour off me, but there was really no recovering from this.

'I saw your door propped open, so I stopped to say hi,' he explained. 'I'm Henry.' He looked like he was going to shake my hand but then, as if he remembered that I'd just sneezed, he dropped it back by his side.

'I'm Susanna,' I said with a sigh as I grabbed the ball of dough and dumped it in the garbage.

'You're the niece,' he said. 'I heard some rumblings in town about you.'

'Oh yeah?'

'Something about you loving the musical *Annie*?' He raised his eyebrows questioningly at me.

'That doesn't sound like me,' I said, somehow managing to keep a straight, innocent face. 'You must be confusing me with someone else.'

He looked suspicious. 'There's not a lot of new people in town to confuse you with.'

'So, what do you do, Henry?' I asked, in what I hoped was a smooth change of subject.

'I work at the nursing home.' As he spoke, he walked into the kitchen and washed his hands. 'The people there are great, but it's like I have eighteen grandparents always trying to "help" me make my life decisions.' Without missing a beat, he was over at the sneeze counter, washing it off.

'What are you doing?' I asked.

'The shop is supposed to open soon, and...' He waved his hand over the counter where I had all the ingredients lined up. 'There are no pies. I thought maybe you could use a hand.'

'You bake?' I asked.

'Oh yes,' he said with a smile. 'Erma is one of my many surrogate grandparents.'

Part of me wanted to shoo him away. 'I can do it myself,' had been my motto ever since I was a little kid and had read a *Sesame Street* book by that same title. But I glanced at the clock, and he was right. The shop was supposed to open in a couple hours. I had a feeling the town wouldn't respond well to me just putting the ingredients in the display case and trying to sell them as a DIY pie kit.

'Thanks,' I said, a little reluctantly. I started peeling the apples.

He tossed the ingredients into the mixer, barely glancing at the recipe I had out on the counter. In no time, he had the ball of dough on the counter and was dividing it up.

'Ah, ah,' he began as if he was going to sneeze, then dazzled me with a smile. 'Just kidding.'

I was tempted to throw a handful of flour at him, but I settled with fixing my withering glare towards him. I wasn't quite ready to laugh at that yet.

'So, tell me more about life at the nursing home,' I said, as I slowly peeled my second apple.

'They've all discovered social media,' he said, darkly.

'Really?' I laughed.

'Yup,' he nodded. He had all the crusts prepared and had moved on to helping me peel apples. 'Life used to be easy. I just had to set up bingo games and card tournaments. Now everyone is constantly handing me their phones and asking me to help them take selfies.'

I laughed. He was already on his fourth apple, and I was still struggling with my second. Tomorrow I would be sure to pick recipes that didn't involve peeling anything. I wondered if with all the genetic engineering out there if you could buy peel-less apples.

'That's not even the worst part,' he said. 'Betty asked me to explain sexting to her.' He shivered in horror at the memory.

'Wow, no wonder you're hiding out in here,' I said.

'I'm not hiding,' he said, a little indignant. 'I'm just doing a community service. The town needs their pie.'

He helped me make the apple pies and prepare the crusts for the blueberry pies. Soon the place was smelling like the pie shop it was.

'I should probably get going.' Henry headed towards the back door. 'Remember to reduce the temperature in fifteen minutes.' He pointed at the timer he'd set. 'And here's this just in case.' He held up a handkerchief and set it on the corner of the desk with a wink before sliding out the back door.

I found myself still smiling after he left. I tried to wipe the smile off my face as I mixed the blueberries and sugar together. Sure, he was cute and he could bake, but I had to focus on the pie shop. Who knew how long I'd be here anyway?

I had a habit of ending up with boyfriends when I was lonely. Usually I chose them without much discretion. My mother disapproved of anyone I dated, so I had learned to accept her disapproval early on. As a result, it often took me longer to recognize when I disapproved.

I was startled out of my daydream by a meow, and to my horror I saw the same silver cat from yesterday sitting on the floor by the pantry. I lunged at it. Why had I left the door open? The cat smoothly sidestepped my grasp. I could hear Mitzy barking from behind the door at the top of the stairs.

Thank goodness I hadn't unlocked the front door yet. The last thing I needed today was the health inspector stopping by while I chased a stray cat around the kitchen. I followed it as it ran under the kitchen island and around to the front of the shop. I stretched out my arms and felt the fur slip through my fingers. I grunted when I fell on my knees and prayed that Flora wasn't looking in from her window just then. The cat disappeared under the display case. Out of breath, I dropped to my stomach and peered underneath expecting to see blue eyes staring back at me, but I couldn't see anything. I ran back and found my phone so I could use the flashlight on it. I shined the light across the dark corners and saw nothing but a few dust bunnies. Mitzy continued to bark her encouragement from upstairs.

'Here kitty, kitty, kitty.' I tried to use a soothing voice. 'I have tuna.' I felt slightly guilty for lying, but I reassured myself that it was for a good cause. Where did the cat go?

I reached my hand underneath, cringing slightly as I imagined cat teeth taking off a finger. I felt nothing. Did she move when I wasn't looking? I found that hard to believe, but as I flashed the light back and forth, I couldn't figure out where she had ended up. I did four more laps around the kitchen dropping to the floor to check every nook and cranny. She must have gone out the back door when I wasn't looking.

I closed the back door and locked it for good measure, then finished making the blueberry pies. Every now and then I thought I saw something out of the corner of my eye, and I turned my head expecting to see a cat. It was always my imagination.

I found the plates in one of the upper cupboards, all stacked and clean. I stood on my tip toes and carefully pulled the whole stack down. Whew, no problem. I balanced the plates in my hands and turned to bring them out front.

Something wrapped around my foot. *Oh no, it's the cat*, I thought. I danced around trying to free myself before I realized that my computer was sliding precariously towards the edge of the kitchen island. I was tripping over my computer cord. Instinctively, I lunged to save my computer, dropping all the plates I had in my hands. The crash was still ringing in my ears as I froze, holding my computer. Every single one had broken. 'Into a million pieces' didn't seem at all like an exaggeration. I crunched through the plate bits and found the broom and dustpan. I swept it up all the while wondering what I was going to serve pie on today.

With the pies still in the oven, I couldn't run to the store to buy paper plates so I searched the cupboards for the second time today. The best I could come up with was a stack of pie tins. I was hoping that word would get out that I was quirky and fun with my innovative idea of serving pie in pie tins instead of the truth that I was a bumbling butterfingers.

My phone beeped and I jumped for it. It was a text from my friend, Michelle, asking if I wanted to go out for a drink tonight. Michelle and I had been friends since college when I helped her fix the desk in her dorm room. It had broken after she'd danced on top of it during an overly enthusiastic round of karaoke.

She considered it her job to make sure I got out on the town at least one night a week. I guess we hadn't talked for a couple days. I explained where I was.

'Whoa, that's major. Keep me posted,' she wrote back. We texted back and forth a little more, and I already felt homesick as our exchange reminded me how nice it was to talk to someone who knew me so well. 'I have to go, but hurry home and bring pie,' she wrote.

'Will do.' I blinked back tears as I set down my phone. Flora, Lena, and Mr Barnes quite literally danced into the shop that morning. Mr Barnes was singing a Frank Sinatra song and twirling Lena as he walked through the door. Then he dipped her. I was amazed at their grace considering she was almost twice his size.

'Pie's on me this morning, ladies,' he said, pausing his singing for a moment. 'I'm just lucky to have three such beautiful women in my life.' He looked up at me. 'Would you like to dance?' he asked, extending his hand in my direction.

'I think I'll just stick to serving pie for now,' I laughed.

They all ordered blueberry pie and insisted that I sit with them again. I tried to turn them down as I still had a lot of baking practice to do today, but in the end, they wore me down. I was hungry, and anyway, it's pretty much biologically impossible for me to turn down pie.

Flora said that the pie tin plates were fun, but she gave me a look that made me think she knew what had really happened. She probably heard the crash all the way over at her shop.

'Who cleans the kitchen at the pie shop?' I asked. They all froze with their eyes wide, forks poised over their slices of pie.

'What do you mean, dear?' Flora asked. She set down her fork and adjusted the napkin on her lap.

'Last night when I went to bed, the kitchen was a disaster zone, and this morning when I woke up it was sparkly clean,' I said.

'Oh, that's just...' Lena began and then paused.

'Minerva,' Mr Barnes said just as Flora said, 'Jane.'

'Right, Minerva and Jane,' Lena said. 'They clean the kitchen every night.'

'What time do they come?' I asked. I wanted to be ready so I would know not to be panicked if I heard noises coming from downstairs. It would be best to know when to write it off as the cleaners and when to call the police.

'They come different times each night,' Mr Barnes said. 'Usually when you're sleeping.'

'Like Santa Claus,' Lena offered with a forced laugh.

'OK,' I said. I wondered why they were so acting so strangely. It seemed like a simple question.

My attention shifted, and I watched them all closely as they took their first bites of pie.

'Did any of you read today's "Ask Elodie"?' Flora asked. She put her first bite into her mouth and sucked her cheeks in for a second before chewing. She glanced at me and gave me a big smile when she saw I was watching. Maybe I should have steered them all away from the blueberry pie and towards the apple pie that Henry had made.

'Yes, of course,' Mr Barnes said, and Lena nodded. They turned to me, and I stared at them all blankly.

'It's a column in the local paper,' Flora explained. 'It's fantastic! Elodie gives out amazing advice.'

'There's usually a little gossip about the happenings in town too,' Lena said. 'Which of course we all love.'

'That Elodie seems like a real spitfire,' Mr Barnes chimed in taking his first bite and chewing only twice before swallowing.

'Seems like?' I asked. 'Don't you know who she is?'

Flora shook her head, 'No, it's a big mystery!'

'Every now and then, Crazy Jackie claims it's her, but that woman couldn't find a shoe in a shoe store, much less give coherent advice like Elodie,' Lena said. When she took a bite, her eyebrows rose for just a fraction of a second.

'Anyway, we talk about her columns a lot, so you should probably keep up with them,' Flora told me.

'Of course, I'll start to read them,' I said, hoping that I would remember to do it when the day was over. It felt like it was non-optional homework. I took a bite of my blueberry pie, and slowly chewed as all the wrong flavors burst into my mouth. This didn't taste like Aunt Erma's pie. It was too sweet and the crumble topping wasn't crumbling at all. It was too hard and crunchy. I would have to try a different recipe tomorrow. Or maybe I would have to just practice more.

When there was a lull in the conversation, I asked questions about Aunt Erma. 'Didn't she give you any idea where she was going?' I asked.

'I'm sorry, but she didn't say,' Flora said.

'Don't worry, she'll probably be back before you know it,' Lena offered.

'But how did she sound when she left?' I asked, remembering the anxious pitch of her voice in the message on my phone.

'I didn't actually see her before she left,' Flora spoke slowly. 'She taped the note for you and one for me on the back door of my shop.'

'But you didn't see her?' I was hoping Flora would tell

40

me that Aunt Erma seemed just fine and had a perfectly logical explanation for leaving me here alone. 'What did she say in the note to you? Can I see it?'

'She wrote that she had to go take care of something. I think I tossed the note out, but don't worry, she sounded very calm and said she'd be back soon,' Flora explained. She glanced over at Mr Barnes.

I wanted to believe her. I got up to serve two customers some apple pie.

'It's in a prime spot. It won't be empty long,' Lena was saying when I sat back down at the table.

'What's a prime spot?' I asked.

'There's an empty storefront in the town square. It used to be McCullen's Dress Shop until Stewart ran off with that woman who was passing through. What did she do for a living?' Lena asked.

'Pinball machine maintenance,' Flora chimed in.

'That's a job?' I began to wonder how many pinball machines there were in the world, how often they broke down, and how one would train to become a pinball maintenance person.

The conversation slid along while I pondered these things, leaving me no time to ask my suddenly burning questions about pinball machine maintenance.

'I hope it's a pet store,' Mr Barnes said. Apparently, the only thing holding him back from getting a cat was the lack of easy access to pet supplies.

'He's been using that excuse for ages,' Lena said. 'He's never going to get a cat.'

'There's a cat that's been hanging around the back door. You could probably adopt her,' I offered.

'I think I've seen that cat. The one with the silver fur?' Flora said.

'Yes!'

'I hadn't seen her until recently but I don't think she's a stray. She looks well cared for,' Flora said, shoving the last of her pie into her mouth and washing it down with a big gulp of coffee.

'I wish she'd spend more time at her home then,' I grumbled.

'Maybe it will be one of those fancy wine bars. I've always wanted to sniff and swirl a glass of wine and talk about the various subtle flavor notes,' Lena said.

'I just hope it's not another bookstore,' Flora said. 'It's a tough market already.'

'Even if there were a hundred bookstores in town, yours would still be the best,' Mr Barnes said, patting her arm.

'I just hope that whatever it is, they're ready to deal with the idiosyncrasies of this town. That takes a special person,' Lena added. 'Like Susanna.'

I nodded, giving them a weak smile as I thought about my packed bag upstairs.

Chapter 4

Day 3 — Friday, November 4th

Dear Elodie,

I just started a new job, and it's not going well. I'm over-motivated and under qualified. I feel like everyone is watching, waiting for me to make a mistake. Unfortunately, I give people a lot to talk about with all the mistakes that I make. Should I just go back to my old job? Or should I stick it out and hope that I get better?

Sincerely,

A Success at Failure

Dear A Success at Failure,

'Fake it till you make it' is a phrase for a reason. You can succeed at your new job. It just might take a little time, and even though you may not realize it, there are people around you who want to see you succeed and will be happy to help you. Put a smile on your face and move forward with confidence. I have

no doubt you'll be successful at anything you put your mind to.

Ask and I'll Answer,
Elodie

I could still see the flames dancing behind my eyelids every time I blinked. Day two of baking my own pies was not going better than day one.

'The fire extinguisher is right here. Try to remember that next time.' A man with cropped blond hair pointed to the red canister on the wall while two other firefighters opened the windows to air the place out. I certainly hoped there wouldn't be a next time.

'Yeah, I see it now. Thanks.' I couldn't keep the edge out of my voice, and my hand shook as I brushed the hair out of my face. I vaguely remembered seeing it there, but I had never been one to react well in a panic situation.

When I'd first started working at Hal's Handyman, I drilled a hole in a water line when I was hanging some pictures in a bathroom. Water was spraying out of the wall, and I ran around in circles yelling and slipping in puddles until my friend and coworker Josh walked in and calmly turned off the water at the shutoff valve. Josh was one of those people who never got riled up about anything.

'I heard this little guy whimpering at the top of the stairs.' The redheaded firefighter came over carrying Mitzy. She handed me the wide-eyed dog.

It had happened so fast. Smoke poured out of the oven. The smoke detectors screeched loudly. When I opened the oven door, the bottom was on fire. I ran to the sink and filled my hands with water and splashed it inside, which of course did nothing. So, I'd grabbed a towel, got it wet, and threw it on the flames. It wasn't wet enough because it ignited immediately. Finally, I got a bowl of water and managed to douse the flames, but not before getting a visit from the friendly neighborhood fire department.

'Could you turn the flashing lights off?' I asked. A crowd had begun to gather in the street.

'Yes, but everyone in town will still know we were here within the hour,' the guy said.

'Don't worry. They'll have something else to talk about tomorrow.' The last firefighter came over carrying a clipboard. He took his helmet off and tucked it under his arm. His gray hair was slicked back, and his piercing blue eyes gave me a good-natured wink.

I'd found Aunt Erma's sales records in one of the files in the bottom drawer of her desk. My first day in town, when everyone came to gawk, I had sold more than she did on an average day. Yesterday, I had only done about a quarter of the business she usually did. I was hoping I could do better today. I was not off to a good start.

After the firefighters left, I set Mitzy on one of the red chairs out front and surveyed the kitchen. I coughed a little. The smoke was thinning now that they had all the doors and windows opened.

I could still hear the excited chatter of the lookie-loos outside. Why didn't they just go home?

I finished putting together and baking the other pies. I

stared through the window of the oven, panicked that some juice might spill over and start an oven fire. I couldn't have the fire department out twice in one day.

The Morning Pie Crew were my first customers of the day. Mr Barnes and Lena teasingly sang a few rounds of 'Ring of Fire.' Flora, with her brow wrinkled, kept asking if I was OK. Finally, they changed the subject.

'The Fall Festival is next week!' Flora said, clapping her hands.

'I know! I can't wait!' Lena squealed. 'I heard that they are going to have dueling pianos as the entertainment this year. There's something about two people playing the piano that really gets me going. I'll be ready to shake my money maker!' She wiggled a little in her seat, giving us a preview of things to come.

'What's the Fall Festival?' I asked.

'It's our town's celebration of fall,' Mr Barnes offered helpfully. 'Really, just an excuse to eat mini donuts and drink Lena's special lemonade.' He gave her a wink.

'My lemonade will put hair on your chest,' Lena added.

'Erma's Pies has a booth there,' Flora told me. 'You should probably start preparing in case Erma's not back in time.'

My eyes widened. How could I prepare for this when I could barely keep the pie shop running?

'Erma made eighty pies last year,' Lena chimed in. 'And she sold out before noon!'

I tried to speak, but I think I just let out a little squeak. Eighty pies? At the rate I was baking, I would have to start now to be ready ... for next year's festival.

'Remember six years ago when the clown snuck up on Gerald?' Lena hooted. 'Gerald is the town wrestler,' she explained to me, as though 'town wrestler' was an actual title that should make sense to me.

'Oh yes,' Mr Barnes said with a chuckle. 'Gerald is a big guy, as you can imagine, and he ran screaming from the town square. We had to send out a search party! We finally found him in the lilac bushes behind the old church.'

'You guys shouldn't be laughing at him,' Flora tsked. 'Fear of clowns is a legitimate thing.'

'Even Gerald laughs at it now,' Lena said. 'Though we haven't had a clown at the festival since.'

I stopped listening as I began to wonder how I could make enough pies for the festival. On the plus side, my baking wasn't as good as Aunt Erma's yet, so maybe I wouldn't sell as much. Perhaps I could get by with baking forty, or maybe even thirty pies. But the thought of baking even thirty pies all at once made my head spin. When I finally tuned back into the conversation, they had moved off the topic of clowns and phobias.

Just before closing time, a customer came in. She was much shorter than I was and very muscular. She wore a bright yellow workout shirt with the name Gina's Gym embroidered in the corner. I greeted her with a smile.

'What can I get for you?' I asked. 'The blueberry crumble has been mighty popular today.' I tried my best sales pitch even though most customers today had only come in to order coffee so they could ask me about the fire.

At that, she wrinkled her nose. How dare she? Who

wrinkled their nose at blueberry crumble pie? I could already tell that she and I would not be friends.

'I'm not here for pie,' she said. Clearly, she wandered through the wrong door. 'I'm here to discuss the possibility of you serving healthier options at your establishment.'

'What?'

'The town is participating in a statewide weight loss challenge,' she told me. 'It's going to be great publicity for my gym, but so many people have been coming into your shop every day and overindulging on empty calories that we're having trouble making much headway.'

I stared blankly at her, which she took as a sign that she should continue talking.

'I'm certainly not suggesting that you close your doors completely,' she said, though the look on her face made me think she would like to suggest that. 'I'd just like to recommend you try some of these recipes for healthier alternatives.' She pushed a booklet across the counter towards me. I read the title: *Fat Free Pies and Desserts*. She had to be kidding. I wanted to throw her out, but despite my height advantage, I was pretty sure she could take me. So, I tried a different approach instead.

'I'll have to discuss it with my aunt when she gets back. She is the owner, after all. I don't really have the power to make these decisions,' I told her with a forced smile.

'Well, every day counts,' she said brightly. 'Maybe you could call your aunt and then start implementing some changes. After all, obesity is a growing epidemic, and we all need to do our part to keep our town healthy.'

'Pie makes people happy,' I said through gritted teeth.

'Ah, you're one of *those* people. You probably eat chocolate when you're sad too.' She sized me up, her eyes rested for a moment on my thighs.

'Oh look, it's closing time,' I said, even though there was still twenty minutes to go. 'I have to lock up. Thanks for stopping in.' I was unable to keep the hint of sarcasm out of my voice for the last part. I forced a polite smile, straining my cheek muscles, as I ushered her out the door. I picked up the booklet she left by the corner as though it might bite me and carried it directly to the garbage. I was pretty sure Aunt Erma wouldn't be changing any of her famous recipes to low fat options. Even the thought made me shudder.

I was relieved to flip the sign at the front door from open to closed and lock up as soon as the clock switched from 5.59 p.m. to 6 p.m. I waved to Flora who was sitting in the window of her bookshop. Her open sign was still lit up.

Upstairs, I found Mitzy drooling on the newspaper that had been sitting on the kitchen table from this morning. She cracked an eye open when she heard me come in.

'Oh, come on,' I said, pulling the newspaper out from under her. She stood up with a sniff and stretched. I brought her outside, fed her, and took her outside again. She seemed to enjoy lying on my stuff, and I was worried what else she might do if given the opportunity.

After I was convinced Mitzy's bladder was empty, I decided to stop at Flora's bookshop to see if I could find a cookbook. Maybe something there would spark my inner Aunt Erma that I couldn't seem to find on the internet. The sun was beginning to set on my short walk over to Flora's, giving the streets a nice orange glow.

A bell tinkled as I walked in the door.

'Hi Susie,' I heard Flora's voice call to me from somewhere.

'Hi Flora,' I called back, looking around, but I didn't see her anywhere. How did she even know it was me?

'Go ahead and look around. I'll be there in a minute,' Flora's voice called.

The shop had floor-to-ceiling shelves crammed full of books. The shelves weren't set up in straight aisles like I was used to. They twisted and turned around the shop, creating quite the maze. Within minutes I wasn't sure if I'd find my way back out again. I wished I'd left a trail of breadcrumbs. How would I locate the cookbook section? Every now and then, there was a small break in the shelves where an overstuffed chair sat as an invitation to curl up with a good book.

I was startled when I heard a snort and rounded the corner to see a white-haired man sprawled over a chair sleeping. His glasses were askew, and a book about relaxation techniques rested on his chest. That was an advertisement if I ever saw one. I wondered if Flora knew he was in here.

Halfway down one of the aisles I stopped when the word 'pie' caught my eye. There was a stack of books on baking pies sitting there as though it were waiting for me. I examined the covers and flipped through the pages ogling the photographs of pies next to each recipe. I decided almost immediately to buy all five of them.

I clutched the stack to my chest and walked a little further, eyeing a few books all while trying to remind myself that I didn't have a lot of disposable income right now. I was somewhere near the back of the shop (I think) when a door caught my eye.

The door was smaller than most doors and rounded at the top. I would have to bend over, but Flora would probably fit through it without ducking. I took a few more steps towards it and felt a tingling sensation run up and down my spine. What was behind that door? I glanced around. No one was in sight. I reached for the knob.

Flora suddenly appeared by my side. 'Did you find everything you needed?' she asked.

I dropped my hand and held up the books.

'I bet you'll find some of the answers you need in those,' she said.

'What's back there?' I asked, nodding towards the door.

'Just some storage. It's a real mess.' She put her arms around my shoulders and ushered me away, but before we got too far, I could have sworn that I'd heard a thump come from behind the door.

'Hey, Flora?' I began as she rung up my purchase.

'Yes, dear?'

'Are you sure you don't have the note Aunt Erma left for you around here somewhere?' I asked, glancing around the counter behind the cash register. I was hoping she had included something more in Flora's note than she had in mine. Maybe a phone number or some more specific information about where she went or when she'd be back.

'I'm sorry, but I don't have it. It didn't say much. I'm sure she told you everything she told me.' She took my money.

'Should I be worried?'

'No, your aunt is a very strong woman. I'm sure she's just fine. She just had a few things she had to take care of.' Flora handed some coins back to me, but didn't meet my eyes.

'OK, thanks.' I grabbed my books. When I got to the door, I glanced back, and Flora was staring at the cash register as though lost in thought.

When I got back to the apartment, I found Mitzy in the kitchen sink licking off the dirty dishes I'd left in there. I couldn't fathom how that tiny dog had leapt up that high. I had to set up a camera to see how this dog pulled these things off.

Chapter 5

Day 4 — Saturday, November 5th

I grabbed the newspaper from outside the front door and shuffled through the pages quickly trying to find Ask Elodie. I was hoping to get the gist of it before the Morning Pie Crew came in. Before I could find it, something caught my eye and I turned back a page.

The headline read, 'Beloved Pie Shop Left in the Hands of a Beginner.' My mouth fell open as I read the article underneath.

Residents of Hocus Hills were surprised when Erma Crosby, a leader in the community, disappeared on a business trip earlier this week leaving her pie shop in the hands of her niece, Susanna Daniels, 31 years old, who doesn't seem to know a rolling pin from a bowling pin.

Erma's pies have been a daily staple for many in town. It's often claimed that they have an almost medicinal quality to them. Several residents are concerned that

Susanna won't be able to achieve that same high quality that we all know and love. Stay tuned readers – we'll be updating the story as we learn more throughout the week.

I crumpled the paper up and threw it down on the table. I longed for the quiet anonymity that I had in the city. Back home, the list of people who knew my name or cared about what I did was short. My mother, my friends Josh and Michelle, and a couple baristas at the local coffee shop. I was good at my job, and no one printed updates about it in the local paper.

I flattened out the paper a little to check the byline. It simply read, 'Elodie.' Who was this Elodie anyway? What gave her the right to write about me?

I finished setting everything up, slamming any cupboard door that got in my way. This wasn't exactly the pep talk I needed.

'How's your day going?' Mr Barnes was the first of the Morning Pie Crew to walk through the door.

'Great,' I said, a slight edge to my voice. His eyebrows rose a little.

'I take it you read the newspaper today.'

Just then, Lena and Flora walked in. 'I brought matches so we can burn all the newspapers.' Lena held up her purse.

'No fires,' I practically shouted.

'Oh, right.' She set her bag down on a chair. 'We could all just rip our copies into shreds. That could be satisfying too.'

I considered the possibility as I served us all some pie.

'Whoa,' I said, looking out the window, almost dropping the last piece of pie. 'What is that?' Henry was walking down the street next to a giant gray and brown furry creature.

Mr Barnes glanced out the window. 'That's Henry's dog, Willy.'

'What's Willy? Part dog, part horse?' I had never in my life seen a dog that big. His face was covered with shaggy fur, and his back was taller than Henry's waist.

'He's an Irish wolfhound,' Flora explained. 'Don't worry, he's very gentle.'

'What does Henry do if Willy sees a squirrel?' I asked.

'Willy doesn't really care for chasing squirrels,' Flora said.

'But he does love ice cream,' Lena chimed in. 'Remember that time Willy took off chasing the Miller kid who was eating an ice cream cone? That boy took off as fast as his little legs would carry him. Willy was close at his heels licking the air in anticipation, and Henry was being dragged behind grasping the leash with both hands.'

Lena and Mr Barnes hooted. Flora gave them a disapproving glare, but I noticed the corners of her mouth twitched.

I was relieved that Mitzy wasn't the size of Bigfoot, but I felt a twinge of disappointment that Henry wasn't coming into the pie shop as I watched them disappear around the corner. I glanced back at the Morning Pie Crew and Lena gave me a knowing look. I hurried back to the table and changed the conversation to Elodie.

'Someone has to know who she is,' I said. 'She's publishing articles about me. I want to talk to her and get a chance to set the record straight.'

'Willard Jefferson runs the paper, but he's always been very tight-lipped about Elodie,' Mr Barnes said.

'Where's the newspaper office?' I asked, still determined to get to the bottom of it.

'In the basement of the bowling alley,' Flora said.

I let the conversation drift into more important topics like whether or not the gazebo should be repainted the same shade of blue or if it should be painted two shades lighter.

'It should match the sky,' Lena said.

'It's been the same shade of blue for a hundred years,' Flora said. 'Tradition is important.'

Mr Barnes seemed decidedly undecided about the issue.

I realized I'd left my phone upstairs in the apartment. I excused myself to go fetch it in case Aunt Erma called. While I was upstairs, Mitzy gave me her big puppy dog eyes and I was guilted into taking her outside again. I was almost back to the front of the pie shop, when I heard the Morning Pie Crew speaking in hushed tones. I paused out of view in the kitchen doorway when I heard my name.

'If she suspects something, she's a great actress,' Lena whispered.

'Erma made it very clear that we're not to talk about it,' Mr Barnes said.

'Poor thing, she doesn't even know...' Flora began.

'Shh, I think I hear her coming,' Lena said.

I made a big show of entering the front of the pie shop. I hoped I wasn't smiling too brightly.

They all spoke at once about how busy their days were and then they paid for their pie and left. I assumed their conversation had something to do with the article in the paper, or maybe they were talking about my pie baking abilities. Either way, I felt knots forming in my stomach as a feeling of loneliness settled over me.

I scooped a small slice of cherry pie onto a plate for a snack. My phone rang, and I saw Josh's name on the caller ID. My finger left a sticky smear on the screen as I answered it.

'Where have you been?' he greeted me. Josh was one of my coworkers and a good friend. He had heard my Aunt Erma sob story more than once. Usually it was after a bad day at work or a fight with my mother and a few beers.

'Are you OK?' he asked when I finished telling him that Aunt Erma was gone. I felt a lump form at the back of my throat. I nodded because I couldn't speak even though I knew he couldn't see me.

I took a deep breath. 'Actually, I'm kind of making a mess of everything.' I told him about my baking disasters and the judgement from the townspeople.

'You went to a strange town to do a new job, and even when your aunt wasn't there, you stayed. She's lucky to have you. You're the most fearless person I know,' he said.

I smiled into my phone. 'Thanks.'

'Now go be the best pie baker you can be, and we'll grab a beer when you get back,' Josh said. We said our goodbyes, and I tried to hold on to the confidence he had given me.

The rest of the day was fairly quiet. A few people wandered by and peered in the windows, amplifying my feeling of being a fish in a bowl. With all the time alone with my thoughts, my loneliness was soon replaced by frustration towards Elodie.

Mitzy and I were walking off some of that frustration after dinner, the cold breeze sweeping through the streets fueling my anger. I was relieved that there weren't many people out and about. 'Doesn't know a rolling pin from a bowling pin?' I said to Mitzy, and she wagged her tail a little as she struggled to keep up. 'It's not my fault Aunt Erma abandoned me here to do all this work. Why won't she call and check in?' I grumbled. 'Doesn't she have a cell phone?' I paused to let Mitzy sniff a leaf.

'I'm sorry. Do you require some sort of assistance?' A voice behind me made me jump. I turned and saw a woman about my age. Her frizzy blonde hair was held back by a thick navy headband that matched her leggings. She had a long thin bag slung over her shoulder and was evaluating me with slightly wide blue eyes.

'No, I'm fine,' I sighed.

'You must be Erma's niece,' she said, noticing Mitzy. I introduced myself. She told me her name was Holly, and she ran the grocery store. 'I'm on my way to Mr Barnes's yoga class. You should come with me. You look like you could use a little yoga right now.'

'I think I need a drink more than yoga,' I said. 'Know where I could find one?'

'Sal's is the best and basically only place for a drink in town, but it's closed tonight,' she said, leaning down to pet Mitzy who was demanding some attention.

'Closed? On a Saturday?'

'His kid's in a play at the elementary school tonight, so he shut down to go watch it. The liquor store is closed too. Nancy's kid is in the same play. Welcome to a small town,' she said with a laugh. She looked at her watch. 'I gotta run, but it was nice to meet you.'

I said goodbye then rounded the corner by the barber shop and saw Henry sitting on a bench in the town square looking up at the sky. Willy lay on the ground next to him. Even lying down, Willy looked gigantic.

'Finding any answers up there?' I asked, which seemed to startle him back to earth.

'Just daydreaming. Or night dreaming, I guess.' He smiled.

Mitzy shamelessly leapt up into his lap, and he stroked her head. I took that as an invitation to sit next to him. Willy stood up and sniffed Mitzy. His tail wagged, and he put a paw up on Henry's lap.

'Oh no, there's not room for you too,' he said. Willy gave me a hopeful look, and I crossed my legs. He reluctantly settled back on the ground.

'How are things at the nursing home?' I asked.

Henry's brow furrowed. 'It was kind of a rough day.'

'I'm sorry. Do you want to talk about it?' He looked so

distraught. Part of me wanted to hug him, but since this was only our second meeting, I settled for resting my hand on his arm. He put his hand on top of mine, and I felt a little jolt of excitement run through me. His hands were so warm.

'No thanks. Enough about me. Let's talk about you,' he said. 'How are things going at the pie shop? Sneeze on any dough balls today?'

'Of course not. Things have been going quite smoothly.' I skipped telling him about the fire, the crazy gym owner, and the newspaper article. He probably had enough going right now that he wasn't plugged into the gossip mill. I did tell him a very light and amusing anecdote about blueberries though.

'How are you adjusting to this small town of ours?'

'Well, I was going to stop at the liquor store, and I've just discovered that nothing is open because there's a play at the elementary school,' I said. 'So that's where I'm at.'

'Ah, yes. Most of us know to plan ahead and shop around these major events.' He removed his hand from mine and his warmth was replaced by the cold night air. I stuck my hand in my pocket. 'For example, if you're looking for a bottle of wine,' he said, reaching into a canvas tote that was sitting next to him, 'I happen to have one on me.'

I stared at him open-mouthed. His big brown eyes blinked brightly back at me. He might actually be the perfect man.

'Why are you carrying a bottle of wine around with you?'

'I had book club tonight, and it was my turn to bring the wine.'

'The bottle is almost full.'

'It was the fourth bottle.'

'How many people in the club?'

'I'd rather not answer that question,' he giggled.

'I'm guessing three.'

He answered with a wide smile and a wink before handing me the bottle. 'Here. Consider it a welcome to town gift.'

'Thanks,' I took the bottle. 'Pink. My favorite flavor.'

'Not really a wine connoisseur, huh?'

'I consider myself to be more of a wine enthusiast than a connoisseur,' I said.

We sat in a comfortable silence for a few more minutes before Mitzy jumped off Henry's lap and gave me her patented 'are you coming?' look.

'I guess it's time for me to go. I'll see you around.'

When we were several steps away, I turned back to give him one more look. He was watching me go.

Mitzy and I strolled around the edge of the mostly deserted town square. Apparently, everyone was at the play. As we rounded the corner near the diner, I saw a blinking neon sign advertising the bowling alley. Without any plan whatsoever, I marched over to the bowling alley and found a dark staircase that lead to a red door. A small plaque next to the door said 'Hocus Hills Gazette.' This was the place. A tiny bit of my gumption had evaporated upon arrival, and I hesitated at the door. I glanced down at Mitzy who looked even more unsure of my actions.

'We have to find out who this Elodie is,' I rationalized with her. She sat down defiantly. 'C'mon,' I said, gently tugging her leash as I took a couple more steps towards the door. I could hear something happening inside and I wanted to see. It would make sense if Elodie was in there right now. If her identity was such a secret she would probably work at night. 'Come on, we have to see. Quick, before anyone comes,' I urged Mitzy, and she reluctantly got up and followed me down steps to the door.

I cracked the door open. I could hear something inside. It sounded like printing presses running. And something else. A popping sound, almost like popcorn. Strange noises, but not dangerous sounding.

I was just about to push the door the rest of the way open when a man appeared, blocking my path.

'Hi,' I said, taking a flustered step backwards. I could see half of his glasses and some curly strawberry blond hair on top of his head. He didn't open the door any further. He just peered out the opening at me with one eye for a moment. Was this Willard Jefferson?

'Can I help you?' His voice was gruff and the fact that he was still masked by the darkness inside and the half-closed door made me take another step back. Then I remembered the newspaper article about me, and my righteous indignation returned.

'I'm looking for Elodie,' I said, clearing my throat when my voice wavered.

'Not in.' He started to close the door, but I stuck my foot out to stop him.

'Are you the editor?' I asked. 'I'm Susanna Daniels.'

He opened the door a little further. I could tell I had piqued his interest. I tried to look around him to see what was happening inside or if Elodie was in there, but his body still took up most of the opening, and I couldn't tell if anyone was behind him.

'Would you like to comment on today's story?' He whipped a notebook out of his pocket, his pen poised over the paper ready for a quote.

'No,' I said flatly. 'I just want to talk to Elodie.'

'No one talks to Elodie,' he said, and with that, he shut the door in my face.

'This isn't over yet,' I said to the closed door. But Mitzy and I trudged back up the stairs and out to the town square to continue our walk.

I paused in front of the empty store front. This must have been the place the Morning Pie Crew was talking about. I peered in the window. I could make out stacks of boxes and a large floor mixer like the one in the kitchen at the pie shop.

'Can I help you?' A woman's voice behind me made me jump. I turned and saw a plump woman in her mid-sixties. Her dark hair was streaked with gray, and she wore it in a pile of curls on top of her head. She had sharp blue eyes.

'My name is Susanna.' I stretched out my hand.

'Alice.' She shook it with a crushing grip, and I tried not to wince.

'Are you opening something here?' I asked, hoping that

it was going to be something that would stay open past 8 p.m. For once, maybe I would have fresh gossip to share with the Morning Pie Crew.

She sized me up and looped her fingers through the straps on her denim overalls before answering, 'Just setting up my cookie shop. Hoping to open in a couple days.'

'Oh, that's great,' I said, trying to hide my disappointment. Not only did it sound like a place that would close early, but it also sounded like competition. I tried to force my most neighborly smile, thinking it would be what Aunt Erma would want me to do. 'I'm new in town too. I work at the pie shop down the street.'

I could have sworn her eyes narrowed for a second before she smiled. 'That's wonderful,' she said. 'I'm looking forward to stopping in and trying your pie.'

'Come on in anytime,' I said.

The silver cat appeared by Alice's feet, and she scooped her up. The cat yowled.

'This is my cat. I named her Cookie,' she said. How original, I thought. She stroked the cat's head while it struggled slightly in her grip.

'I've seen her around,' I said.

'Are you planning to enter the baking contest at the Fall Festival?' she asked.

'I don't know. I'm still honing my baking skills,' I said.

She nodded sympathetically. 'I wouldn't bother if I were you. My cookies are definitely going to win.'

My eyes widened. She had to be joking, but if she was, nothing on her face gave it away.

'Well, it was nice to meet you.' I hurried off down the street, not sure what else to say.

'You too,' she called after me, making my skin prickle.

When we got back to the apartment, I immediately flopped down on the sofa, the exhaustion of the day setting in. Then I sat straight up and grabbed my computer and found the online form to sign up for the baking contest. I hit the keyboard a little too hard as I entered in my information. I sat back, satisfied. I tried to picture the look on Alice's face when I beat her.

Chapter 6

Dear Elodie,

Let me open by saying I do not like cats. They're creepy and hairy and their eyes always look angry. All my nightmares usually feature a cat. They are truly horrifying, even when they're kittens. That being said, in general, I am quite the animal lover. What I don't love is when people let their animals run free. There is a cat in the neighborhood that just wanders the streets. She apparently has a home, but the woman who owns her can't keep her contained and doesn't seem to understand what a huge problem that is. I keep seeing the cat outside my door, and she's not bothered when I try to shoo her away.

Should I call animal control or just suck it up and accept that I'm going to be tormented by this cat on a regular basis?

Sincerely,

Crazy Cat-less Lady

Dear Crazy Cat-less Lady,
You didn't say if you've directly spoken with the cat's owner. Maybe you can explain to her your concerns for the cat. You could also try recommending that she find a new home for it if she doesn't have the time to take care of it properly. Calling animal control seems a little extreme. Perhaps you should also consider talking to a professional who can help you work through your deep dislike of cats.
Ask and I'll Answer,
Elodie

The next day started out with a bang, quite literally. I heard a loud crash in the kitchen and went running downstairs in my polka dot pajamas with Mitzy close at my heels. I slid down the last few stairs and fell through the door at the bottom.

I startled a twenty-something year old man who was stacking boxes that had fallen off his dolly. He let out a little squeak and jumped back making his straight brown hair flop into his large green eyes.

'Who are you?' I demanded as Mitzy, the ever-helpful guard dog, hid behind my feet.

'I'm Stan,' he said, composing himself.

'Why are you in my kitchen, Stan?' I demanded, searching the counter tops for a weapon, but the kitchen was obnoxiously clean. Thanks, mystery night cleaners.

'I'm the delivery guy. You must be the niece.' He spoke in a soft voice, and I had to lean in a little to hear him. He extended his hand, ignoring my hostile tone. He was very tall and very skinny. I wondered briefly if I could get him to check the attic space in Aunt Erma's apartment for the pie recipes I still hadn't found.

'Oh,' I said, feeling a little silly. I had seen 'Delivery Day' written on Aunt Erma's calendar, but I assumed the delivery would happen during my waking hours. I shook his hand, which was a little cold and clammy, and he went back to stacking up the boxes and sacks of flour. 'You deliver on a Sunday?'

'We might be a small town, but this is still a pretty happening place,' he said.

'What are you delivering?'

He glanced over at the clipboard he had set down on the counter. 'Flour, sugar, brown sugar, blueberries, strawberries, apples, chocolate, cream, eggs, butter, coffee, and canned pumpkin.' He ticked them off. 'I will have to get some of these things in the fridge right away.'

'Why does that one box say "frozen peas" on it?' I asked, pointing.

'Oh, fiddling fiddlesticks,' Stan exclaimed. I tried to hide my smile at his very G-rated agitation. 'I must have grabbed the wrong boxes this morning,' he explained. 'I'm going to have to go back to the warehouse to get the right ones.'

He began to stack the boxes back on his two-wheeler. For such a skinny guy, he seemed to be very strong, lifting large boxes as though they were empty.

'Wait, that one says butter on it,' I said, pointing at the box he was holding. He flipped it around to read it.

'Oh, you're right. I must have gotten some of the right boxes. Hurray!' He sorted the boxes into two piles. One to return to the warehouse, and one to leave with me. In the end I got the flour, the pumpkin, half the order of strawberries, and one stick of butter. I don't know how it happened, but the large box labeled butter only had one stick inside. Stan made notes amending the delivery on his sheet, and I signed it. He left after assuring me that he would return with the rest of the order for the pie shop, eventually.

He said he had to get Bob his delivery because 'you know how Bob can get,' and then he would swing by the next six stops because they were right on the way back to the warehouse. Somewhere in there he figured he would probably need lunch because when his blood sugar got low he forgot to use his turn signal and apparently Sheriff Buddy had been ticketing people lately for not using their turn signal.

After he left, I grabbed the sack of flour to put it away and fell over because it was so heavy. How did Aunt Erma do this at her age? Mitzy, well-trained in health code regulations, understood that she needed to stay out of the kitchen and sat watching me from the bottom of the stairs where I had left the door open after my less than graceful entrance.

I checked my supplies. I was not going to get through the day without the rest of the delivery, but Stan didn't inspire a lot of confidence that he would return in a timely fashion. I was going to have to venture out to the grocery store.

At the store, I grabbed a cart and frantically began throwing things inside. Apples, bananas, blueberries, sugar, butter. Anything that looked like it might go into a pie went in my cart. I wondered if the same person who kept cleaning the kitchen would also assemble these ingredients into delicious pies. Like the story, *The Elves and the Shoemaker*. I could try leaving all the ingredients on the counter tonight and maybe I'd wake up to completely baked pies. I could almost hear Aunt Erma gasp in horror when I grabbed an armload of frozen pie crusts and tossed them in the cart. On a whim, I threw in a frozen pizza for dinner tonight.

'You seem to be doing a good job on the fruits, but your cart could really use a few more leafy greens.' I heard a voice say behind me. I turned around and saw a woman in a Basil's Market apron studying my cart. Her name tag said, 'Luanne.' She was an older woman, probably around Aunt Erma's age, with chin-length gray hair that had a bright blue streak through it. She was thin and looked like someone who had spent a lot of time doing yoga.

'What?' I asked.

'I could grab you some kale, maybe a little romaine. Then you could make a nice salad to go along with your dinner.' She motioned towards the frozen pizza.

'Mom, leave her alone.' Holly appeared from around the corner, also wearing a Basil's Market apron.

'Humph.' The older woman stomped off, grumbling.

'Sorry about my mother,' Holly said. 'She thinks everyone is her child.'

'No problem,' I laughed. 'She's right. I don't get enough vegetables.'

'How are things going at the pie shop?' she asked.

'I haven't burned the place down yet. That's about the extent of my accomplishments so far,' I said.

'You sound like you need a night out. Want to grab drinks with me on Tuesday?' she asked. 'Sal's should be open.'

'Sounds great,' I said. We made plans to meet up in a couple of days, and I hurried to finish my shopping.

I dumped all my groceries in the kitchen and ran upstairs. I poured myself a giant mug of coffee, got a quick pep talk from Mitzy and her tail, and rushed back down to get to work.

I lined up all the ingredients for the first pie on the counter. With a deep breath, I tried to channel my inner Aunt Erma. I left the back door unlocked, but not open. I was hoping Henry would stop by. I could use both his company and his baking expertise today.

The pumpkin pie recipe looked easy enough, so I began with that. The only thing I found a little confusing was the evaporated milk. I pulled the gallon of milk I had bought out of the fridge. How in the world do you evaporate milk? After a quick search on the internet I found that I could have just bought cans of something called evaporated milk. I let out a frustrated sigh. I should have been watching the cooking channel more often.

Luckily there were also recipes for turning regular milk into evaporated milk. It didn't look hard, and I decided it would be easier than heading back to the grocery store. I didn't want another lecture from Holly's mother. I measured the milk and put it on the stove to simmer and turned my attention back to the other ingredients. I mixed things together for the pumpkin pie filling. The preparation time listed at the top of the recipe mocked my slowness. At least the pie crusts were already prepared. I thought of the frozen ones in the freezer.

I was daydreaming about being back in my pajamas when I noticed a burning smell. I turned around just in time to see the milk boiling over onto the stove. It happened so fast. Boiled milk spread all across the stove sizzling as it hit the hot burner and filled the shop with a terrible smell.

On a positive note, this could probably be considered one of the regular tests of the smoke detectors that the firefighters advised me to conduct. The ear-piercing beeps filled the shop as I turned off the stove and frantically waved a towel at the ceiling. They turned off quickly, but I called the fire department just to make sure they wouldn't come out again.

A woman with a raspy voice answered. I explained what had happened. I heard a strange noise. Was she laughing?

'Hold please,' she said. She must have just put her hand over the receiver because I could hear her recounting the story I had just told her.

'She should open an ice cream shop for the safety of everyone in town,' someone shouted. More roaring laughter.

'I'm still here,' I shouted into the phone.

The woman came back on the line and asked me if I was sure there wasn't any fire anywhere.

'No, nothing. I'm sorry to bother you,' I said a little bitterly.

'Talk to you tomorrow,' she said and hung up.

I was running out of time before the shop was supposed to open, and all I had was six half-made pumpkin pies. I grabbed my coat off the hook and took off through the back door towards the grocery store. As I ran, people stopped and stared, but I didn't have time to worry about that now. I rushed through the aisles of the store until I found the evaporated milk. I grabbed an armful of cans and headed to the checkout where Luanne was waiting for me.

'Back again?' she asked.

'Yup,' I said breathlessly.

'You know what you need to try?' She carefully examined each can before scanning it.

A grocery store with a self-checkout lane? I thought. 'What?' I asked, trying to keep the edge out of my voice.

'You should try using almond milk as a substitute for evaporated milk.' She paused and held the second to the last can she needed to scan in her hands. 'I've heard that you can boil it down and not only is it healthier because it's plant based, but I bet it would give your pies a lovely nutty flavor.' She was still holding the can in her hand.

'I'll keep that in mind. Thanks.' I held cash in my hand, hoping it would speed her up.

'Would you like to run back and grab some almond

74

milk now?' she asked earnestly. 'It's just right back there next to the regular milk.'

'No, thanks.' I was hopping from one leg to another as my impatience grew. 'I'm kind of in a hurry.'

'Oh.' She looked offended. 'I just thought you might like a little friendly advice, that's all.' She scanned the can in her hand. One more to go. 'You could probably try it with soy milk too,' she offered.

'Maybe next time, thanks.' I threw my money down on the counter and grabbed the cans she had scanned.

'Wait, I can bag those for you,' she said.

'No need,' I called over my shoulder, and with that, I was out the door. More heads turned, and people pointed as I ran down the street. They were probably just marveling at my speed. I ran on the cross-country team for a few weeks in high school. As I recall, I could hold my own. I eventually quit the team though because I realized how boring it was to run for longer than ten minutes at time.

The pie shop still smelled like burnt milk when I got back. I considered lighting a candle, but couldn't risk having an open flame.

I froze as I caught a glimpse of my reflection in the stainless-steel refrigerator. I was still wearing my purple sparkly apron. Even more horrifying, I was still wearing my hairnet. Great, now I was going to be the crazy hairnet lady.

I didn't have time to worry about that now though. I opened the back door all the way to air out the smell and quickly got to work. I had six pumpkin pies completed by the time I was unlocking the front door. They looked a little lumpy, but I figured I could cover that up with a heaping pile of whipped cream.

I wrote pumpkin pie in big letters on the chalkboard out front and mentally practiced my spiel selling it so by the time I was done people wouldn't even want any other kind of pie.

I greeted each customer that came in with a, 'Doesn't this chilly fall day make you crave a piece of pumpkin pie?' With most people, it worked. A few scrunched up their noses and left. I assured them that there would be a wider selection tomorrow. I hoped that was true. The Morning Pie Crew was very supportive.

'I was craving pumpkin pie,' Flora said.

'Me too,' Lena chimed in.

'It's a perfect choice to get us in the mood for Thanksgiving,' Mr Barnes said.

But I saw the concerned glances they exchanged when they thought I wasn't looking.

'Are you giving these out?' A woman with dark curly hair walked in holding a bright pink flyer. 'There's a box of them outside your door.'

She handed it to me, and I read the words, 'Cookie Castle Grand Opening tomorrow! We have so many delicious options to choose from! Bring in this flier for a free cookie.'

'No, I'm certainly not giving these out.' I threw the flyer down on the counter. I noticed her pick it up, fold it, and stick it in her purse. I hurried outside and sure enough there was a large box of brightly colored fliers sitting next to the front door. I picked it up, grunting under the weight, carried it back through the kitchen, and dropped it on the floor by the desk.

Alice was going to hear about this.

I was washing dishes in the apartment while my pizza baked, wishing the mystery cleaners would clean upstairs, when my phone rang in the living room. I quickly dried my hands on a towel and threw myself across the sofa to reach my phone, answering it just before it went to voice-mail. I was desperately hoping to hear Aunt Erma's voice on the other end of the line.

'Susie, where are you? We need you back here now,' Hal's booming voice demanded. I kicked myself for answering my phone without checking the caller ID first.

'Sorry, Hal. I still need a few more days,' I said, heading back to the kitchen.

'The Steadmans picked different door knobs for their addition, and they want you to install them,' he said.

'Have Josh do it,' I suggested.

'They asked for you.'

'I know they're a big client,' I moaned.

'Our biggest.'

'I'll call them and apologize,' I offered.

'If you're not back at work tomorrow, I'm going to have to fire you,' Hal said.

I took a deep shaky breath. 'I'm not going to be back tomorrow.'

'I'm sorry, but you're fired,' he barked, not sounding sorry at all.

I hung up, tempted to throw my phone at the wall, but settled for letting out a frustrated growl instead.

I ran to the oven, suddenly remembering my pizza.

'Son of a...' I began and growled again instead of finishing that sentence with the intended expletive. I pulled it out of the toaster oven and picked around for a minute thinking that maybe I could find one corner to munch on to soothe my growling stomach, but nothing. The cheese on the top of the pizza was burned beyond edibility, and that was saying something because I wasn't picky.

I had to get it out of the apartment. The burning smell was filling the space quickly. Even Mitzy looked disgusted and I had just seen her licking a place that certainly couldn't smell like roses.

I grabbed the burnt pizza, carefully balancing it on the piece of cardboard and stomped down the stairs and out the back door. I threw the pizza in the dumpster and slammed the lid twice for good measure.

'Whoa, what did the dumpster do to you?' Henry appeared next to me, his eyes a little wide.

'Trust me, he had it coming,' I said. 'Let that be a warning to you. Don't get on my bad side.'

'I'll keep that in mind,' he said. His dark eyes twinkled with amusement and I stared into them perhaps a second longer than social convention allowed. He shifted the large tote bag he was carrying from one arm to the other. 'How's your night going? Do you want to talk about it? Or should

I just tell you where all the other dumpsters in town are so you can beat them up too?'

'I got fired from my job back home, I'm terrible at my job here, and I burnt my dinner,' I said, motioning to the dumpster. 'So that's how my night's going.' I sighed and leaned back against the brick wall, crossing my arms against the cold. 'Is the grocery store still open?' I asked hopefully. If it wasn't, I would have to eat pie for dinner. I knew no one was going to cry any tears for me over that, but I was really hoping for a good meal before the dessert portion of the evening.

He grimaced. 'Sorry, they closed an hour ago.' Of course they did. 'But here,' he said as he eagerly reached into his bag and produced a couple containers. 'Take some of this food.'

'I couldn't,' I said, but I smiled at his sweet, earnest offer.

'No please, take some. There are a couple women at the nursing home who insist on cooking for me because I'm a single man, and despite the fact that I've cooked several meals at the nursing home when our cook calls in sick, they still don't think I'm capable of doing anything with food other than eat it.' He handed me the containers. 'It's a little old-fashioned if you ask me, but I haven't been able to change their minds after all these years, and my freezer is full.'

'OK,' I agreed, after what I hoped was a polite hesitation.

'And another plus,' he added, 'is that their food is always really soft, so you barely have to chew. That can be a nice bonus if you're tired.'

I smiled. Whatever was in those containers had to be better than the stale crackers I had eaten as a snack this afternoon. I took the containers out of his hands.

'Thank you. This is so nice,' I said. He hesitated for a minute, and I wondered if I should invite him up. My head was still spinning after being fired and I wasn't sure I was in the best mood for company, so I let the moment pass while wondering if I would regret it later.

He said goodbye and promised to stop in the next day for pie.

Chapter 7

Day 6 — Monday, November 7th

Dear Elodie,

I'm trying to launch my music career, but it turns out there's not a lot of interest in Pig Latin rap these days. I know in my heart this is what I'm meant to be doing. My family is trying to make me give up and go to school for engineering.

So, what do you think? Should I go back to school or should I ollowfay ymay reamsday?

Sincerely,

Appingray Reamerday or Engineer?

Dear Appingray Reamerday or Engineer?

I know it's easy to follow the path that your family lays out for you, but real bravery and happiness comes from following your dreams.

Sometimes you have to take some side jobs to make ends meet, but never lose sight of your goals. Happiness is so important. Never give up on yourself.

Ask and I'll Answer,
Elodie

The next day the Morning Pie Crew came in first thing in the morning. Little did I know at the time that they would be the only customers who would walk through the door all day.

'Do you think I should talk to the police?' I asked.

Lena pursed her lips.

'I don't think it's come to that yet,' Flora said. 'Erma probably just got caught up longer than she expected. I wouldn't worry about it.'

Mr Barnes put his hand on my arm, and I felt wave of calm wash over me.

'OK,' I agreed before I could stop myself.

'Who is the Pig Latin rapper in town?' Flora asked, pulling out her newspaper.

'Probably the Warner kid,' Lena said. 'Janet is always crowing about how her little David is going to be an engineer.'

'It could be that woman who works at the diner sometimes. What's her name? The one who pushes her poodle around in a stroller,' Mr Barnes said.

'Nina,' Lena offered.

'Right, Nina. I've heard her speak in Pig Latin after a few beers at Sal's,' he said.

We spent a long time discussing whether or not parents should pressure their children to do one job if their children wanted to do something else. My mother wasn't thrilled with the idea of me going to trade school to become a handyman, but she couldn't argue that I was really good at fixing things. She always thought I should become a lawyer like her instead of following in my dad's footsteps. I could never complain to her about work because she would always use the opportunity to tell me I would have been happier in a more 'elite' job. I was never sure what an 'elite' job would get me besides less comfortable work clothes.

Once they were gone, I wandered around aimlessly for a while before wiping off all the tables ... again. Then I stared out the window. I tried to imagine what Aunt Erma would do when the shop was empty. Then I wondered if that ever happened to her or if, because her pie was so amazing, there was a constant line of people wanting more.

I looked around the shop. A broken table leg caught my eye. Now there was something that I could fix. Relieved to be back in my comfort zone, I found a piece of paper and wrote a to-do list, including things I would need from the hardware store. Besides the table, there were a few small holes in the sheetrock, a leak under the kitchen sink (a problem Aunt Erma had solved by putting a coffee tin below it), and the small table the cash register sat on desperately needed to be repainted. I grabbed the 'Back in 10 minutes' sign and hung it on the door.

I was making the walk to the hardware store just two doors over, when curiosity got the best of me. I went to the end of the street, tiptoeing as I approached the corner and peered around it.

Just as I feared. There was a crowd around the cookie shop.

Was that Tanner O'Connell playing the harmonica out front under the grand opening banner? He paused his playing to sing a few lines about the delicious wonders you could find in the cookie shop.

Just yesterday, I had given him an extra dollop of whipped cream on his pumpkin pie. Didn't a dollop mean anything to anyone anymore?

People milled around happily munching cookies, many holding bags with more cookies. I could hear the loud 'yums' from here. I felt slightly guilty for wishing they would all end up with food poisoning.

I turned back down the street to the hardware store. Lena greeted me cheerfully when I walked in.

'Missed me already?' she asked.

'Of course,' I answered.

I surveyed the shop and felt at home. Shiny new tools lined the shelves. The shelves were painted varying shades of purple, which it turned out was Lena's favorite color. I could see bottles of different flavored soft drinks selling for seventy-five cents each in the window of a vending machine by the front door. A sign above the vending machine read, 'Enjoy a pop while you shop.' There was a row of shiny new red snow blowers displayed near the front.

With Lena's help, I searched through bins of screws and aisles of wall patch, light bulbs, and spray foam. She mixed up a couple colors of paint for me, one to match the table and one for the walls. Then she showed me the corner that had scrap wood, and I was able to find the perfect piece to fix the table.

'Erma's going to be so happy with the work you're doing,' Lena said with a glowing smile as she rang me up.

I forced a smile, hoping Aunt Erma would only see the things I fixed when she got back. Perhaps some new paint would distract her from the fact that I'd lost all her customers. I tried to push the image of the crowd outside the cookie shop out of my mind.

I carried my purchases back over to the pie shop. It didn't look like anyone had missed me while I was gone.

I was in the zone for the next few hours, fixing every broken thing I could find as I listened to Nineties pop music. It was pure bliss. Well, mostly bliss. Occasionally lyrics from a song would remind me of Alice and her stupid cookie shop. The table soon stood on four solid, even legs. I brought the stack of encyclopedias that had been keeping the table upright upstairs to put on a bookshelf and groaned when I saw Mitzy laying on one of my sweatshirts. I could have sworn that sweatshirt had been in my still zipped suitcase.

I shooed her off, and Mitzy reluctantly moved. I had to admit, she looked pretty proud of herself though. I shook off the fur and hung the sweatshirt high on a hook in the bathroom before going back downstairs.

As closing time approached, I was only mostly exhausted, a huge step up from the days before. I was cleaning off some paint brushes when the phone rang. It was Henry.

'I really hate to bother you, but I haven't been able to get away today. I was wondering if you would mind bringing five pies to the nursing home? I would really owe you!' He sounded desperate.

'No problem,' I assured him, even though my feet were protesting the idea of walking anywhere other than upstairs to the sofa.

'Great.' He sounded relieved. 'Things can get really ugly over here if people don't get their Monday night pie.'

He gave me directions to the nursing home. I didn't even have to write them down. It was easy to remember directions in a town the size of a thimble.

I finished closing up, gave Mitzy some food and attention, and changed out of my flour covered clothes before packing up the pies and heading to the nursing home. I could smell the pies through their boxes, and my stomach growled. I had three custard and two cherry. I had sampled both kinds earlier in the day. The cherry had a crumble topping made of brown sugar, flour, and butter, and that had gotten a little too hard when I accidentally left the pies in the oven too long. I overcompensated with the custard and took them out too early which resulted in a slightly squishy filling. They were all edible, I repeatedly reassured myself on the walk.

I got there quickly. There was a wooden sign out front with 'Enchanted Woods' stamped on it in thick gold letters. It was a large brick building that looked more like a mansion than a nursing home. I walked up the ramp to the door, and as soon as I stepped inside, I felt the heat.

How warm did they keep it in here? It had to be at least 85 degrees!

A pleasant blonde woman at the front desk directed me toward the dining room down the hall. I thanked her and headed in that direction. I noticed it didn't smell like most nursing homes I had been in before. When I was growing up, my grandfather had been in a nursing home for six years. I used to visit him a couple times a week to read to him. That place smelled like depression and death. I would try to take shallow breaths until my nose got used to the smell and didn't notice it anymore. This place smelled like orange blossoms though. I peeked through doorways half expecting to see a grove of orange trees.

The dining room was inviting, and I stood just inside to take it all in. A fire crackled in the corner and fresh flowers filled vases at the center of five round wooden tables. The whole back wall was a shelf crammed full of books. There were a few residents talking and laughing. A man in a maroon sweater vest and large glasses, whose face was more wrinkled than not, was juggling flaming batons. I felt my heart begin to race. No more fires, I thought. Somehow the fire department would blame me for this.

Henry was standing near a table with three little old ladies. He turned to the juggling man. 'Harold, I said no fires,' he called. I don't know how Harold doused the flames, but the fire disappeared, and he was juggling rainbow colored balls instead.

Henry went back to the group of ladies. He was very animated, telling a story with lots of big hand gestures. He spoke loudly and distinctly. At one point, he filled his cheeks up with air and the whole table hooted. I smiled as I walked closer with my stack of pies. He looked up and noticed me.

'Susie, we're so glad you're here!' he exclaimed. 'I'd like you to meet Sandy Kay, Bernie Clausen, and Claire Sprinkles.'

'Hello everyone!' I said. 'Ms Sprinkles, that's such a wonderfully unusual name!'

'It was my stage name, dear,' she told me with a dazzling smile. She had bright red hair and teeth so white I almost had to look away.

'Oh, were you an actress?' I asked her.

'Of sorts,' she said as she wiggled her eyebrows at me.

I didn't understand until Sandy leaned over to me and stage whispered behind her hand, 'She was more of a dancer.'

'A pole dancer,' hooted Bernie.

'And I was good,' Claire told me. 'This one—' she pointed at Henry '—gets embarrassed when I start to talk about my old life, but if you ever want to hear any of my stories, I have some really spicy ones.'

The other women nodded in agreement. My smile froze.

'I see you brought our pies. Let me take those from you.' Henry smoothly switched the topic and carefully grabbed the stack from my arms. 'I'll just get these all set up on the buffet table, and then I'll walk you out.'

'Great,' I said.

Residents had begun to gather in the room and most of them were closely watching the boxes of pie. I put my hands on my hips in an attempt to keep the sweat from accumulating under my armpits.

'Have a seat,' the woman named Sandy said as she pulled out a chair for me. 'Tell us what it's like to be young!'

I laughed and sat down. They began to grill me with questions about myself, my job, and my love life. How long did it take for someone to slice and set out a few pies? Sandy was telling me about her son. The nicest young man you could ever meet, a doctor, and he was just waiting for a lovely young woman like me to settle down and start a family.

'Oh, your son isn't a real doctor. He's just got his PhD in some business psychology mumbo jumbo,' Ms Sprinkles said. 'Plus, she's too young to settle down. She needs to be out there sowing her wild oats.'

Every part of this conversation was making me uncomfortable. I casually backed up my chair a little bit and looked over towards the buffet. Henry was still carefully serving up the pies and arranging the slices in neat rows on the table.

'Maybe I should go and help Henry serve the pie,' I said as I began to stand up. Bernie, who had been pretty quiet up until now, grabbed my arm and pulled me back to my seat. She was surprisingly strong for being such a small, frail-looking woman.

'Nonsense! He's fine,' she said to me. She took a deep breath, her eyes closed, and her tone changed. 'You need to dust the cat.' She released her grip on my arm, and her eyes fluttered open. 'Don't forget what I told you,' she said forcefully. The other two women exchanged an uncomfortable look, and I wondered if Bernie was slipping into dementia. I smiled at her.

'Thank you. I'll get right on that,' I assured her.

Just then, Henry came back. 'If you're ready to leave, I can walk you out,' he said.

'Well ladies, it's been a pleasure talking to you.' I stood up and backed away quickly.

'Remember if you need any tips on how to please a man, just come and see me. I had them install a pole in my room upstairs, and I can show you some of my best moves,' Claire Sprinkles said with a little shimmy of her shoulders. My eyes widened.

'I'll show you a picture of my son next time you come,' Sandy said with a wink.

'Don't forget about the cat,' Bernie said, her brow furrowed.

I waved goodbye and rushed out of there with Henry close behind me.

The woman at the front desk was gone. I turned to Henry. He was looking into my eyes and I felt a little shiver run through me. He was really quite handsome.

'How are you?' He had the kindest eyes, and I felt like he wanted a genuine answer.

I automatically answered, 'Good,' and then I paused. 'Well, I think I'm OK,' I amended. He encouraged me to go on and I spilled my guts about the cookie shop and my fears of failing Aunt Erma.

'This is just a small bump in the road,' he said. 'I haven't known you very long, but I already know you're brave and amazing, and I have no doubt you'll be able to get all the customers back and then some.'

I felt a lump at the back of my throat. His kind words were exactly what I needed to hear tonight.

'Thanks,' I said softly.

'Thank you so much for delivering the pies,' he said. 'It has been an absolute madhouse here today!' He gave my arm a gentle squeeze.

'No problem,' I said but hoped he wouldn't need me to do it again anytime soon. I was terrified at the prospect of Claire dragging me up to her room to pole dance.

I was startled out of my pie high that night when my cell phone rang. I sighed when I saw it was my mother's home number. Ignoring her calls had become a habit since I'd got to Hocus Hills, but if I didn't answer soon, she was bound to make a police report or send out search parties.

I muted the drama-filled reality show I was watching, where the guy was so in love and the girl was just playing him, and sat up straighter on the sofa. Mitzy sensed my movement and assumed it meant I dropped food. She leapt to her feet and eyed me intently.

'Hello,' I said, trying hard not to sound like I was annoyed.

'Susanna, finally.' My mother's exasperated voice hit me. 'I've been trying to call you for days.' I could almost hear my mother pacing around her bedroom upstairs on her cordless phone.

'What's up?' I was eager to get this conversation over with.

'What's up? What do you mean, "What's up?" Where have you been? I tried to stop by your apartment, but you weren't there. I have been calling you, but no answer. I've been worried.' My mother said it all in a tone that indicated her worry was a huge inconvenience for her.

'I've been busy.' I played with the fringe on the corner of the purple blanket. Mitzy had decided I was not about to feed her pie and curled up on my lap. It was soothing. I was beginning to see the benefit of having a dog.

'Susanna Penelope Maxine Bennett Daniels,' I cringed as my mother used all five of my names. Who gave their kid five names? What kind of baggage was that for them to carry around their whole lives? 'I want to know exactly where you are and what you've been doing! Are you on drugs? Have you joined a cult?' Her voice lowered in horror. 'Are you a Scientologist now?'

'No, Mom, nothing like that.'

'Well, what then?' she demanded.

'I am at Aunt Erma's,' I said, reassuring myself silently that I was a grown-up who could make these decisions without her mother's approval. My shoulders still tensed as I waited for her reaction.

'Why?' she demanded. Her voice reached the low angry tone I had only elicited a couple times in my life ▢ once when I lied about spending the night with a boy, and once when I had punched a girl on the playground in middle school.

'She needed help in the pie shop. She had to go away for a while.' I decided to keep my explanations short and simple. It was the safest way with my mother.

'She's not there? Where is she?' she demanded.

'I don't know,' I answered truthfully, but it sounded like a lie even to my ears. 'What happened between you two? Why won't you tell me?'

'Because it's none of your business,' she said. 'But trust me, you need to stay away from her.'

'I told her I would help. If you can't give me a real reason why I should leave, I'm going to stay,' I said.

'Why would you do this?' My mother was almost hysterical now.

'Do what?'

'Just come back to the city,' she insisted.

'I'll be back when I can,' I tried in a soothing tone, but my mother's frustration was palpable through the phone.

We hung up, and I went back to my pie. I chewed, not really tasting it – tragic. I had even more questions than answers now.

Well, at least now my mother knew where I was.

Chapter 8

Day 7 — Tuesday, November 8th

Dear Elodie,

You'll never believe what my niece did today. She went into my room and stole my favorite teddy bear. I know I'm 42 and she's only 7, and I should be an adult about this, but I just hate when other people touch my stuff.

I took my teddy bear back from her and explained the importance of boundaries. Now my brother is angry. He thinks I should just let my niece have the bear, but I think it's important for her to learn young that she can't always have everything she wants.

Who's right? Should I give my niece the teddy bear and risk her growing up to be a selfish monster? Or do I keep it and risk my brother cutting me out of their lives?

Sincerely,

My Bear or Share Bear?

Dear My Bear or Share Bear?

I understand where you're coming from. Kids shouldn't just be given everything they ever wanted. However, is a teddy bear really worth destroying your family over? Maybe you could give her the teddy bear (either that one or a different one if that particular one holds sentimental value) and then ask her to give you something in return. Make it a fun game that will teach her the joys of sharing.

Ask and I'll Answer,
Elodie

I turned the page of the newspaper and groaned when I saw an ad for Alice's cookie shop in big bold letters. 'Sick of having the same old boring pie for dessert day in and day out? Come to the Cookie Castle where we have fresh exciting new flavors every day! There's something for everyone, even your dog or cat! Stop by today!'

I had to admit that the picture of cookies at the bottom of the ad was tempting, but that didn't stop me from ripping the page out of the newspaper and tearing it into tiny bits. Wasn't that psychiatrist on television always saying that you needed to find healthy expressions of your emotions instead of keeping them inside. This was healthy, wasn't it? I pounded the confetti pile of paper into the table with my fist. Healthy expressions, I told myself.

I drummed my fingers against the display case. No one had come into the shop today except for the Morning Pie Crew. That left me with plenty of time to consider my options to boost business. I grabbed a piece of paper and a pen from the desk in the back. I doodled several pictures of hammers and screwdrivers and a few daisies before jotting down a few ideas, including making a specials board for the sidewalk. I headed towards the hardware store.

I took the long way there, attempting a casual stroll as I rounded the corner to the town square so I could see if the cookie shop was as busy as yesterday. The line was out the door again. I don't know why I tortured myself like this.

With a new wave of determination, I turned and quickly walked back towards the hardware store. Thanksgiving was only a couple of weeks away, and I knew my customers would come back. Pie was tradition. People liked tradition. I just had to keep the pie shop going until then.

'This is becoming a habit,' Lena greeted me when I walked through the door.

I walked past a couple who was heading out the door carrying a paper bag. They both had graying brown hair. The man gave me a small nod and smile, but the woman gave me an icy stare. Her sharp green eyes sent a shiver through me.

As soon as they were out the door, Lena went into full on gossip mode. 'Those were Stan's parents. They come in a few times each year to visit from the big city,' she began with a meaningful nod as though that should be enough to elicit some kind of reaction from me.

'Oh, sure,' I said uncertainly.

'His mother always goes on and on about how "charming" it is here. I hate when people call our town "charming." Even the word "quaint" was bandied about.' She rolled her eyes. 'They might as well call all of us residents "cute" too.' She contorted her face into such a look of disgust that I couldn't help but giggle. 'His dad just wanted to know where he could get the best pizza in town, as though we have more than one option for pizza. Then they bought a wrench and some mason jars.'

Lena helped me find everything I needed, then I paid for the supplies. When I got back to the shop, Alice was lurking in the alley.

'Hi Alice,' I greeted her flatly.

'Susanna, I'm so glad I caught you.' Her smile was warm, but I didn't trust her.

'What can I do for you?' I tried to keep the edge out of my tone as I set down my supplies.

'I just wanted to stop by and bring you some cookies.' She held up a white paper bag that had the words 'Cookie Castle' stamped on the side in gold letters. 'I know we got off on the wrong foot, and that's probably my fault.' I almost snorted. *Probably*? 'I just wanted to drop these off and say that I hope we can be good neighbors, and I can't wait to meet your aunt if she ever returns.' The 'if' didn't slip past me unnoticed.

'Thanks,' I said, unable to keep a hint of sarcasm out of my tone as I took the bag from her.

Just then, Alice's cell phone beeped. She glanced at the screen. 'I really have to get back to the shop. I don't have the luxury of coming and going all day from my shop like you do. It must be so relaxing,' she said. 'Enjoy the cookies.'

I fumed as I watched her go. I opened the bag. There were cookies shaped like turkeys in there. She was trying to take the Thanksgiving market. I was angry with her and furious with myself for thinking they looked delicious. Maybe just one bite?

Then I remembered the box of flyers Alice had left in front of the pie shop, and I took one of the cookies out of the bag and set it on the floor. I found my hammer and carefully hammered it into a million tiny crumbs. Healthy expressions of rage, I told myself, sweeping up the crumbs.

I left the rest of the cookies in the bag on the desk and went to work building a chalkboard sign that could be set out on the sidewalk. I would call this phase one of my plan. In my imagination, one of the phases involved taking a bulldozer to the Cookie Castle.

The sign looked good when I was done. I used all the colors of chalk to write out today's pie flavors. I'd even drawn a picture of a pie that wasn't half bad. I set it out on the sidewalk and stood there for a minute half hoping that a horde of people would come running over for pie. When that didn't happen, I went inside.

A little while later I saw Sheriff Buddy in front of the shop looking at the sign. The sign was working! He was probably trying to decide what to order. Maybe he'd even get a whole pie. I stood behind the display case waiting for him to come in. Then he pulled out a tape measure and measured from the building to the edge of the sign. What was he doing?

He saw me watching him and stepped inside.

'Hi Sheriff, what can I do for you today?' I pointed to the pies in the case. 'Anything look good?'

'Sure, they all look good, but I still have a few more pounds to go before I meet my goal for the weight loss challenge,' he said, patting his stomach. I groaned inwardly. 'I'm here on business anyway.'

'What's wrong?' My heart began to race. Was he going to tell me something bad had happened to Aunt Erma? I felt tears prickling at my eyes.

'You need to move your sign.'

I blinked. 'What?'

'According to the city code, there has to be a four-foot walkway between the building and the edge of the sidewalk. The way you have your sign placed right now, there's only a three-foot, ten-inch walkway,' he explained. 'We've had some complaints, so I had to come check it out.'

I had a couple ideas about who might be complaining.

'So, you want me to move my sign over two inches?' I asked.

'Yes,' he said, perfectly serious. 'Otherwise it's a safety hazard.' Some incoherent staticky mumblings came through his walkie talkie and he responded, 'I'll be right there.' Then he turned back to me. 'I have to go. A fight broke out at the cookie shop over the last snickerdoodle. I'll check back later.'

After he left, I grudgingly went out and nudged the sign

over a couple inches. Stan's mother was at the end of the street watching me. I waved, but she just kept staring. I shivered a little and went back inside.

Dear Elodie,

My good friend recently discovered that she has a snake infestation in her house. She assures me that the snakes are harmless, but I am terrified of them. She's even started to name them. The other day I was at her house for tea, and I went to the bathroom. While I was in there, a snake slithered out from under the bath mat. It would have scared the you-know-what out of me if I hadn't already gone to the bathroom. When I screamed, she said, 'Oh that's just Goomba being Goomba.'

I told her I won't come over anymore until she deals with this horrific situation. She has more of a live and let live philosophy and said the snakes will move out when they're good and ready.

What should I do? I hate to lose my friend over this, but I hate snakes even more.

Sincerely,
Scared of Slithering

Dear Scared of Slithering,

Everyone is afraid of different things. Maybe your friend sees them as family, or maybe she wants them to keep her insect population in check. Either way, if she isn't willing to deal with them for your comfort, suggest that you meet at a restaurant or invite her over to your house. This doesn't have to be a deal breaker in your friendship.

If she insists on bringing her snakes with her to the restaurant or to your house, that might be a deal breaker.

Ask and I'll Answer,

Elodie

Later that day I heard the bell out front tinkle and jumped up from my spot where I was catching up on past Ask Elodie columns.

A woman in a dark green knitted hat stood out front. Her light brown curly hair poked out the sides. She was weighed down by two canvas bags.

I greeted her with a wide smile, so excited to have another customer. 'What can I get for you?' I asked.

'Oh honey, I don't need any more desserts. My bags are already full of cookies from that delightful shop. Have you tried it? I sampled every flavor they had and then proceeded to buy a dozen of each kind. I'm going to give them to all my friends back home. I'll be the star of the knitting club!' she babbled on excitedly. 'I was just wondering if you could give me directions to the grocery store. I want to buy some milk to go with all these cookies.'

I didn't even bother hiding my annoyance as I gave the woman directions, but she didn't seem to notice. She just kept smiling and peeking inside her bags to check on her cookies.

With a cheerful, 'Toodles,' she was off, and that was the last time the bell over the front door rang for the day.

A Slice of Magic

I pushed open the door to Sal's Bar. It was an eclectic place with creaky wooden floors and bright, sparkly pictures hung on the walls. There was a pool table in the corner, and the bar was long and made from dark stained wood.

I looked around and didn't see Holly. Not really surprising since in my eagerness, I had arrived ten minutes early.

A man in a green flannel shirt with slicked back sandy brown hair stood leaning against the corner of the bar like he owned the place. I guessed he was Sal.

'It's made from parts of the Titanic's hull,' Sal said rubbing his hand along the side of the bar when he saw me eyeing it.

'I thought the Titanic was made from steel,' I said, narrowing my eyes at him.

He paused, sizing me up. 'You got me there. It's made out of pieces of the Barnaby's old barn. You're pretty smart. Most people believe me.'

'Most people just think you're crazy and don't want to upset you.' A woman with thick curly blonde hair came out from the back. 'Is he trying to tell you that Titanic crap?'

I nodded.

'Oh, Sal.' She shook her head at him. 'You really need to work on some new material. He has a thing for Leonardo DiCaprio,' she told me.

'What can I say? That movie spoke to my soul,' he said. 'I have to stop watching before the end though. I can't stand it when the boat sinks. Tragic.' He looked down, letting out a deep sigh.

'Buck up. I can suggest some good movies with happy endings,' I said, patting him on the shoulder.

Holly walked through the door. We ordered margaritas and talked as though we were old friends. I told her about being fired from my job back home.

'It was kind of soul sucking, but at least I was good at it,' I said. She gave me the, 'you're better off without them, and they'll regret losing you,' spiel. Then she told me about her kooky mother and her secret life as a novelist.

'Romance novels, huh?' I said.

'Yeah, my biggest fans are my mother's friends.'

'I want to read your books!' I said.

'You might notice a few copies at your local grocery store.'

'Can I buy them tonight?' I stood up.

'It's closed now, you'll have to wait until tomorrow.' She pulled me back to my seat, laughing.

'I will buy them all first thing tomorrow,' I said.

'Maybe you should start with just one and see how that goes.' She took a large gulp of her margarita. 'I heard Gina's giving you a hard time,' Holly commented.

'What is with that woman?' I asked recalling my encounter with the muscular gym lady.

'She takes the word intense to a whole new level. We dated for a few months, but she broke up with me when I refused to sign up for a triathlon with her. Can you believe that? Who breaks up with someone for that?' she asked. My mouth dropped open. How could someone as nice as Holly date someone like Gina? 'Anyway,' she said, shaking her head, 'I heard the cookie shop opened.'

I nodded and carefully licked a little salt off the rim.

'Personally, I was hoping for a dance studio. I've been wanting to take tap for ages.'

'I wish it was a dance studio,' I wailed. 'The Morning Pie Crew is going to have to start ordering ten pies apiece if I'm going to keep the place in business until Aunt Erma gets back.'

'Cookies are just a fad, pies are forever,' Holly declared, holding her nearly empty glass in the air to accentuate her proclamation.

The server came to our table. 'Another round?' she asked

'Yes, please,' we chorused.

'Did I hear you say something about cookies?' she asked Holly.

Holly nodded, her mouth full of the last sip of her margarita.

'I was at that new shop today, and it was amazing! The best dessert I've ever had. Did you try the rocky road cookies? They were just to die for!' she gushed while collecting our empty glasses.

I saw a look of interest pass across Holly's face at the mention of rocky road cookies, but she quickly switched to indignance. 'No way, I prefer pie,' she said.

'Do you know anything about this new woman, Alice?' I asked after the server left.

'Look at you. Saying "new woman", as though that wasn't you just a few days ago,' Holly said.

I glared at her.

'She's kind of a mystery, actually. I've heard a lot of different theories around town about where she came from and why she's here,' Holly said. 'I think she's a spy.'

'Who's she spying for?' I asked.

Holly shrugged.

'I think she's running from the law,' I said.

'She could be a con artist. She has this quality about her that seems to attract people to her.'

'Yeah.' I glumly took a sip of my margarita.

'Don't worry about it.' Holly patted my arm. 'Erma's Pie Shop is a staple in this town. The cookie excitement will wear off after a few days.' She looked like she believed her words about as much as I did.

By the time I had finished my second margarita, I was feeling pretty good about my new life. So what if my pies were more of an acquired taste? This town had some really nice people in it, and as soon as Aunt Erma got back, she could teach me how to bake as well as she did.

I left Holly at the table and wandered back to the bathroom. To get there I had to go down a narrow hallway that was lined with paintings. I could have sworn that the man holding a dog in one of the paintings winked at me. I stopped and studied it for a second, but he didn't move again. It must have been the alcohol playing tricks on my mind.

It was quiet in the two-stall bathroom compared to the loud buzz of the bar. I could faintly hear the beat of the country music coming through the door. I don't know if it was the alcohol or the fact that I'd made a new friend, but my confidence was through the roof. I washed my hands and looked at myself in the mirror.

'Watch out world!' I said, 'You are looking good!' I did a little dance for my reflection. Then I heard a toilet flush.

Alice appeared in the doorway of the other stall. 'Don't let me interrupt,' she said, making her way to the other sink.

'Hi Alice,' I said through slightly gritted teeth. I was determined to be pleasant and not let her ruin my happiness.

'Did you eat the cookies I brought you?' she asked.

I thought about the crumbs in the garbage. 'No, I didn't. Sorry,' I said, unable to keep the sarcasm out of my voice.

A look of disappointment flickered across her face before she smiled angelically as she scrubbed her hands. 'You look great. Really well rested. Me, I'm exhausted. Nonstop customers today. I think it's great that you're able to be so upbeat, dancing and smiling, with everything that's happening. Did you pick that up in one of Mr Barnes's yoga classes?'

My jaw dropped, but no words came out. This was always how it was for me. I rarely came up with a good comeback on the spot, but give me three or four hours, and I would have a zinger ready to throw back at her. I turned to leave.

'I'm sorry if that came out the wrong way. I'm sure you'll give me a run for my money in the baking contest. After all, Erma must have taught you some of her baking secrets, didn't mustn't she?' Alice asked.

I gave her a noncommittal shrug. I wasn't willing to give her the satisfaction that I was pretty much flying blind here.

'Have you found the secret ingredients yet?' She pulled a paper towel out of the dispenser and carefully dried every finger.

'What are you talking about?' I turned back towards her, wondering if she was just trying to mess with me.

'Hm,' she said, sizing me up.

'What have you heard?' I hated that I was asking her for information.

She picked up the small blue porcelain soap dispenser that sat next to the sink. She sniffed it and tucked it in her purse.

'We all have secrets, dear.' Then she brushed past me and was out the door before I could say another word.

I was out the door half a second behind her, but she was nowhere to be seen. I looked up and down the narrow hallway, but she had just vanished into thin air.

Chapter 9

Someone was in the apartment. I sat straight up. My brain still felt fuzzy from the margaritas. The fairy lights cast a dim glow around the room. I held my breath. I didn't hear anything besides the beating of my heart and Mitzy snoring softly. Her head rested on one of the cookbooks I'd bought. She had somehow managed to pull it off the shelf and drag it over to her bed.

'Psst.' I crept over to Mitzy's bed and nudged her shoulder. She cracked an eye open. When she didn't see a treat, she closed it. I nudged her again. Despite her tiny size, I wanted back up as I checked the apartment for intruders. She began snoring comically loudly. Was she *pretending* to be asleep? After a few more nudges, I gave up.

The sun was starting to rise, and it was getting brighter in the apartment with each passing minute. I grabbed the remote control and a coaster and crept around the perimeter of the apartment. I rounded every corner spy-style, pressing myself against the wall, and then quickly turning into each room brandishing my remote ready to throw it at an intruder's head. All the rooms were empty, except for the little brown spider that had built her web in the corner of Aunt Erma's bedroom two days ago. I had named her Mavis and had a stern talk with her to make it clear that she was not, under any circumstances, to crawl into my mouth while I was sleeping.

Once I was convinced that Mavis, Mitzy, and I were alone in the apartment, I made coffee and sat down at my computer. I checked my email, scanning through countless ads, hoping to see one from Aunt Erma. I found the email she had sent to me before I came, and replied to it. Just a simple how are you, where the heck are you, and when in the world are you going to be back? *Please reply right away*, I thought, touching the necklace she left me through my shirt with one hand and crossing my fingers with the other. I refreshed my email ten times, but no response yet. So, I grabbed Mitzy's leash, and she led me outside.

The early morning air was crisp. I hurried Mitzy through the alley so we could stand in the sun by the street. That stupid silver cat was there, standing at attention as though she'd been waiting for us. Before I could stop her, Mitzy was in front of the cat licking her face with her little tail wagging faster than I'd ever seen.

'No Mitzy,' I cried, half expecting the cat to claw at her face. I stopped myself from pulling the leash back when the cat just closed her eyes and purred. Then she put her paw on Mitzy's shoulder as though petting her. What kind of strange love affair was this?

A Slice of Magic

The cat looked up at me with her big blue eyes, then came over and rubbed against my leg. Mitzy followed the cat wagging her tail, just trying to be a part of it. Despite my general aversion to cats, it felt nice, and I bent down to pat her head.

Flora had hung Christmas lights in the window of her shop and around the front door. A little thrill ran through me.

I still felt traces of that magical feeling that surrounded Christmas when I was a kid. My parents would let me spend all of Christmas day in my pajamas. Aunt Erma would come over with stacks of sugar cookies and tubs of frosting. We would decorate them while watching whatever Christmas movies were on television. I was allowed to eat as many cookies as I wanted while we decorated. Usually I ate too many and got a stomachache, but I never complained because I didn't want the grown-ups to tell me I couldn't have as many cookies next time.

The last Christmas we were all together, my dad was sick and my mom was snapping at everybody. After Mom had yelled at me for licking my fingers and then touching the cookies, Aunt Erma ushered me into the kitchen to help her bake a pie for dinner. I tried to blink back my tears as Aunt Erma began pulling out all the ingredients.

'Did I ever tell you about the time I met one of Santa's elves?' she asked me.

I shook my head, swallowing the lump in my throat.

'I was hanging up Christmas lights all over my house. When I got done, I plugged them in and not one of them lit up. I plugged them in and unplugged them and thought

I was going to have to take every last one of them down and then I heard some bells tinkling, and I turned around to see a woman dressed in bright red from head to toe. She asked me if she could help me with anything. I said, "No thank you." It was cold out and I wasn't sure what she could do besides stand there and help me test every bulb. She said, "Let me try plugging it in." I didn't know why she wanted to try. I was pretty capable of plugging things in, but I let her. The whole yard lit up. Lights I hadn't even hung sparkled in the trees. I marveled for a minute, and when I turned to thank her, she was gone. All I heard were sleigh bells ringing.'

I had watched Aunt Erma breathlessly. She'd told the story all while putting together a beautiful pie. By the time I had helped her pinch the top and bottom crusts together, a specialty of mine, I had forgotten all about my mother yelling at me.

I shook my head to bring myself out of my daydream. I told the cat to go home, a little more gently than usual this time, and Mitzy and I went inside.

Dear Elodie,

All of my friends have gotten into rock climbing. Suddenly it's all they ever want to do. I've tried going with them, but I don't get any enjoyment out of hanging on by my fingertips, only being held up by my own strength and what seems to be to be an all too skinny rope. Should I keep trying and risk falling to my death?

Sincerely,

Not a Rock Star

A Slice of Magic

Dear Not a Rock Star,

It's hard when our friends go in one direction and we go in another. It can happen to the closest of friendships. Try inviting your friends to occasionally do activities that you enjoy. They're still probably going to spend a lot of their time rock climbing, but maybe you can compromise so you can maintain your friendships. I would also encourage you to join some groups, maybe a curling team or a book club, so you can make some more friends who enjoy doing the same activities you do.

Ask and I'll Answer,
Elodie

I began to feel like I was honing my baking skills. I had finally figured out how to make a French silk pie that wasn't crunchy.

That was why, when I overheard Flora telling Lena and Mr Barnes that my pies were getting better, but were still missing that 'little something,' I felt deflated. I searched my brain for anything Aunt Erma might have taught me. Any special thing that she did that no one else knew about. It had been over twenty years since she taught me things in the kitchen though. I couldn't even remember what I'd learned on the news last night, much less any potential baking secrets from my childhood.

Everyone I asked said that she was very tight-lipped about her recipes. They were a family secret they told me. *Hello! I'm family*, I thought. I found myself wishing several times a day that Aunt Erma would come back. What if she died? I wondered. Would I be left here disappointing people forever because I could never live up to the standards she set?

My pies were always 'missing something.' I heard it time and time again. Usually it was not-so-quietly whispered, but every now and then someone would tell me I was getting close to Aunt Erma's baking, but I was just missing 'something.' If only I could find a jar of that 'something.' A note, a recipe, a can of 'something.'

I had checked the bookshelf a hundred times since I'd arrived, always hoping to see some magical cookbook appear. The one I expected to be labeled 'Secret Family Recipes.' I hadn't found it yet, but maybe the one hundred and first time was the charm, I thought, staring at the book spines and willing something to appear. When nothing did, I grabbed one of the cookbooks I'd bought from Flora and flipped through the pages. Today I was going to try something different. Triple chocolate pumpkin pie.

With a deep breath, I imagined I was starring in my own cooking show. I measured ingredients quickly, only occasionally glancing at the recipe before casually adding a dash of this or that.

Holly came in shortly after the first set of pies came out of the oven. I wasn't going to win any awards for presentation but I brought a pie out front to show her.

'It looks good,' she said. Her words said, 'supportive friend,' but her tone and darting eyes said, 'please don't make me eat that.'

'I'm doomed,' I groaned. 'In just over a week, I'm going to run the pie shop into the ground.'

Holly looked at my forlorn face for a minute. 'I'll take a piece of your pie,' she said throwing down the money before she could change her mind.

'Great.' I quickly cut a generous slice and handed it to her. She perched herself at the closest table and took a bite. I watched her face. A look of horror flickered across it before she composed her features back into a neutral expression.

'Susie, I don't know if we know each other well enough for me to be this honest with you, but that's not so good.'

'I was afraid of that.'

I tried to give her the money back, but being the sweet person that she was, she refused to accept it. She told me I could keep the money as long as I didn't make her eat any more of it. Maybe this was my new way of making money, forcing people to eat gross pie until they paid me to let them stop. After a couple more minutes of chatting, I went back to the kitchen to try again.

I was in the middle of scraping a gloppy mess of chocolate and cherries into a pie crust, another new recipe, when Stan appeared at the back door.

'Hey Stan,' I said, carefully using the spatula to wipe a blob of chocolate off the side of the pie tin. 'It's not delivery day, is it? Are you here for pie?' I asked hopefully. I could really use another sale or two – or fifty. He was peering around the kitchen. What was he looking for?

'Nah, but I know I didn't deliver enough cinnamon last

time.' He held up a crumpled brown paper bag. 'I thought I'd drop some off so you didn't have to go to the store.' He was fidgeting and still looking around the kitchen.

Could he be a spy for that inspector, Violet? Was he trying to look in to see if Mitzy was chewing on a rolling pin or if I'd left milk out on the counter? Was Violet ready to burst in and shut me down?

'Thanks,' I said, grabbing the bag from his hand. 'I saw your parents yesterday.'

He looked me in the eye for the first time, and I took a step back. His green eyes had a trace of the sharpness that I saw in his mother's eyes at the hardware store. I shivered. Was it the chill in the November air, or was there something about Stan? Who was I kidding? Stan was about as sinister as a bunny.

'I'm always glad to have them visit and even happier to have them leave,' he said with a good-natured shrug.

'Do you have any big plans while they're in town?'

'Nope. See you later,' he said, turning abruptly and heading out the back door.

Later on, I was just plopping a large dollop of whipped cream on a piece of apple pie a la mode for Mrs Lanigan, when Gina burst through the door.

'What do you think you're doing?' she spat at me. I froze, mid-dollop.

'Playing the banjo,' I said, a phrase my dad always used when I would ask him what he was doing and it was really obvious. I handed the piece of pie to Mrs Lanigan, who thanked me and then went to sit in the corner to watch the scene that was about to unfold in front of her. She didn't even try to hide her curiosity. In fact, she had pulled a notebook out of her purse and watched us over the top of her half-moon spectacles. She was looked ready to take notes. I wouldn't be surprised if this was the front page story in the gazette tomorrow.

'Look at this.' She waved her hand angrily at the display case. She was wearing her gold Gina's Gym tank top and her arm muscles bulged as she waved them. I briefly considered how glad I was that Mrs Lanigan was there because Gina could kick the crap out of me if she wanted to.

'Looks delicious, doesn't it?' I felt confident with my witness in the corner.

'You didn't take a single one of my suggestions.' Her voice rose in anger.

'Gina,' I began slowly as though I was explaining something to a small child. 'This is a pie shop. People don't come here for the cardboard flavored low-fat option.'

'We need to win this weight loss challenge. The prize is $20,000, and I would finally be able to get those deluxe rowing machines.' She leaned in close to me, lowering her voice, which oddly enough turned out to be way more terrifying than when she was yelling. 'I want those rowing machines.'

The bell rang, and I looked up to see Alice walking through the door. Perfect.

'Hi Alice.' I gritted my teeth and tried to smile.

She surveyed the place with disdain before greeting me. 'Hello Sue. I just came to check out the competition.' Her laugh grated my ears. Nobody called me Sue.

'What can I get you?' I asked. She stared at the case through narrowed eyes, the corners of her mouth slightly turned down.

'Alice offers low-fat cookies,' Gina chimed in. Of course she did.

Alice smiled warmly at Gina. 'I just want to make sure there's something for every single person in town to eat at my shop,' she said.

Gina returned her gaze with pure admiration. Finally, Alice chose the peach pie. 'Just a small slice, thanks.' She and Gina stood at the front talking loudly about how great it was to have a new dessert place in town that offered such a wide variety of delicious options. Of course they were talking up the cookie shop in front of my customer. Alice took small careful bites as though analyzing the ingredients of the pie.

I was wiping down the top of the display case when Gina turned to Mrs Lanigan and said, 'You should really go to Alice's. She has so many different kinds of delicious cookies and her prices are really reasonable.'

'That's it,' I said, throwing down the rag in my hand. 'You need to go.'

'And you need to offer some low-fat options!' Gina turned to leave.

'Thank you for the pie,' Alice set down the plate with her half-eaten piece on it. 'It was…' She paused for a minute.

'Unique.' They left the shop together whispering conspiratorially.

I tried taking one of those deep calming breaths Mr Barnes was always talking about. While my back was turned, Mrs Lanigan slipped out, leaving some money and most of her pie sitting on the table.

Apparently watching *Lady and the Tramp* three hundred times as a kid did not leave me qualified to make decisions such as how often a dog should go out. Mitzy greeted me with indignant prancing the second I opened the door of the apartment. I followed her downstairs and put on her leash. She refused to look at me even when I said her name.

I jumped when I saw a figure standing on the corner of the alley leaning against the brick building across the way. The streetlight on that corner had burned out, and I couldn't see very well. I could just see a silhouette. The hair on my arms stood up. I had seen a movie once where a vicious attack had happened in an alley. Why did we need alleys anyway? Why couldn't we just have streets or no streets. What was with this in between stuff?

'Hi,' I said, my voice a little too high-pitched. Mitzy growled. Didn't she realize she was the size of a football? The figure silently took a couple menacing steps towards me before heading off in the opposite direction. I stayed frozen in place until the figure was well out of sight. If Mitzy wasn't still growling, I would have almost been able to convince myself that I'd imagined the whole thing.

'Mitzy,' I said disapprovingly. For the first time tonight,

she looked at me. She stopped growling for a second before turning back in the direction where the figure had disappeared and started up again. Finally, she must have decided that he or she had gotten far enough away, and she quietly took care of her business.

We headed back inside. Mitzy paused at the door, sniffed the air, and let out a final warning growl before turning to walk inside. I still felt a little strange. Maybe it was being in a strange town in a strange apartment with a strange dog or maybe it had something to do with the person in the alley. Either way, I double checked that all the doors and windows were locked.

Later that night I was pacing around the apartment. Who was that creepy person? Why was Gina always harassing me? Where was Aunt Erma? Why didn't she leave me with any recipes or special instructions? How could I make Alice and her cookies disappear?

Mitzy watched me, her head following me back and forth from her perch on the arm of the sofa. I stopped to stare out the window.

All of the shops on the block were dark. The streetlights cast a warm glow around them – except the burnt-out streetlight on the corner by the pie shop. I wondered who I could contact about that. I could see a few lights on in the apartments above the shops up and down the street. Flora's light was on, but her pink curtains were closed. I was just about to turn back to my pacing when the front door to Flora's shop opened, and Lena slipped out.

She glanced up and down the street and went over to

the dark streetlight. In the shadows, it looked like she reached out and touched it. What was she doing?

The light lit up, brightly illuminating the street. Lena gave a satisfied nod and walked away. I stepped back from the window, my mouth hanging open. Maybe there was a secret switch on the side of the pole, or perhaps it was just some strange coincidence.

So many things in this town just didn't add up.

Chapter 10

Dear Elodie,

I feel like the universe is trying to tell me something. Last week I tripped over a rock on the sidewalk and spilled my coffee. The puddle of coffee on the sidewalk looked like the silhouette of a dog. I think that means the universe is trying to tell me that I should get a dog. My family thinks I'm crazy, but I don't want to ignore such a clear sign as this one. What do you think? Should I get a dog? Or should I listen to my family and ignore the sign?

Sincerely,

Canine in the coffee?

Dear Canine in the coffee?

I think your heart is trying to tell you that you want a dog. Maybe you can start with fostering before making a commitment to a dog. Then you can decide if you're ready and if it's everything you hoped it would be. Sometimes the universe sends us mysterious messages and it can take a long time to decode them. Good luck!

   Ask and I'll Answer,
   Elodie

I made the mistake of flipping through the paper again as I drank my first cup of coffee. My name in a headline caught my eye.

Susanna Daniels Flakes Under Pressure By Elodie

   It's been a tough week for our newcomer, Susanna Daniels. Business at the pie shop has dropped off as she struggles to create edible creations. At the time this paper went to press, there was no word on when Erma Crosby would return. One witness claims that Ms Daniels has been exchanging hostile words with the new cookie shop owner in town, Alice Baker. The anonymous source also states that Ms. Daniels was seen throwing customers out of her establishment. It makes us wonder if she wants the pie shop to succeed or if she's trying to run it into the ground. Will Erma get back in time to save the pie shop?

It was as though someone had taken all of my worst fears and printed them in the paper for everyone to read. How about including some of the things Alice and Gina said in the pie shop last night and the fact they poached my customer? This was one-sided reporting if I ever saw it. Was Mrs Lanigan actually Elodie? She was the only one, other than Gina and Alice, in the pie shop last night. I brightened a little at the possibility of cracking the case of her secret identity.

I took a few deep breath, poured myself another cup of coffee, and got to work. Aunt Erma wouldn't want me to let this bother me.

Slowly rolling the pin back and forth across the flour covered crust brought me back to the days when Aunt Erma would spend the night at our house. Even though she only lived a couple miles away from us, she would come stay in the guest room for a few nights before and after every holiday and birthday.

On the night before my seventh birthday, I woke with a start in the middle of a nightmare. My parents were right. I shouldn't have watched the scary movie with the witches in it. Thirsty for a drink of water, I grabbed my stuffed rabbit for protection and crept downstairs. The lights were on in the kitchen and I peeked around the doorframe wondering if the witches had found me. I was relieved to see Aunt Erma in there, humming as she mixed blueberries and sugar together in a large bowl. I'd heard my mother talk about how Aunt Erma couldn't sleep through the night so she would sometimes get a head start on the baking. I'd never actually witnessed it before.

Aunt Erma saw me and immediately came over, scooped me up, and twirled me around singing silly songs about pie until my nightmare was a distant memory and I couldn't stop giggling. Then she set me down on the chair she had already pulled up next to the counter. It was almost as though she had been waiting for me to wake up. I helped her make the crumble topping for the pie by measuring the sugar while she mixed in the butter and spices. Then she let me sprinkle it on top of the pie with my hands. I piled it extra high on one part of the pie and asked if I could have that piece. She laughed and said I could.

While we waited for the pie to bake, Aunt Erma found some cards and we were playing a game of war when my dad stumbled in wearing his bright green and orange floral pajama pants. My mom had bought them as a joke, but the joke was on her because my dad wore them all the time. He joined our game and before long, my mother wandered in wearing her maroon robe with curlers in her hair.

'What's going on in here?' she demanded, but I could see the smile tugging at her lips. She joined us in our card game. On a whim, I instituted a rule that everyone had to talk with a British accent. I didn't really think that anyone other than Aunt Erma would comply, but everyone did, even my mother. We were all giggling hysterically by the time the pie came out of the oven.

We waited as long as we possibly could for it to cool, which was not as long as the recipe recommended. The filling was runny and hot, but still delicious.

I fell asleep in my chair and later woke up in my bed with happy thoughts in my head and a small blueberry stain on the sleeve of my pink nightgown.

I had a plan when the Morning Pie Crew came in. But first I wanted to share my theory about Elodie.

'I think I know who it is,' I said triumphantly as I set the last two slices of peanut butter pie on the table.

They all looked at me expectantly.

'I think Mrs Lanigan is Elodie,' I announced, after a dramatic pause. I waited for their gasps of agreement, and their praise for my brilliance.

Instead, they burst out laughing. Not exactly the stroke my ego was looking for.

'Nice try, kiddo,' Mr Barnes said, composing himself. 'But until last year Mrs Lanigan lived in Paris, so I'm afraid she is not our Elodie.'

'Oh.' I tried to hide my disappointment.

'Don't worry about that article today though,' Flora said. 'It was pure garbage, and I'm sure everyone will see it that way.'

Lena nodded in agreement. 'Your pies are delicious.' I would have believed her if she hadn't smiled quite so hard at me.

'Thanks,' I said, and then changed the topic because I couldn't get the image of Lena and the streetlight out of my head.

'There's a light bulb burned out in that fixture over there. Could one of you help me with it?' I asked. I had loosened the bulb earlier that day.

'I think Erma has extra bulbs in the upstairs closet,' Mr Barnes said.

'If you can't find them, you should come visit me later.

I have some nice energy efficient bulbs on sale this week,' Lena offered.

'Thanks,' I said. Well, that had backfired. I was probably being silly anyway. Surely it was just a fluke that Lena touched the lamp post and it illuminated.

'Did you guys hear about Mac's new tattoo?' Lena asked.

Soon there was excited chatter about the giant tattoo of Mac's cat that went across his back.

'I have a tattoo of a book,' Flora told me.

'Really? Why haven't I ever seen it?' I asked.

'It's not really in a place most people see very often,' she said with a wink.

My smile froze. 'Oh, OK.' I prayed she wouldn't offer to show it to me so I quickly changed the subject.

Later that day, I was on my way home from the grocery store. I had taken advantage of the afternoon lull to pick up some snacks and a few things Stan had forgotten to bring.

The afternoon lull was lasting longer each day I was running the pie shop.

'Whoa!' I jumped back after almost walking into the opening door of the hair salon.

'Hi,' Henry said stepping outside. 'Sorry, did I almost get you with the door?'

'It's my fault. I wasn't paying attention. A lot on my mind.' I was still trying to come up with ways to bring more customers into the pie shop. 'Your hair looks beautiful,' I said, motioning to the salon.

'Thank you for noticing.' He struck a pose. 'Actually, I'm here with Bernie. She gets her hair done every other Thursday at noon. She's just finishing up, and I've caught up on my gossip for the week, so I thought I'd come out here and work on my tan.'

'Great idea,' I said. He had the pale skin of someone who burned easily.

We chatted for a bit. He caught me up on all the latest gossip he'd just heard. Apparently, Mrs Boddington had gone to the city for a spa day and came back three cup sizes bigger. Then, could you believe the Salem sisters are trying to sell knitted toilet paper cozies in their basement? Who in the world would buy such a thing?

He was just finishing up a story about how Stella's bad hip was going to keep her from teaching this week's Learn to Polka class, when Bernie came out of the salon. Her white hair was curled into perfect little ringlets.

'Bernie, you remember Susanna from the pie shop, right?' Henry said. Just then, his phone rang, and he excused himself to take the call.

Her eyes widened and she took a step towards me. Unintentionally, I took a step back.

'Do you remember what I told you?' She reached out and grabbed my hand tightly between both of hers.

'Yes.' I tried to smile, but I could feel my brow wrinkle.

She closed her eyes, still clutching my hand. 'Dust the cat. The time will come soon, and you have to remember this.'

I looked over at Henry. He was still on the phone, his back turned towards us. 'I'll remember,' I assured her.

'Good.' She patted my hand and released it. 'It's time for my nap then.' With that, she turned on her heel and teetered off so fast that Henry had to hurry after her.

'I'll see you tomorrow at the pie shop,' he called over his shoulder.

I waved, still feeling a little weird after my encounter with Bernie.

I gathered my bags and closed my eyes turning my face up to take in the sunshine. My eyes flew open. Suddenly I was drenched. It was raining! How in the world had that happened? A minute ago there wasn't a cloud in the sky and now it was raining so hard I thought I might need scuba gear just to make it back to the pie shop.

I ran to the nearest awning. It was strange. No one else was running. In fact, they had all stopped and looked as though they were taking in the rain. It was the weirdest thing I had ever seen. I looked around to see if anyone else thought the scene was strange. I noticed the gray cat pressing herself against the window behind me and realized I was standing in front of Alice's shop. She was inside standing behind the counter glaring at me with such intensity that I decided I'd rather brave the rain than her. I stepped out from under the awning and just as quickly as the rain started, it stopped. The sun was shining again. The streets glistened with the rain. People began to bustle about as though nothing had happened.

I felt as though something important had just happened, but I didn't know what it meant. Like I had gotten up in the middle of a movie to go to the bathroom, and when I came back everyone was gasping, and I didn't know why.

After several persistent invitations, I had finally caved and gone to one of Mr Barnes's yoga classes with Holly. Flora and Lena had invited me to go with them, but they liked to go to the 6 a.m. class. They had all failed to mention that it was hot yoga. The room felt suffocating, and I began dripping sweat the moment I walked in.

I looked at all the contorted bodies around me. Maybe I didn't need new friends this badly.

'Doesn't it feel good in here?' Holly rolled out her mat in the front row of the class. There were lots of words I could come up with to describe how it felt in here, but good wasn't one of them. I reluctantly unrolled my rented mat next to her and gazed longingly at the back row where I belonged.

Class began. Mr Barnes spoke in such a confident and soothing voice that I almost believed I could do yoga until the poses began to get a little more difficult and I started to slip in puddles of my own sweat.

I looked at my arms and then back at Mr Barnes, trying to copy the way he was twisted up. He had called it eagle pose, but in all my years on earth, I had never seen an eagle in a pose like that. The rest of the class consisted of me trying to copy the crazy contortions, all the while being told repeatedly to breathe. My breathing was coming out more like groans, and I prayed that I would be able to get out of bed the next morning.

I thought that yoga class mostly consisted of people sitting cross legged in a circle while gossiping. Apparently, all my knowledge of yoga came from late night sitcoms.

I looked at the clock. Only twelve minutes of the hour-long class had gone by. I peeked over at Holly. Her eyes were closed.

'Do we get a break?' I whispered to the woman next to me who made the mistake of glancing in my direction. The woman wore a blue and pink tank top and shorts set that perfectly matched her yoga mat. Her reddish-brown hair was piled into a bun on top of her head. She sized me up as though trying to decide if I was joking or not. I wasn't.

She shook her head with a curt smile and went back to staring straight ahead.

Finally, the class ended with us laying on the floor with our eyes closed. Why couldn't the whole class have been like this?

'What did you think?' Holly asked once the class was dismissed with a chorus of 'Namaste.'

I groaned as I struggled with the exhausting task of rolling up my mat. 'I liked the last part,' I said.

'Trust me. After a few weeks of classes, you'll feel amazing,' she said with a serene smile.

I didn't have the heart to tell her that there was no way I was going to make it through a few weeks of this torture. Holly excused herself for a minute to go talk to a woman across the studio about a special order that had just come in at the grocery store, and I busied myself trying to dry off my feet enough to put my socks and shoes back on. As

I debated about what to eat first when I got back to the apartment, pie or pizza, I began listening in on the conversation happening right behind me.

'I think she's in on it,' a woman's voice said.

'It's too much of a coincidence that the spells have been altered and are showing up in other communities right after she got here,' a man's voice said.

Did he say spells?

'For everyone's safety, I think they should just arrest her until Erma comes back,' another woman said.

Then I heard someone pointedly clear their throat. I glanced back at the group, and they were all staring at me. I quickly slipped on my other shoe, and went to return my mat and find Holly. I thought about asking her about what I'd overheard, but I didn't want her to think I was suffering from heat stroke. I tried to sort out myself what I'd heard in my head, but it just didn't make any sense.

When I got back, my head felt fuzzy. I put on a pot of coffee, but no amount of coffee seemed to help.

I went back to the kitchen and began digging around in the cupboards, continuing my unending quest for Aunt Erma's recipes. I heaved large bags of sugar and flour across the shelves to see if there was anything behind them. Clouds of flour poofed out through the edges of the bags and surrounded me. I even felt along the backs of the cupboards and along the floor in case there was a trap door that led to a secret compartment where she kept all of her recipes. Aunt Erma was the trap door and secret compartment type. I was blindly reaching behind a stack of pie tins on the top shelf when I felt a box. *Finally*, I thought as I pulled it out.

It was a solid wooden box about the size of a loaf of bread, painted purple and covered in a glaze that made it sparkle. I ran my finger over its swirled carved designs, and I felt a strange tingling run up my arm. I unlatched the two bronze clasps on the front and opened it up. There were twelve glass bottles inside. I picked up one that was filled with a tan powder. It was labeled Spice #7 in curly green handwriting that I recognized as Aunt Erma's. I pulled the stopper out of the top and sniffed. It smelled like cinnamon and nutmeg and something I couldn't quite put my finger on, but it made my mouth water. Maybe that was what my pies were missing. Aunt Erma's special spices. These looked different from the ones that sat on the counter. I vaguely remembered her telling me about them once as I helped her clean the kitchen after Thanksgiving. I had stood next to her at the sink, carefully drying the steaming plates as she handed them to me. She was explaining the importance of different spices and how if they were combined correctly, they could create magic. Just then, my mother had bustled into the kitchen and swept me out. She told me to go help my dad find some playing cards so we could get our traditional group solitaire game started. It wasn't until I went to college that I discovered most people considered solitaire to be a solo activity. In my family, it was a fast-paced game where everyone played on everyone else's aces. As I headed towards the living room, I could hear angry whispering from my mother and Aunt Erma's dismissive responses, but

I kept moving because I was too afraid to get caught eaves-dropping.

It was late. I thought tonight would be the night that I would meet Minerva and Jane, the late-night kitchen cleaners. I paused for a moment to listen for them unlocking the door, but nothing. I carried the box of spices to the bottom of the steps and glanced back at the kitchen, surveying the mess one more time and grateful to have kitchen cleaners even if I didn't know who they were.

I brought the box upstairs so Minerva and Jane wouldn't move it somewhere. I couldn't risk losing it again. I sat at the kitchen table and sniffed the contents of each bottle while Mitzy surveyed me with interested eyes. Each one smelled delicious and vaguely familiar. I wondered if they would be able to work their magic to make my pies taste more delicious.

Chapter 11

Day 10 — Friday, November 11th

Dear Elodie,

I think my sister is on drugs. We own a duplex together, each living on one side, and lately I've heard her singing loudly and often. Then the other day she suggested I come over and we order a pizza at nine o'clock at night. Nine o'clock! Of course, I didn't go at that hour. Finally, I've seen an unfamiliar car parked out front at all hours of the day. I can only assume the car belongs to her dealer.

I've started to avoid her because I'm afraid of being sucked into her drug world. Should I stage an intervention? Or should I just move to avoid the problem?

Sincerely,
Sober Sister

Dear Sober Sister,

Far be it from me to question your take on your sister's actions, but it sounds to me like she's possibly just in love. Try inviting her over for pizza at a time that's acceptable for you and ask her what's going on. Maybe she'll be inspired to share her secret love affair with you. Either way, I think you should spend less time at the window watching your sister. If she is on drugs, there are support groups out there who can help you find the right path.

> *Good luck!*
> *Ask and I'll Answer,*
> *Elodie*

I woke up feeling hopeful. Finding the spices felt like a sign that things were going to get better. Maybe Aunt Erma would even come back today. I imagined her bustling around the kitchen. It was always so natural for her.

I admired the spotless kitchen and surveyed the contents of the refrigerator. For once, Stan had gotten most of my order right. Containers of cherries, blackberries, and blueberries lined the top three shelves. He had forgotten the lemons, so I had to scrap my idea to make lemon meringue pie today.

Flora called and apologized up and down when she told me that the she and Lena had to help Mr Barnes with a project so they wouldn't be able to come in today.

'We'll each buy three pieces of pie tomorrow,' she promised.

'Let me know if you guys need any help with your project,' I offered, even though she hadn't told me what it was. I was a little relieved that I had a day to test my new secret ingredients before the Morning Pie Crew came in to judge.

I pretended I was Aunt Erma and all this baking stuff came naturally to me. I mixed together ingredients and rolled out pie crusts. It felt ever-so-slightly easier than before. I kept the box of spices sitting on the counter next to me. First, I made four cherry pies. I pulled a couple of bottles of spices out and smelled them before selecting Spice #4. It smelled a little like cinnamon and ginger. In my excitement, I sprinkled a healthy dose on the top of each pie. I noted on a piece of paper which spices I used in which pies. Next, I made blackberry pies. For those I selected Spice #7. I thought the cinnamon and nutmeg mix would bring out the flavors of the blackberries. I used an oatmeal, butter, brown sugar crumble topping on both the cherry and blackberry pies and put them in the oven before moving on to make banana cream and French silk pies.

As the fruit pies baked, delicious aromas filled the whole shop. Maybe I was getting the hang of this after all. I had sixteen pies ready to go by the time I was unlocking the front door.

The first customers of the day were a family of four. The mother's red hair was reflected in the children and the father's sandy brown hair was held back with a green baseball cap. The parents were both busy on their cell phones as the little boy and girl vied for their attention. They all ordered a slice of the cherry pie. Then they crowded around a table as I served their pie, all the while the kids loudly arguing over how they were going to spend the rest of their day. The little girl, who couldn't have been more than five, would punctuate the end of every sentence with a toss of her pigtails. Things got quiet when I set their pie in front of them, and the parents lowered their phones as they took their first bite. The only sound was the occasional, 'Mmm,' that the little girl let out.

I headed back towards the kitchen, but curiosity got the best of me, and I stayed out front to see if they were going to finish their pie. Not wanting to seem too creepy, I pretended to arrange the pies in the front case. They were about halfway through their pieces when the laughter began. It started with the dad �口 a little chuckle that turned into a full-on belly laugh. The mom looked at him surprised for a second, then she burst into a fit of giggles and soon tears were running down her cheeks. Both children had thrown their heads back and were laughing so loudly it almost sounded fake. I crouched down a little lower behind the bakery case. What was wrong with this family?

They tried to keep eating their pie, but every bite was interrupted by more laughter. Suddenly feeling self-conscious, as though they were laughing at me, I slunk back into the kitchen. I didn't dare go too far just in case their erratic behavior escalated.

Finally, they finished their pie. I went back out front to clean up as they headed for the door, gasping for air.

'I don't know what it is, we just can't stop laughing,' the red-faced dad said to me.

'Enjoy your day,' was all I could respond. Despite the strangeness of the family, I was pleased to see that they had eaten every crumb on their plate. The spices must be the secret ingredient after all!

I remembered one year when my parents had fought with Aunt Erma about something 'grown up' before Christmas dinner. Everyone had eaten in complete silence, except for me who kept asking what time Santa would come. 'When you're asleep,' Aunt Erma finally responded, and my mother let out an angry sigh. After dinner, pie was served and within a few bites my mom and Aunt Erma were giggling and sharing stories about their ice-skating adventures when they were kids. My dad shared a funny story about seeing Santa when he was about my age. Everyone was laughing, and I felt warm and happy.

A few minutes after the giggle family left, a middle-aged man in a blue cabbie hat wandered in. After seriously pondering the bakery case for a minute, he ordered a piece of blackberry pie. He sat at the table by the window, chewing each bite slowly as he stared out the window. I wandered back into the kitchen to pick out some recipes for tomorrow. As I debated between coconut cream or peanut butter cream, I heard a soft singing coming from out front. I froze for a second as it grew louder. I went out front. The man was grasping the shiny napkin holder and serenading it with an enthusiastic, albeit off-key, rendition of 'My Heart Will Go On.'

A young couple opened the door, but when they saw the man singing to the napkin holder they quickly backed out. Not willing to lose any business, I chased after them as the man held the last note of the song.

'Please, come back in,' I said when I caught up to them a couple shops down the street. They still looked a little wide-eyed. 'He's just an actor rehearsing for a part. He's very committed. You know how actors can be.'

They seemed to accept my explanation and followed me back. 'Good, I really had a pie craving,' the young man said.

'He just caught us a little off guard,' the young woman said with a laugh.

'You guys from out of town?' I asked. They both nodded. 'Yeah, we have some characters here. Everyone's very friendly though.'

I led them through the front door, and much to my relief the man wasn't singing. Instead he was talking to the napkin holder in a soft, loving voice.

'You're more beautiful than a sunset,' he cooed.

The young couple ordered a couple pieces of banana cream pie and squished themselves as far away into the back corner as they could. I think they were afraid they might catch his craziness.

The man continued to talk to his napkin holder, and the couple talked to each other in low voices, frequently casting glances at the man that ranged from curious to anxious. I didn't want to leave them alone with Mr Napkin, so I stayed out front wiping off the same spot on the display case.

Soon the couple's voices grew louder, and I was startled out of the daydream I was having in which I was running a very successful pie shop where everything was going as it was supposed to.

'You always sing so loudly in the bathroom. Singing 'Twinkle Twinkle Little Star' at the top of your lungs. What's up with that? Learn a new song!' the man said to the woman.

'I have to sing loudly to drown out the sound of your feet clomping on the floor. You don't weigh 3,000 pounds. How do you manage to walk that loudly?' she spat back at him.

'You're probably hearing me trip over the shoes you always leave in the middle of the living room.'

'You chew so slowly!'

'You drink water too loudly!'

'You say "thank you" too much!'

I was staring at them with open curiosity now.

The man at the other table had stopped singing and now clutched the napkin holder close to his chest as though to shield it from the hostility. He got up and went over to the other man and nudged him.

'Hey, you need a woman like this in your life,' he loudly whispered, holding up the napkin holder.

The woman got up and stormed out, knocking over a chair in her haste to leave.

'She's never left me,' the man with the napkin holder said.

After a brief hesitation, the other guy got up and went after the girl. The napkin holder guy went back to stroking the side of his napkin holder unfazed. He finished reciting a poem and looked at me.

'Would you mind if I take her home with me?' He held up the napkin dispenser.

'Please do. You two have clearly bonded,' I told him. I decided I'd rather buy a new napkin holder than incur the wrath of such a delusional man. I glanced around for a second after he left, half expecting a camera crew from one of those prankster shows to come popping in.

I was thrilled to finally have a steady stream of customers, most of whom took their pie to go. They said the smell from the street drew them in. Maybe I wouldn't run the shop into the ground after all.

I was happily exhausted when the afternoon lull hit. I sat at the desk in the kitchen with my feet propped up on an old cardboard box and drank coffee while reading recipe books. The bell over the front door rang. I reluctantly stood on my sore feet, not sure I was ready to deal with another nutty customer quite yet. I was relieved to see that it was Henry.

'Hey, I'm glad to see you,' I said.

'Oh yeah?' He looked so flattered I didn't have the heart to tell him that it was because I needed a little normal in my day. 'Tough day at the office?'

I smiled. 'You could say that! What can I get for you today?'

He held up a book in his hand. I recognized it as one of Holly's books. I hadn't pegged him as a romance reader. 'Well, I'm on break, so I thought I'd read while eating a piece of pie for myself first.' He pondered the display case for a minute. 'How about a slice of French silk.'

I scooped his piece and left him to his book. After fifteen minutes, I popped back out front to see if he was ready to order pies to bring back to work.

'How's everything going out here?'

'Just wonderful. The pie was delicious!'

I was pleased to see that he had completely cleaned his plate, possibly even licked it clean. I smiled a little and grabbed his plate off the table.

'Oh no, let me do that for you.' He pulled the plate out of my hand and headed back towards the kitchen.

'Um, Henry,' I said as I followed him back to the kitchen. 'I can do it. Really. I'm sure you have work to get back to.' But he was already washing his plate. *Well, I tried,* I thought as I went to make a fresh pot of coffee.

Henry looked up and saw me heading for the coffee pot. He dropped the plate, it clattered in the bottom of the sink, and he rushed over to my side with soap suds still on his hands.

'Are you making coffee?' he asked eagerly. 'I can do that for you!'

'Really, it's OK, Henry. I love making coffee! And drinking it,' I said with a laugh. He'd already wiped his hands dry on a nearby towel and was cleaning out the old coffee from the pot. Wow, he was acting strangely. I wondered if someone had slipped him some medication at the nursing home. 'Henry, the five cups of coffee I had earlier are catching up to me. I'm just going to run back to the bathroom real quick.'

'Oh, I can do that for you!' He dropped the bag of coffee.

'No!' I practically yelled at him. This had just gone from pretty weird to really weird. He looked a little startled, but just went back to his coffee making. I fled to the back. First, I went to the bathroom. I went quickly, afraid that Henry would bulldoze through the door after he finished making coffee to help me wash my hands. When I came out, I grabbed my cell phone and called Holly.

'Hey Pie Lady,' she answered the phone on the second ring.

'Something strange is happening,' I whispered, not even bothering with a greeting.

'What?'

I gave her a brief account of my day so far. I was just finishing the part about Henry when he rushed into the kitchen carrying a cup of coffee.

'Here.' He handed it to me. 'Do you have phone calls to make? I can do that for you!' He reached for my phone.

'I'll be right over,' I heard Holly say before Henry grabbed the phone from my hand.

'Who do you need to call?' Henry asked, his finger poised to dial.

'No one,' I grabbed my phone back. 'I was just about to mop the floors and make dinner.'

'No, no, let me do that for you.' He headed for the closet to grab the mop.

Don't judge me. If there was going to be a crazy man in the store, I figured I might as well take advantage of it a little bit. As he passed by the oven, he turned it on. I wondered what he'd make for dinner.

'Sit down,' he said as he filled the bucket with hot water. I still had the coffee that he'd given me in my hand, so I took it out front and waited for Holly. Henry was still mopping (sadly, no dinner yet) when Holly arrived.

'So, interesting day?' she smiled.

'You could say that!' I sighed.

'I'm going to go talk to Henry in the back for a minute.' She grabbed Henry, pulled the mop out of his hand, despite his protests, and dragged him back into the kitchen. Being the nosy person that I am, I tried to listen. They were rudely quiet though, and all I heard was a strange sound, like popcorn popping. A few minutes later they both emerged from the kitchen. Henry looked a little confused.

'Sorry, Susie. I don't know what got into me.'

'No problem,' I said.

'I'll get him out of your hair.' Holly guided him towards the door. 'I think he's just really sleep deprived.'

Henry nodded feebly as he headed out the door.

'See ya,' I called.

Violet powered through the door just before closing time.

'Can I get you some pie?' I asked, even though I knew what the answer would be.

'Is Erma back yet?' She ignored my question.

I shook my head.

She pursed her lips. 'I don't think you're taking this seriously.'

'Taking what seriously?' This woman was a mystery to me.

She narrowed her eyes, but nothing else on her body moved.

'Are you sure you don't want some pie?' I asked, gesturing to the display case. I knew the healing power of pie.

'I need to smell the pies,' she said, ignoring my question.

'Um, OK.'

She came around, and I opened the display case for her. She pulled each one out and took a big whiff. 'What did you put in them?' she demanded.

'Nothing,' I said innocently.

'I need to confiscate these,' she said. She began to gather the remaining slices of pie. There was only a handful of slices after the busy day I'd had.

'All of them?' my voice came out a little squeaky. 'Why?'

'You haven't been following the regulations. We might have to shut this place down until we can track Erma down.' Her sharp words took my breath away.

'What?' A thousand thoughts raced through my mind. How could I have messed this up so quickly?

'Erma needs to take our allegations seriously and be here to answer for them,' Violet continued. She dumped the pieces of pie out of their tins and into a plastic bag she pulled out of her briefcase. I was tempted to ring them up on the cash register and try to charge her for the pie. She spun on her heel to leave.

'Wait!' I raced out from behind the counter and grabbed her arm.

Violet stiffened even more under my hands and she looked at me sharply like she might punch me. 'What?' Her voice was cold.

All I could hear in my brain was static. 'You can't close

down the pie shop,' I pleaded with her. She looked me up and down. 'You're at least required to give the proprietor written reason for a forced shutdown.' I tried to sound official, like I knew what I was talking about, and it seemed to work.

'Fine,' she said, but her tone made it sound like it was anything but. 'We'll hold off shutting the place down.' She turned to leave. 'For now,' she added before storming out the door.

I breathed a sigh of relief. I closed up the shop and trudged upstairs. Mitzy glared at me when I walked in to show her disapproval at my recent neglect. I took her on a long walk. I noticed Flora on the other side of the town square. I was going to go say hello, but I realized she was talking to Violet. I couldn't see Flora's face, but she was gesturing emphatically. Violet's expression remained neutral. At the end of their conversation, Violet nodded once, and they both went their separate ways. Flora was gone by the time we walked across the square.

Back at the apartment, I tried to buy Mitzy's affection by giving her a couple slices of apple as a treat and throwing her squeaky toy around, but she really knew how to hold a grudge.

Drink. I needed one. Mitzy watched with wide eyes as I turned to leave her yet again.

'I'll be back soon,' I promised, wishing she didn't have the power to make me feel so guilty. 'Maybe I can pick up some extra treats on the way home.' That seemed to perk her up a bit.

Sal's was quiet. Just a few regulars scattered around. I sat on a stool at the bar and let my head drop into my arms.

'Here, you look like you could use this.' Sal slid a beer across the bar.

'Thanks.' I looked up and grabbed the pint.

He stood in front of me wiping down the bar. 'Rough day?' he asked, clinching the cliché.

'Weird day,' I said.

'Weird is what we do best around here,' he said.

A tall scruffy guy in a blue baseball cap sidled up to the bar to order a drink, and Sal went over to serve him. I sipped my beer and watched the football game on the television without really seeing it.

I could sense someone standing behind me, and I turned to see Alice. Inwardly, I groaned. Outwardly, I gave her a simple head nod, which apparently she took as an invitation to sit down next to me. I was annoyed that she smelled like cookies.

'How'd things go at the pie shop today?' Her tone was light, almost friendly.

'Fine.'

'I heard your pies have become more and more delicious. Have you been trying new recipes? New ingredients?' she asked, leaning in.

I wondered how many drinks she'd had to make her so friendly. 'Nope,' I lied. The bar wasn't a relaxing place to be anymore. I swallowed the last of my beer and threw some money on the bar.

She grabbed my arm, her grip was strong.

'Wait, are you sure you didn't do anything different today?' Her voice was tinged with desperation.

I wrenched my arm free and stumbled back a few steps. Everyone in the bar was openly staring now. I had to get out of here. The last thing I needed was for people to say I got into a fight with Alice. I was pretty sure she'd be able to spin the story and make herself come across as the victim.

'Have a good night, Alice.' I turned and rushed out the door.

Chapter 12

Day 11 — Saturday, November 12th

Dear Elodie,
  I have two older sisters. We all live together in an apartment. My oldest sister and I get along wonderfully, but I have a huge problem with my other sister. She always borrows my books. That's not the problem, books are meant to be read, but she writes in them. Sometimes it's a note to herself, sometimes it's a note about the book, and sometimes it's a grocery list. Then to top it off, she folds the pages in half to mark her spot. I'm not talking about just folding the corner down, she folds them completely in half.
  I've tried giving her sticky notes and bookmarks, but she never uses them. I told her she can't borrow my books, but she does anyway.
  How can I handle this situation before she destroys all of my books?
  She hates frogs with a passion. I know it's immature

of me, but I'm tempted to put a bunch of frogs in her bed.

Sincerely,
Revenge of the Frogs

Dear Revenge of the Frogs,

Don't put frogs in your sister's bed. I repeat, do not put frogs in your sister's bed! It won't accomplish anything.

Try talking to your sister again. Explain your feelings and ask her why she does those things to your books. Maybe she's frustrated about something you're doing and damaging your books is her way of seeking revenge. Sometimes in roommate situations, it's the small annoyances that fester until they consume you. You both need to talk about it or this could become an all-out war and no one will win.

Ask and I'll Answer,
Elodie

It was still dark outside when I was startled by a knock at the front door. I had been up for hours prepping for the Fall Festival. I peeked out from the kitchen, and Flora was standing there with her nose pressed against the glass. When she saw me, she waved enthusiastically. I unlocked the door to let her in.

'What are you doing up so early?' I asked.

'I'm like a kid on Christmas. I can't sleep when it's Fall Festival day,' she said, stepping inside. 'I thought maybe I could help you with a few things.'

'Um, OK. Come on in.' I led her back to the kitchen and offered her some coffee. She said no. I poured her some anyway, and she began to drink it. I went back to prepping the pies. She watched me closely.

'You discovered Erma's spices,' she said after a moment of silence.

I paused, holding a cup of sugar over a bowl of blueberries. 'Yes.'

'We thought maybe she had taken them with her. She had some very strong spices, and some people react very strangely to them. You know how chamomile can make people feel calm? Some of Erma's spices make people feel happy or loving,' she explained.

'OK,' I said slowly, still holding the cup of sugar. I wasn't sure I really believed all that hippy dippy stuff, but I couldn't deny that people had acted strangely yesterday. Maybe there was some correlation to the spices.

'I can help you add the perfect amount of spice,' she offered.

'Sure,' I said. A little extra help wouldn't hurt on a crazy day like today. On the off chance that she was right about the spices causing people to feel certain ways, I didn't have enough napkin holders to do it wrong again.

I had spent extra time on one of the blueberry pies. I wanted to make the perfect pie for the baking contest. I made sure the berries were heaped to the right height, the crust was perfectly smooth and flakey, and the brown sugar crumble topping was evenly distributed. I admired my work of art when it came out of the oven, even snapping a picture of it on my cell phone. I sent the picture to Henry before realizing he might not be up yet. He texted back right away though. 'Looks amazing! I see first place in your future!' I grinned at my phone. When I looked up Flora was looking at me, her eyebrows raised and a smile playing on her lips. I quickly set down my phone and got back to work.

Once Flora was satisfied that we'd added the proper amount of spices to all thirty-seven pies I'd made, she went to get herself ready.

I was so hopped up on caffeine and nerves that I was singing into a wooden spoon by the time Holly arrived. She had offered to help me set up my booth. We began to haul the first load of pies and decorations to the town square. I had been warned that the town took the Fall Festival very seriously, and I was beginning to see how true that was.

There were people on ladders hanging giant glittering paper leaves from trees and stringing twinkle lights across the square. Despite the fact that we were still hours from the start of the festival, it looked like everyone already had their booths mostly set up. We were assigned a spot in the corner – not prime real estate, but not a bad location. We were just past Flora's booth and kitty corner from a fortune teller booth. Flora had stacks of books on display. I was hoping for a break today so I could go page through all of them.

The fortune teller already had little crystal balls hanging from the top of the booth with a giant one sitting in the front. I did a double take. I could have sworn I saw Aunt Erma's face flash across all the crystal balls. I stared for a minute, but they just sparkled. It must have just been a reflection.

'Hey, are you going to help with this?' Holly nudged me as she began pulling decorations out of the box. First, we hung the 'Erma's Pies' sign on the front. I'd found that along with some colored lights in the back of the closet when I was looking for recipes. Our final decoration was a paper leaf chain that I'd made myself. I had found the idea online, and I was proud that it only took me six tries to make it into something that I wasn't too embarrassed to hang up.

We'd made several trips back and forth between the festival and the pie shop to get all the pies and supplies. Despite the fact that I was wearing my most comfortable tennis shoes, my feet were begging me to sit down and put them up already. Holly had just finished writing the menu out on the chalkboard when people started to wander through. Soon we had a long line, and we were serving pie fast and furiously. On the plus side, I didn't have time to think about my feet anymore.

I noticed Henry at the end of the aisle. Bernie, Sandy, and Claire, as well as a couple of other residents from the nursing home whose names I didn't know, crowded around him while he held up different cardigans that were on display from Bonnie's Boutique. I couldn't help but notice how cute he looked in his blue jacket and bright yellow hat. A long multi-colored scarf was wrapped around his neck. No doubt a gift from one of the residents. He said something, and they all laughed. I turned my attention back towards my own booth and the line had gotten twice as long.

'Bless you for being here,' I said to Holly. I smiled when I heard several people say, 'Oh yum,' as they took their first bite on their way out of the line.

'I'm happy I could help,' she said, scooping a piece of strawberry rhubarb into a paper bowl. 'Just remember this when I ask you to do some research for my next book.'

'Wait. What?' I asked freezing with a five-dollar bill in my hand and turning away from the customer standing in front of me. How could I help with research for a romance novel?

'Don't worry about it.' She waved a hand dismissively at me and handed me the pie. 'I'll tell you later.'

With all of the ups and downs at the pie shop this week, it felt good to have a line of people wanting to eat my pies. I exhaled feeling a little relieved when we finally got a break in the action.

'I'm hearing rave reviews out there.' Mr Barnes came up holding two cups of coffee. He handed one to Holly and one to me.

'What's the haps at the rest of the festival?' Holly asked him. I gratefully took a large gulp of coffee and felt some energy start to flow through my veins again.

'Gina's booth is certainly an intense place to walk past,' he said.

'Is she force feeding people fat-free mini donuts?' I asked.

'She has people doing pull ups in front of her booth. They're pure muscle. I'm pretty sure they've never eaten an ounce of fat in their whole lives, and they look angry about it,' he said.

'I'm all about staying healthy, but everyone needs to enjoy life too,' Holly said. 'Pie is a necessary part of the living process.'

'Everything in moderation,' Mr Barnes said. 'That's what I teach in my yoga classes. That and how to stand on one foot while saying "om".'

'Do you want to go to sunrise yoga tomorrow morning?' Holly asked, turning to me.

'Um, well,' I stuttered. 'Do we need more forks? Maybe I should run back to the pie shop and get some.'

'Don't worry, we have a few more boxes under here.' Holly pulled them out and set them on the table.

Luckily the line of questioning ended when more customers came, but I had a feeling I wasn't totally off the hook yet.

'You're Stan's parents, right?' I greeted the couple who was studying the pies.

'Yes, I'm Dennis and this is Brenda.' Brenda gave me a thin smile that didn't reach her eyes. No wonder Stan was such a nervous fellow. His mother was terrifying.

'It's nice to meet you. What can I get you?' I asked.

'Could you tell us what you put in your pies? Brenda's allergic to some spices.' Dennis studied the chalkboard.

Brenda stared at me with such intensity that I shrank back a step.

'We mix a lot of different spices together. If you're concerned about an allergic reaction, it's probably best to steer clear of the pie,' I said. Also, I had no idea what was in Aunt Erma's secret spice mixes.

'Maybe we'll just take one slice then.' He picked the cheesecake, and as he walked away, Dennis took small careful bites while Brenda hovered over him.

'I think I understand Stan better now,' Holly said from her perch in the corner of the booth. I nodded in agreement.

Gina stalked up to our booth and glared at our choices.

'Hi Gina.' I attempted a cheerful hostess tone, but my hand gripped the pie server tighter.

'Still nothing low-fat, I see,' she said.

'Blueberries are pretty healthy with all those antioxidants,' I offered.

'Not in a pie filled with sugar, with a crust that's full of fat.' She wrinkled her nose.

A couple walked up with their young daughter, smiling at the pie choices.

'Are you sure you want to indoctrinate your daughter into the culture of obesity?' Gina asked.

My mouth fell open and the couple hurried away with their sad, confused little girl.

'What are you doing?' I asked. Anger swelled in my chest, and I gripped the tin of the apple pie in front of me tightly. I was tempted to throw the whole thing in her face.

'If you're not going to meet my demands, I am going to be your worst enemy,' she threatened, narrowing her eyes at me.

I almost laughed at her words. My worst enemy? Were we in a superhero movie?

Chapter 13

Day 11 — Saturday

I'd never entered a baking contest before. Come to think of it, I'd never even seen a baking contest outside of a television show. The Hocus Hills Baking Contest was a serious event. There were nine of us who had entered. We all stood in a circle, each next to a little table that held our dish.

After an opening ceremony during which the high school dance team performed and far too many children played solos on violins, the judges were sworn in. Each judge had to solemnly repeat that they hadn't accepted any bribes and they would only favor their favorite flavors. By this point I was stifling a case of the giggles. I glanced around the circle and saw that everyone's face was solemn. Alice stood next to me looking calm and confident as a wave of irritation passed over me. I closed my eyes for a second and willed my pie to win.

Lena had given me the lowdown on the five judges. 'Fred Lund is a soft-spoken man who began judging all kinds of town contests after his wife died. He's probably the fairest person I know. Joe Turner is drunk with power when he's a judge. He thinks he's king of the universe and would prefer that everyone bows down before him. You can probably get by with a head bob though. Felicity Clayborn loves the color red, so make sure you wear that red polka dot apron. Janice Brent is a rabid fan of John Denver, so you can probably win her over if you hum one of his songs while she tastes your pie. And Ginger Robinson is just a cranky old bat, so there's really nothing you can do there.'

The judges began six people down from me. A tall thin middle-aged gentleman stood over a round cake covered in chocolate frosting and decorated with whipped cream and cherries. My mouth watered a little as I looked at it. It was hard to see the judges faces when they tasted it, but based on their nods to each other, they seemed to be enjoying it. The man looked pleased and turned to give a woman behind him a thumbs-up.

The next contestant was a young woman with long blonde hair. She had made little cheesecake bites that she presented with a flourish of her perfectly manicured hands. I noticed Felicity Clayborn wrinkled her nose a little as she bit into it. I tried not to feel happy about that.

I daydreamed about winning while the judges made their way closer to me. I thought of how proud Aunt Erma would be and the ways I could subtly rub it in Alice's face while still appearing gracious. It certainly wouldn't hurt if it drew more customers into the pie shop too.

The judges started to line up in front of me and I began quietly humming 'Take Me Home, Country Roads.' I gave them a head bob and brushed off my apron, just to make sure Felicity noticed that it was red. Then I presented them each with a piece of pie and watched their reactions. Every one of their faces went from pleasantly surprised to horrified all at once. Janice spit her piece out and it fell into a gooey blob on her plate. Fred's face had turned a deep shade of red as he struggled to swallow. Ginger began gagging, and the other two had their faces squished up into such looks of disgust it would have been very funny if it wasn't happening in front of me.

'What's in that?' Joe asked.

'Um, blueberries?' I said, uncertainly. I wasn't sure what he expected me to say. Strychnine? Cow dung?

'Keep practicing, honey,' Fred said, setting down his plate and drinking the glass of water someone handed him.

'Get rid of these,' Felicity handed her plate to a woman standing off to the side and the others followed suit.

'But, I … what?' I stuttered through words unable to make a full sentence. I had practiced this pie for hours. Even if my baking wasn't up to Aunt Erma's quality yet, I didn't think it was spit out worthy. The judges ignored my stutters and moved on. Joe was wiping his tongue off with a napkin.

Alice was next. I glanced over and she was positively glowing, which made my blood boil even more. She lifted her tray of cookies and presented them to the judges. She gave a humble shrug as they oohed and aahed over the sparkly frosting she had used to decorate them.

As though that wasn't bad enough, as each one of them

took a bite out of their cookie, they let out loud exclamations of delight.

I kept my head down as the judges finished making their rounds. I just couldn't figure out what went wrong. I waited until I thought no one was looking and grabbed a blueberry out of the pie tin and popped it in my mouth. It tasted fine to me.

I glanced over at Alice, and she gave me a smug smile. I wanted to strangle her, but there were too many witnesses.

The judges disappeared for a few minutes to confer and came back carrying a set of ribbons. After a speech about all the wonderful entries (well, almost all of them, Janice muttered glancing in my direction), they had decided to award first place to Alice. She beamed as the judges presented her with the ribbon and everyone clapped.

'Oh, thank you, thank you!' she gushed. 'In honor of this win, my cookies will be half off all next week. Please stop by and enjoy!' The cheers in the audience grew louder.

Second place went to the man with the chocolate cake, and third place went to a woman who had made cookie dough cupcakes.

I was still a little in shock about what happened when Holly came up behind me. 'Are you OK?' she asked putting her arm around my shoulders.

'I'm confused,' I said, holding my pie up. 'Will you try a bite?'

She looked nervous, but then to her credit, she said, 'Of course.' What a good friend. She grabbed a fork and shoved a bite in her mouth.

She chewed it thoughtfully for a minute.

'Tastes good to me,' she said with a shrug. 'Who knows what's wrong with the judges? Don't worry about it though.'

'Don't worry about it?' I screeched a little louder than I intended, and a few heads turned. Then I lowered my voice. 'The whole town just saw Janice Brent spit my pie out. How many customers do you think will come into the pie shop now?'

'Maybe we can design a new ad campaign for you. Or write a jingle for the radio.' She began to sing, 'When you're feeling sad and saggy, stop by Erma's pies, it won't make you gaggy.'

'What?' I asked.

'It's just a first draft.' She looked at my face, 'What? Too soon? I was just brainstorming. I thought this was a safe space.'

'I think Alice did something to the pie,' I whispered.

'What do you mean?' she asked.

'I think she sabotaged me so she'd have an easier time winning.'

'Why would she do that?' Holly had a concerned and sympathetic look on her face.

'She's been out to get me. She wants to be queen of desserts in Hocus Hills. Don't ask me to explain the insane,' I said.

'Maybe.' She nodded doubtfully. 'Let's get back to the booth.' Holly grabbed my arm and gently led me away.

'I'll meet you there,' I said. 'I just have to grab something.' Holly uncertainly watched me go.

I found Alice walking back towards her cookie booth. The intricate paper lanterns and professional banner that hung in her booth made my paper chain look juvenile. I stepped in front of her, and she looked surprised for a second before the smug smile returned to her lips.

'That was fun, wasn't it?' Alice asked. She reached up to scratch her shoulder with the hand that held the blue ribbon so it dangled in front of my face.

'Did you do something to my pie?' I demanded. I tried to keep my voice down. Maybe the pressure of running the pie shop without Aunt Erma really was getting to me.

'I'm sorry the contest didn't go better for you,' she said with sarcastic sympathy.

'What did you add to it?' I was determined to get to the bottom of this.

'I can't believe you would accuse me of tampering with the baking contest,' Alice spoke loudly, and people turned to stare.

'I'm going to prove that you messed with my pie,' I hissed, then flashed a smile at the gawkers.

'I'd be happy to give you some baking lessons if you want.' She gave me a charming smile. I felt the blood rise to my cheeks, and I gripped the sides of my apron to keep myself from punching her. I turned and stormed back to my booth. Lena and Mr Barnes were standing there talking to Holly. I wanted to throw something or kick something, but I settled for stomping my foot. I don't know what I expected. Of course, Alice wasn't going to just admit to ruining my pie. I would have to prove it.

'How's it going?' Lena asked slowly.

'Great, just great,' I said.

'Don't you worry about the contest, dear,' Mr Barnes said. 'There are plenty of people around here who didn't see it.'

'Oh, but they'll hear about it soon, I'm sure,' I said.

They continued their cheerful chatter, and I daydreamed about the different ways I could prove Alice's foul play.

Things slowed down drastically after that. I think maybe word was spreading about how the baking competition had gone. We took inventory of what we had left.

'We're almost out of paper plates and chocolate banana cream pie,' Holly said.

'I definitely have more plates, and I might have one more pie in the fridge back at the store,' I said. 'I'll run and get them. Can you handle things here?'

'No problema, chica,' she said. 'I'm just going to eat this piece of pie right here that flipped over when I tried to scoop it out of the tin. You can't serve pie like this. I'm really doing a public service here.' She sat down on the folding chair in the corner and took the first bite off the fork. 'Mmm,' she sighed. 'You're welcome.'

I laughed and made my way through the groups of carefree people enjoying all the booths. I took a deep breath, hoping to inhale the fun and exhale the knot that had formed in my stomach after the contest and wouldn't let go.

'Hey,' I heard a voice and turned to see Henry had fallen into step next to me. I smiled at him, forgetting for just a second about the disastrous contest.

'I saw the contest,' he said. Thump, the memory hit me harder. The sympathy in his eyes made me realize it was, in fact, as bad as I thought.

'You win some, you lose some,' I said with what I hoped was a breezy shrug. He watched me for a second. I could tell he knew how upset I was, but he didn't push.

'Well, I got you something,' he reached into his coat pocket and pulled out a small blue flower made out of ribbon. 'I bought it at one of the booths. I thought you deserved a blue ribbon for all of your hard work.' His eyes were bright and cheeks slightly flushed as he handed it to me.

'Thank you,' I said. I swallowed hard, horrified to find myself choking up at his kindness. Don't cry, I scolded myself. That would be the one thing that would make today even more embarrassing.

'I better get back to the nursing home residents,' he said, and I was relieved I didn't have to try to hold it together any longer. 'When I left them Sandy was arguing with Bonnie over the best way to knit a hat. I should probably intervene before anyone gets stabbed with a knitting needle.'

'Good luck,' I said. 'And thanks again.' I held up the flower as he waved goodbye.

Then I carefully tucked the flower into my pocket and continued to the pie shop. The sun had gone behind the clouds making the streets dark and cold. There wasn't another soul in sight. The sounds of the crowd at the festival grew distant.

The moment I rounded the corner, something felt

170

different. Then I saw it. The small window by the door was broken. Without thinking I turned and ran back to the festival.

'Holly!' I was out of breath and had to bend over with my hands on my thighs for a minute.

'Susie, what's wrong?' She put her hand on my shoulder and bent down.

'Pie shop, broken,' I gasped. Wow, maybe Gina was right. I should work out more.

'What? What's broken?' Holly asked. A few people had started to gather around and I realized I might be making a scene.

'Someone broke into the pie shop.' I was finally able to get out a full sentence.

It was like a noisy mob scene, and I think I was a part of it. Everyone in town seemed to be moving together towards the pie shop. They fell silent when they saw the broken window.

Chapter 14

Day 11 — Saturday

'She probably broke into it herself,' a voice called out. Was that Gina?

'Why would I break into my own shop?' I asked.

'For attention. Sympathy. Everyone knows how well the baking competition went for you. Maybe you're hoping people will come buy your pies if you've been the victim of a break in.' Gina appeared through the crowd advancing towards me.

'That's ridiculous,' I sputtered. I had not expected this.

'You're the only one in town who would break in like that,' she said, pointing an accusatory finger at me.

'What does that even mean?' I asked.

'Come on, Gina,' Holly stepped between us, her hands balled into fists. 'Susie wouldn't break into the pie shop.' Her voice reached a menacing tone I'd never heard from her before and both Gina and I took a step back. 'Just because you're nuts, doesn't mean everyone else is.'

The crowd collectively gasped. Gina's eyes narrowed, and

Sheriff Buddy appeared just in time to stop the verbal attack that Gina was about to launch.

'What's going on here?' he asked and twenty voices answered him. He got the gist of the story from the eager crowd and came over to get my account. 'I'll go in and check it out,' he said to me. Quiet murmurs went through the crowd as we all waited outside. I kept catching people glancing at me and then looking away. I noticed Alice standing at the edge of the crowd surveying the scene. She held the silver cat in her arms. The cat was struggling to get away, but Alice held her firmly. Gina's eyes were boring into me as though she was hoping I would burst into flames. She was probably the one who did this so she could blame me for it. Maybe she was hoping to shut down the pie shop for a few days so she could win her stupid weight loss challenge.

Henry appeared next to me. 'What's happening?' he asked.

'Someone broke into the pie shop,' Holly told him. His eyes widened.

'Are you OK? Did they take anything?' he asked.

I shrugged. 'The sheriff's in there now.'

'Gina's trying to get everyone riled up into thinking that Susie did it,' Holly whispered.

'They're going to pull out torches and pitchforks soon,' I said.

Henry tried to hide a smile, 'I knew you were trouble from the moment you got here.' He gave my arm a playful squeeze. Then with a more serious face, 'Do you want me to go talk to her?' I shook my head.

174

Just then, Sheriff Buddy came back outside, and the crowd was silent.

'No one is inside anymore, but it's a mess in there,' he said.

'Sounds like the work of someone looking for sympathy to me,' Gina said in loud whisper. I ignored her.

'Susanna, will you come inside with me and see if you notice anything missing?' Sheriff Buddy asked.

'We'll be right out here waiting for you,' Holly said, squeezing my arm. I followed the sheriff through the front door. Broken glass crunched under my feet. I wanted to sweep it up before going any further, but I resisted the urge and followed him back into the kitchen.

'Where do you keep the cash in here? Is it missing?'

I barely heard him. The kitchen was a disaster. The warm homey feel was gone. I tried to swallow the lump at the back of my throat. Bags of flour had been thrown off the shelf. A few of them had been ripped open, and flour was strewn across the kitchen leaving a layer of white powder covering everything. I walked around, my feet making tracks in the flour, something young Susie would have enjoyed, but old Susie was just thinking about how much clean-up was ahead of me. There were a couple of smashed glass pie pans. They were sturdy so they'd only broken into a few pieces, but someone must have thrown them against the floor to make that happen. They didn't break just by dropping them. I could say that from experience. Everything from the shelves in the pantry had been knocked to the floor. It was a giant pile of cans and bags and bottles. Aunt Erma's favorite flowered coffee mug lay in a pile of broken pieces underneath the shelf at the back of the kitchen. How would I ever explain this to her?

'It was probably just a couple of kids getting into trouble during the festival,' Sheriff Buddy was saying. 'Do you notice anything missing?'

I checked for the cash box in the desk. There wasn't much there because I diligently went to the bank every day to deposit the profits. Every penny was still inside.

I shrugged. 'I don't see anything missing.' Mitzy let out a tormented howl from upstairs. I ran up and opened the door. She practically flew into my arms, shaking.

It looked around the apartment, but everything looked exactly how I left it except for a cookie cutter that was sitting on the edge of Mitzy's bed. That couldn't be blamed on the burglar though.

I went back downstairs where the sheriff was waiting, making notes in his little notebook.

'It's strange that they didn't go upstairs, isn't it?' I asked him.

He shrugged. 'Maybe the dog scared them off.'

Mitzy's mood was bolstered by me holding her, and she wagged her tail at him and let out a low growly bark, all traces of her fear gone. 'Or maybe they weren't looking to do anything besides cause trouble. Or maybe they saw you coming and ran before they found what they were looking for.'

What could they have been looking for here? The pie

shop certainly didn't have a whole lot of valuables inside. Sheriff Buddy asked a few more questions and jotted down some more notes.

'Call me if you notice anything missing,' he said, handing me his card. 'Good luck with the clean-up.' And with that he was gone.

Holly and Henry appeared at the door. 'Whoa,' Henry said looking around.

'The sheriff thinks it was just some kids,' I said. Holly and Henry exchanged a look.

'We'll help you clean up,' Holly offered.

I suddenly felt a wave of exhaustion fall over me. 'No thanks. I think I'll take care of it tomorrow morning. Maybe I'll open a little late,' I said. They seemed to understand my desire to be alone.

'Call me if you need anything,' Henry said, hugging Mitzy and I before heading out the door. Was it just my imagination or did the hug last a second longer than a typical friend hug? Holly's raised eyebrows answered that question for me.

'I'll check in with you in a little bit.' She wrapped me in her arms, careful not to squish the dog between us. Mitzy took the opportunity to lick her face. 'Thanks, Mitzy,' she said, wiping off her cheek with her sleeve. 'I can come back in the morning to help with all of this,' she motioned to the mess as she walked out the door.

I tried to put Mitzy back upstairs so I could put something over the broken window out front, but she protested with such a terrible howl that I let her follow me. It wasn't like the kitchen was sanitary at the moment anyway. I found a piece of plywood, a leftover from one of my earlier improvement projects, and hammered it in over the opening. Then I swept up the glass. With each stroke of the broom my blood pressure went up another notch. Here I was trying to help my aunt, working as hard as I could, and this was how I was treated?

Mitzy stayed close. I went to the pantry to pick up everything that wasn't broken and she settled into the office chair, her wide eyes watching me closely. I was muttering angrily at the cans as I set them down harder than necessary on the shelves. Mitzy tilted her head side to side as though thoughtfully listening to my every complaint. After the pantry, I scrubbed the countertops and mopped the floors until everything sparkled.

My stomach growled loudly. I hadn't eaten since breakfast. We went upstairs, and I filled Mitzy's bowl with food while I reheated some pizza.

Between the break-in and the baking contest disaster, my head was spinning. I was still seething about Alice's sabotage and Gina's accusations when my phone beeped with a text.

It was from Holly. It said, 'Come to the back door.' I trudged down the stairs. Mitzy almost tripped me halfway down with her need to stay as close as possible.

'If you kill me, there will be no one left to feed you,' I scolded her. She backed off a couple paces.

I cracked the back door open and Holly stood there holding up a large bottle of tequila and a shopping bag.

'I'm here to help clean up, and I brought margaritas,' she sang out.

I opened the door wider to let her in.

'How did you get this done so fast?' she marveled at the pristine kitchen.

'I was fueled by anger. Now we can just relax and have that.' I pointed to the bottle.

'Did you read this Ask Elodie?' Holly asked holding up a folded newspaper that I'd left on the kitchen table. I'd fished some old papers out of the recycling so I could catch up on past columns.

'I think I read it this morning,' I said. This morning seemed like so long ago.

'It was the one about the frogs,' she said, seeing the blank look in my eyes.

'Right, it's coming back to me now.'

'I can't believe that person wanted to put frogs in her sister's bed,' Holly said, shaking her head as she cut up a lime, 'That's cruel to the frogs. I'm glad Elodie set her straight.'

'I understand that it's not fair to the frogs, but I totally get the desire for revenge,' I said.

I had offered to help make the margaritas, but apparently they were a secret family recipe. 'You shouldn't even be in the room when I make them,' she told me. I promised not to look.

Holly began jumping up and down, holding the cocktail shaker in her hands. I raised my eyebrows.

'I have to work for my drinks,' she explained loudly, trying to be heard over the rattling ice as she hopped across the kitchen floor. 'So, who are you planning revenge against?'

'Oh, I don't know. Alice, Gina, that kid who works at the coffee shop who always skimps on the whipped cream, whoever broke into the pie shop.' I ticked them off on my fingers.

Holly served us each a drink, and we clinked glasses.

'Wait,' she cried as I put the drink to my lips. I froze. 'I brought straws.' She searched through the bag she'd brought and pulled out a couple of large, brightly colored straws that looped around a few times at the top. 'Trust me. It will taste even better if you drink it through this straw,' she said. I shrugged my shoulders and plopped the straw into my drink.

Wow, it was good.

We began plotting different forms of revenge. Switching Alice's sugar for salt so her cookies would be disgusting. Putting full fat yogurt into Gina's morning low fat yogurt smoothies. Filling the burglar's house with flour.

'I can't believe people think you broke into your own shop,' Holly said. She was sprawled across the armchair with one of her legs on a footstool and one hanging off the side.

'Yeah, why did Gina say that I was the only one who would break in "like that"?' I asked.

'Because you don't know the spell,' Holly mumbled sleepily.

'What?'

Her eyes snapped open, 'Because Gina's crazy.'

'What spell?' I asked. Why did that word keep coming up around here?

'It looks like you could use another round.' Holly grabbed my glass and trotted off to the kitchen.

The night quickly deteriorated into a sing-along of the greatest hits from the Nineties, but I couldn't get Holly's words out of my head.

Holly had made a nest of pillows and blankets on the living room floor, and I was in my usual spot on the sofa. Mitzy was curled up next to Holly's head and I worried that Mitzy would roll onto Holly's face and smother her. I didn't worry for long though because soon I was sound asleep.

Suddenly I was standing in the center of town. There were smashed pies on the ground all around me. I could hear Aunt Erma's voice yelling, 'She took them! She took them!' I started running. Where was she? I had to find her. Crusts and fruit and custards squished under my feet. No matter which direction I ran, Aunt Erma's voice sounded distant. I woke with a start and sat straight up on the couch feeling disoriented, my heart hammering in my chest.

I leapt over Holly's snoring body and ran down to the kitchen. I frantically began opening cupboard doors. Where were they? I searched every inch before finally leaning against the wall, deflated.

The spices were missing.

Chapter 15

Day 12 — Sunday, November 13th

My heart was racing. Maybe I was still a little drunk from the margaritas Holly had brought over, or maybe I had finally been pushed too far. I'd spent my whole life understanding. Every time something went wrong, I was always the understanding one. Not anymore. Now I was going to do something about it. The plan was far from well thought out. I shifted the large bag I was carrying to the other hand.

The streets were quiet except for a light breeze that rustled the last few leaves off the trees. The mannequins in the thrift store window looked menacing with the streetlights casting shadows across their blank faces. Since it was just after three in the morning, I hadn't even bothered to change out of my superhero pajamas. I wrapped my sweatshirt tighter against the damp cold air as I approached Alice's shop.

'What are you doing?' A voice behind me made me jump. I turned around to see Henry and Willy. Henry was wearing his bright yellow knit hat, and Willy wore a matching knit vest.

'Henry. You scared me. I'm just out for a late-night stroll.' My voice sounded strange. 'What are you doing out so late?'

'Willy couldn't sleep.' He patted the dog on the head. 'And when Willy can't sleep, nobody can sleep, so we decided to go for a walk.' A large roll of toilet paper fell out of my bag. Henry's eyebrows shot up.

'I'm just doing some ... decorating,' I said lamely.

He stared at me for a minute, and I thought he might tell me to go home and stop being so immature. 'Want some help?' he asked, picking up the roll. I nodded, and they followed me.

We got to Alice's shop, and I set the bag down. I pulled out a roll of toilet paper and a roll of plastic wrap.

'I'm thinking this for Alice,' I whispered, holding up the toilet paper. 'And this for Gina.' I held up the plastic wrap.

'I'm curious to see how you use that one.' He pointed at the plastic wrap. I gave him a wicked smile and handed him a roll of toilet paper.

We both froze when we heard a noise inside the shop. We listened and heard a meow. I breathed out; it was just the cat. Willy let out a low growl.

'No,' Henry said, and he quieted down immediately. After telling the dog to 'sit,' and 'wait,' both commands he obeyed perfectly, Henry came over to help.

I had never TP'd anyone's place before. We were fulfilling a childhood dream of mine and getting back at Alice. Two birds, I thought as I joyfully wrapped the toilet paper from one pillar to the next in front of the door. The cat appeared inside the window and watched us. I held my finger up to my lips and winked at her. The cat winked back at me. I was beginning to accept that everything in this town was unusual. I looked over at Henry. He was expertly throwing the roll high in the air as he covered one of the trees out front.

Moving on to the bushes next to the shop, I pictured Alice's face when she won the baking contest. That smug smile when she looked down her nose at me made me want to do more than just TP her shop. Then when she agreed with Gina that I must have broken into my own shop, something inside me snapped. Nothing Aunt Erma had taught me had prepared me for this.

I realized I'd been wrapping the same bush for a while now, and I moved on to the next. I threw the last roll haphazardly up. It hooked on the awning. We stood back to survey our work.

'I think it's a huge improvement,' Henry said. I was very aware of the fact that his arm had wrapped around my shoulders.

I felt something wet hit my nose. I looked up. Flakes of snow were falling. It was strange since it was November and had been so warm just yesterday. The moment felt surreal, and I wondered if maybe I was still dreaming.

'Now onward to our next mission,' I said holding out one of the rolls of plastic wrap in front of me to lead the way. The rest were in the bag around my wrist. Henry and

Willy followed as I led them the three blocks to Gina's Gym.

'Now what?' Henry asked.

Gina had two statues out in front of her gym on either side of the door. One was of a woman lifting a large barbell over her head and the other was of a shirtless man posing to show off his bulging muscles. We were standing under an awning, protected from the snow that was now falling heavily from the sky.

'Here, hold this there,' I pointed to the feet of the woman as I pulled out one end of the plastic wrap and handed it to him. I stretched the roll across the front door towards the other statue, wrapped it around his feet and back to where Henry was standing. I continued going back and forth, tightly wrapping layer after layer of plastic while Henry watched. Maybe I would accuse Gina of doing this to her own shop tomorrow. Give her a taste of her own medicine.

Once I got to a point where I couldn't reach anymore, Henry took over. By the time we'd used all the rolls of plastic wrap I'd brought, the front door was completely covered. It would be awfully difficult for people to get inside tomorrow morning. Henry touched the plastic wrap and murmured something.

'What are you doing?' I asked.

'What's going on out there?' a voice from a window called out before he could answer.

'Run!' Henry whispered, grabbing my hand and Willy's leash.

We ran for blocks without looking back. Snowflakes pelted our faces. Finally we stopped, dissolving into a pile of giggles. Willy pranced excitedly next to us.

'Well, thanks for letting us come along,' Henry said once he caught his breath. 'It's late, and we should get some sleep.'

He gently brushed a snowflake off my cheek. I said goodnight as they disappeared into the snowflakes. I couldn't imagine going to bed. I was so amped up on adrenaline, but when I got back to the apartment I lay down and immediately fell into a deep sleep.

I woke up the next morning to the brilliant light shining through the window. While most people grumbled about the cold, I was ready for snow angels and hot chocolate and fleece pajamas.

Holly was gone. She had made a pot of coffee and left me a note reminding me to call her if I needed anything. I called the number from Sheriff Buddy's card and got his voicemail so I left a message about the missing spices.

For once, Mitzy's enthusiasm was a bit more hesitant than mine when we went outside. She paused at the door and then sniffed the sidewalk before looking at me.

'Come on,' I said, giving her a little nudge with my foot. She backed towards the door to the kitchen. 'Come on,' I said, a little more forcefully, giving the leash a tug. She dug her nails into the tile. For such a small dog, she could sure make herself immobile.

I pulled out my cell phone and dialed Holly, 'The furry thing won't step on the white stuff,' I said flatly when she answered.

'What?' She sounded a little groggy and confused.

'The dog, the thing you call a bundle of love. She is ruining first snow day for me,' I said, glaring at Mitzy for good measure. She gazed back at me, innocently batting her eyes.

'Did you put her booties on?' Holly asked, sounding a little more alert now.

'Her what?'

'Her booties.'

'You have got to be kidding,' I said.

'What kind of person kids about dog booties?' she asked in a perfectly serious tone. 'I think Erma kept them in the little wooden chest by the back door.'

I opened the chest up, and sure enough, there were four knitted little red booties lying in there. When I pulled them out, Mitzy's tail began to wag, and she rolled over onto her back sticking all four paws into the air.

'If you really want to make points with her, you could put her scarf on.' Holly was really enjoying herself now. 'I think she likes to wear the blue one on Sundays.'

'I'm hanging up now,' I said, yelling 'thank you' as I hung up the phone and tucked it back into my pocket. I put the booties on Mitzy, and she happily skipped outside and pranced around in the snow.

We walked down the street. I couldn't help myself. I had to go check out our handiwork. A few inches of fluffy snow had fallen, and it muffled my steps on the unshoveled sidewalk. I casually walked by Alice's shop on the sidewalk across the street and tried not to stare as I went by. Stan was outside scooping wet bits of toilet paper into a big plastic garbage bag while Alice barked directions at him. How had she gotten him to do that? A couple walked past pointing and snickering behind their hands. A man stopped to take a picture, and Alice glared at him so menacingly that he quickly put his phone away and hurried down the street.

'Ew, ew, ew,' Stan said, as a large glob stuck to his fingers.

'Stop being such a baby. It's just paper,' Alice said, though I noticed she hadn't touched any of it herself.

I tried not to giggle as I turned down the street to go towards the gym.

My phone beeped with a text from Henry. 'Apparently our artwork is the talk of the town. What are we going to decorate tonight?' I smiled.

I was still half a block away when I spotted Gina with a box cutter angrily tearing through the plastic in front of the door. Two other women were out front with her. One was trying to gather up pieces of plastic wrap that were flying away, and the other one was on the ground doing one armed push-ups in the snow. Every now and then she would switch hands – probably when it got too cold.

A man in a green tracksuit walked up carrying a gym bag.

'What? We can't get inside?' His voice sounded panicked. 'But I can't miss a workout. I still need to lose two more pounds this month.'

Gina growled something incoherent, though I thought I could make out an expletive or two.

He dropped to the ground next to the woman and began doing push-ups with her. I almost felt guilty before remembering Gina's accusations.

Chapter 16

Day 12 — Sunday

Dear Elodie,

I recently started dating someone. Things have been going great so far. We like the same movies, she laughs at my jokes, and she doesn't mind that I yell at figure skaters on TV when they fall. I think this could be the real deal.

The problem is my family. Whenever we plan a date night, my family looks in my date book to see where we're going. I keep a very thorough calendar. Once they find out where we're going to be, they just show up. I planned a fancy date night last week, and sure enough, my family appeared in the middle of our appetizers. To make matters worse, my parents and three sisters pulled up chairs around the table so they could join us. Needless to say, it was too crowded and uncomfortable. After consuming lots of food and drinks, they all disappeared right before the check came.

I've tried talking to them about it. They always dismiss

my concerns. They tell me they just want to better get to know the person I'm dating. They think I'm being too sensitive and that their behavior isn't out of line at all.

How do I get them to back off before they scare away this woman?

Sincerely,
Table for Too Many

Dear Table for Too Many,
Buy a date book that locks or be spontaneous.
Ask and I'll Answer,
Elodie

It began snowing again as soon as I got back to the pie shop. The flakes came down hard and fast while I prepped for the day. I found some Christmas CDs in the back of Aunt Erma's cupboards.

Violet stalked in the second I unlocked the door.

'The spices are missing?' She sounded a little panicked.

'Yes. How did you know that?' I asked.

'All of them?' She ignored my question.

'I think so.'

She then proceeded to question me for the next twenty minutes. She asked if I had seen anyone suspicious around the pie shop or if I had any inkling who might have broken in.

I answered, 'I don't know,' to a lot of her questions. Sure, I might suspect Alice or Gina, but I didn't have any evidence except that I didn't really like either of them. Finally, she left, as frustrated with me as ever.

Flora came in around noon, a little later than the usual time. She wore a bright red hat and snowflakes covered her from head to toe. 'It's really coming down out there!' she said with a shiver.

'Isn't it beautiful?' I said.

'Ah, you're one of those snow lovers, huh?' she said. 'I am still on the fence about this whole winter thing. I've thought about spending winters in Florida, but all my family and friends are local. I don't know what I would do down there. Besides be warm.' She looked a little wistful.

I laughed. 'Would you like a cup of coffee while you wait for the others?'

'I am afraid the others aren't going to make it today. It's a little too far for Mr Barnes in this weather, and Lena is having a run on snow blowers today. I just wanted to check on you after that horrible break-in,' she explained.

'Oh, I'm alright.' I watched her to see if she bought my lie.

'Do you have time to sit and have a slice of pie with me?' she asked.

'I definitely have time,' I said. 'I don't think I am going to get a lot of customers today.' The snow was coming down so hard, I could not even see across the street now.

'The plow will come through eventually,' she said. 'But you know Bob will start work on the ice rink first. The kids get so excited to skate. Plus, Bob likes to ice skate too. You know he used to dream of being an Olympic figure skater back in his youth. He dances around the ice when he thinks no one is watching. He's not half bad either.' She took her coat off, hung it on the back of her chair, and pulled her hat off. Some of her hair had come loose from her bun, and the strands stood straight up from the static electricity.

I ignored the fact that she spoke about Bob like I should know who he was. I had gotten used to that.

'There's an ice rink in town?' I asked. I too had Olympic aspirations. Not in reality of course. I was a complete klutz on the ice, but in theory. When I was a kid I used to perform skating programs with my best friend on the floor of our living rooms. We would dress up and jump and dance and twirl about to different songs. Then we would make our parents award us medals that we'd fashioned out of construction paper.

'Oh yes, it's really close too,' she said. 'You know the clearing just over where the Larsons live?' I stared at her blankly. 'The place where Tommy broke his leg in that pogo stick accident?' I continued to stare blankly. She realized she wasn't going to get anywhere with me. 'You go just down the block here, take a right and before long you'll see it on your left-hand side. It won't take you long to walk there at all.'

'I might have to check it out,' I said. 'But I don't have skates.'

'Erma should have some. I think she kept them in the trunk by the back door. We go out skating every now and then. She can skate circles around me.' She had stopped looking at me and was now looking at the selection of pies. 'I will have a piece of the pumpkin,' she said. 'I feel like I need a little extra vitamin C in my life today. Don't forget to pile on the whipped cream.' I whipped my own whipped cream like Aunt Erma did. At home, I always bought cans of whipped cream because I had forgotten how amazing homemade whipped cream was. I didn't think I could ever go back to that again. I usually found a way to taste test a few spoonfuls of the cream each day under the guise of quality control. It was so good. I served up two pieces of pumpkin pie and went to join her at the table out front with two cups of coffee.

'Just make sure if you go skating, you go after dark,' she warned me.

'Why's that?'

'The little hooligans like to skate really fast and then slide across the ice on their stomachs, but all the kids in town have to be home by dark. It's much quieter and more peaceful if you wait. You might even get the whole rink to yourself,' she said.

'Oh, that would be fun, and probably the safest for everyone. I might slide across the ice on my stomach, but it would be an accident.'

She laughed, but then her face grew serious. 'How are you doing after the break-in?' she asked again.

I shrugged. 'I'm alright.'

'They didn't take anything?'

'It turns out they stole the spices,' I said.

Her face paled. 'All of them?' she asked.

I nodded, 'The whole box was gone.'

'Have you heard anything from your aunt?' Flora asked.

'No. I'm starting to get more than a little worried.'

'I wouldn't worry,' she said. 'Sometimes a woman just has some things to take care of.' Her voice was perfectly calm, but her brow furrowed in the middle a little when she talked.

'Doesn't she have a cell phone?' I had asked this question before, but I couldn't help hoping I would get a different answer this time.

'She doesn't like cell phones. Says too much screen time is turning everyone's brains to mush,' Flora said.

Despite the nagging feeling in my stomach, we moved the conversation along. We gossiped about people in town and the upcoming holidays. I wasn't as plugged into the gossip mill as Lena and Mr Barnes were, so I was not as good at participating in the discussions, but I was an eager listener. It felt homey to be gossiping with Flora – just me and her.

I wanted to ask her about Henry. She seemed to know him so well, but I couldn't figure out how to bring him up without looking like a schoolgirl with a crush. Which, to be honest, was a little bit how I felt.

'I should really get going,' Flora said once her pie was gone.

'Maybe I could visit you at the bookstore later. I've been wanting to spend more time in there, and I don't think anyone will miss me here today,' I said.

'That would be lovely, dear,' she said with a smile.

Flora bundled up and was out the door with a wave. The snow had lightened up a little, so I was able to see her red hat for part of her walk across the street before it faded into the flakes.

I had zero customers after Flora. Was it because of the snow or because of the Fall Festival fiasco? I flipped the sign to 'Closed' later that afternoon and walked over to Flora's bookstore. The snow was just a light dusting of flakes coming from the sky now. Even though her shop was about forty steps from mine, I was freezing by the time I got there.

'You came,' she called joyfully as I stepped inside.

'Of course I came. I had to kick out the fifty people who were inside waiting to pay for pie, but I came here. For you,' I joked.

'Quiet day, huh?'

'Yup, it's only been me and Mitzy since you left us earlier,' I said. 'I organized the books on the bookshelf by alphabetical order. Then I moved on to the CDs and organized them by genre and then by alphabetical order. Then I moved on to the pantry. I instituted a whole new organizational system. Aunt Erma probably won't be able to find anything when she gets back.'

'Oh, I'm sure she'll love everything you've done with the place,' Flora said. 'She'll be so grateful to you for coming.'

I wandered around the shop. I had asked her once how she was able to keep track of everything. The books were stacked so high and so deep. What if someone was looking for something specific? I didn't see a computer to keep track of inventory anywhere in the shop.

'Oh, I have my ways,' she had told me with a twinkle in her eye.

'She always has what people are looking for, and she always knows right where to find it,' Mr Barnes had told me.

Christmas music was playing, and Flora was singing along softly. The place was brightly lit, and she had hung Christmas lights along all the bookshelves and around the cash register desk at the front.

'It's so festive in here,' I said.

'Oh honey, I am just getting started,' she said. 'I am going to make a Christmas tree out of books by the front door next.'

Would I ever figure out the layout of this place? I went down one aisle and over to the next and already I was lost in a maze of bookshelves. One book caught my eye. The young girl pictured on the cover bore a vague resemblance to me when I was a kid. I opened it up and ran my finger over the first page. The paper was thick and had a soft worn quality to it. It was a book of fairy tales. Each one was accompanied by intricate illustrations, all of which featured the girl who was both familiar and not at the same time. I carried it to the front to buy.

'Good choice,' Flora said as she stood up from her downward dog position to ring me up. She hadn't been able to make it to her usual yoga class today, so she was practicing in the shop.

I grabbed my purchase and headed out the door. The snow was coming down heavier again. I heard the rumble and scraping just in time to get out of the street before the plow truck came through. It sprayed snow up covering me from head to toe with slushy ice. I felt like a walking snowman as I tried to dust off my book and myself. I really should have taken Flora up on the offer of a bag. Maybe a bag for my whole body. I felt the dampness seeping through my coat already.

I ran upstairs to take a quick shower to warm up and changed into my pajamas. It was still three hours before the pie shop was supposed to close, but I figured no one would come in. Just in case, I flipped the sign to 'Open' again once I got back downstairs.

I was right. Almost. I was sitting in the overstuffed red chair in the corner when Henry walked in. I was halfway through the first fairy tale in the book, and I was already hooked. It was about an evil queen who turned all of her enemies into squirrels.

'Whoa,' Henry said. 'You blend right into the chair.' I was wearing a long red sweatshirt and red leggings with white polka dots. Mitzy sat on the arm of the chair. 'Red's a good color on you,' he said and my heart fluttered a little.

'You're the second customer I've had today,' I said, prying myself out of the chair.

We chatted for a minute while I boxed up his pies for the nursing home residents.

'I told them I might not make it here today with all the snow, and there was almost a mutiny,' he said with a laugh. 'Mr Macabee said that back in his day he would walk twelve miles to school in three feet of snow with baked potatoes in his boots to keep him warm, and he would eat the potatoes for lunch. Then Mr Cramer shook his fist at me and said, "Bringing us pie is the most important part of your job, so get going."'

'I pay him to say those things,' I teased.

I told him about my plans to go ice skating later. I asked him if he'd seen the rink. He said it was beautiful, that Bob had gotten it all done a couple hours ago, and the kids were having fun shoveling it off. I was excited when he said that Bob had even hung Christmas lights on the trees around the rink.

Later that night, after I had found Aunt Erma's skates exactly where Flora said they would be, I traipsed through the snow to find the ice rink. I was wearing black leggings and a long, thick maroon sweater with lots of layers underneath. My coat was still soaking wet after my walk back from the bookshop earlier in the day. The snow had stopped, the sky was crystal clear, and the stars twinkled. The moon was full, but it was very light considering how late it was.

The ice sparkled in the Christmas lights that hung on the trees surrounding the clearing. I put the skates on. Luckily, they fit perfectly, but they felt strange on my feet. It had been years since I'd been on ice skates. I stepped out onto the ice, pushed off with the confidence of an Olympian, and promptly fell flat on my face. I'm talking full on belly slide. I could almost hear the crowd gasp. Oh wait, that was a real gasp. I looked up and saw Henry peering down at me.

'Are you OK?' he asked concerned.

'Of course,' I said. 'Did you see the triple toe loop I did before that fall?'

'Yes, I definitely did,' he said, hiding a smile. 'It was beautiful, you almost stuck that landing.'

I stood up carefully so as not to go flying again. I guess I was a little out of practice. I always thought visualization was everything, and I often visualized that I was flying around the ice when I watched skating specials on television.

'What are you doing here?' I asked him as I stood with my knees bent hoping that position didn't look as awkward as it felt.

'I was just walking home from work. I didn't dare drive in this morning with all the snow. I saw you down here and came to say hi. Just in time to catch you at the end of a beautiful performance,' he said.

'Thank you, oh so much, for humoring me,' I said. 'Since you're making fun of me, do you have skates?'

'Uh...' He looked uncomfortable.

'Come on buddy,' I said. 'If you have skates, you have to go get them and come out here with me. I want to see you strut your stuff.'

'I think my skates are broken.'

'Yeah, right.' I rolled my eyes.

'They need to be sharpened?'

'Nice try. Go get them.'

'Fine, I'll be back in a bit. But I'm only doing this to make sure you don't break your neck because you're out here alone,' he said turning to head towards his house.

'How very chivalrous of you,' I called after him. I wondered briefly if he would actually come back or if he would just go home, lock all the doors, and turn off the lights.

I skated around the rink. I felt bolder with every stroke. I was cruising around at a halfway decent speed by the time Henry came back. He carried hockey skates, two hockey sticks, and a puck.

'Um, what are you doing?' I asked.

'I figured it would be safer if you had something to hold onto when you skate,' he joked. 'We don't have to play. It was just an idea.' He threw the hockey sticks into the snow.

'I bet I can beat you at hockey,' I said with more certainty than I felt.

'Oh yeah?' His face lit up.

'Yup!' I nodded and went over to fish one of the sticks out of the snowbank.

'Care to make it interesting?' he asked.

My eyebrows shot up. 'How do you suggest we do that?'

'Loser of the game buys drinks at Sal's,' he said as he finished lacing up his skates.

'You're on!' I glided over and shook his hand.

My confidence began to dissipate when Henry got out on the ice. He flew around the rink so fast it was almost as though his blades weren't touching the ice.

'Just need to do a couple warm up laps,' he called out as he sped by me.

I gaped at him, then quickly tried to hide my surprise.

He skidded to a stop, sending a spray of ice into the air.

He grabbed a handful of snow from one of the piles by the ice and began making snowballs.

'We'll put two on each end, and you have to get the puck between the snowballs to score a goal,' Henry explained.

'Yeah, I get it,' I said. 'Now let's get to some hockey playing!'

He took the puck out of his pocket, and the game began. He was playing a very gentlemanly game, but I'll admit, I was out to win. Henry pulled his stick back, ready to shoot the puck into the goal, and I lunged at him. We both fell to the ice.

'Oops,' I said as I landed on top of him. He felt warm and was breathing hard from all the physical activity, I think.

'Oops?' he asked. 'I think you did that on purpose. If there was a ref here, I think he'd call a foul.'

I carefully pushed myself off him and sat up on the ice.

'What?' I asked in mock horror. 'That was a perfectly legal maneuver. I think you need to check your hockey handbook again.'

'Hockey handbook?'

'Yup,' I nodded earnestly at him. 'When one player is playing at the level of Wayne Gretzky, the other player can check said player at any time in order to prevent him or her from scoring a goal. I watched a lot of figure skating growing up which taught me that it's perfectly acceptable to incapacitate your rival in order to win.'

He held his hands up in surrender. We played a little more, and I scored a goal. Since we hadn't decided how many points we were going to play to, I claimed that one was good enough. I did a victory lap around the ice while singing 'We are the Champions.'

'Fine, you win,' he said. 'Let's go get drinks.'

'I can drink a lot,' I said. 'I hope you brought a lot of cash in that wallet. And I don't want to hear from you that any of my playing was "unfair".' I used my fingers to do air quotes.

He laughed. 'I wouldn't dare call any of your moves "unfair".' He mocked my air quotes.

We took our skates off and headed to Sal's.

Henry and I found a table near the bar and ordered a couple of beers. I don't know what it was about the drinks here, but they were more delicious than any drink I'd had anywhere else. I smiled a little when the soundtrack for Titanic came on. We drank in silence for a few minutes.

'How are things at the nursing home?' I asked.

'Good,' he said taking a big gulp of beer. 'Next week they're going to put on a Thanksgiving show.'

'A Thanksgiving show? What does that entail?' I asked.

'Beats me,' he said. 'They wanted to do it without me because they want to surprise me. For my birthday.' He added the last part as an afterthought.

'It's almost your birthday?' That got me excited. I loved birthdays.

He shrugged and glanced at me as though he wished he could take back what he said.

'When? When is it?' I bounced in my seat. He reached over and slid my beer away from me.

'I think we need to cut you off,' he said. 'Maybe you should have a water? Soda? Iced tea?'

'The only kind of tea I drink is Long Island,' I said, reaching over to grab my beer. 'And you can't change the subject. I want to know when your birthday is. If you don't tell me, I'll just find out from someone else. Hey Sal,' I called out towards the bar. 'When's Henry's birthday?'

'Today,' Sal called back.

'Oh yeah? We should sing now,' a woman's voice called out.

'Yeah, let's sing.' I shot at huge smile at Henry who was now glaring at me.

Sal poured a healthy shot behind the bar.

'Happy birthday to you,' I began and everyone in the bar joined in. Sal brought the shot over to the table and lit it on fire. We finished singing, and as Henry blew it out, mouthed, 'I hate you,' then winked, and took the shot while everyone cheered. I reached over and grabbed his arm. 'You're welcome,' I said. 'Now how many shots will it take to make you forgive me?'

'At least two more, and you have to do them with me,' he said.

Sal made us some shots that tasted sweet and lemony and sparkled in the glass. I was feeling loose and giggly.

'Henry, Henry, Henry,' I said, reaching across the table to grab his arm again. 'Tell me about yourself.'

'What do you want to know?' His face was glowing a bit too.

'What do you love about the nursing home?' I asked.

'What are your plans for the rest of your life? How many serious relationships have you had?' I kind of surprised myself with that last question, and from the look on Henry's face, him too.

'Um...' he began. 'I love the people at the nursing home. They're all really wonderful. They're like family. Sometimes they annoy the heck out of me, but usually I truly enjoy being with them. I would like to travel for a while, then spend the rest of my life in this town. It's perfect here.'

'Wow,' I said. 'Why?'

He shrugged. 'I just feel like I belong here. How about you? How long do you think you'll stay here?'

I paused for a minute. I'd been taking things just one day at a time since I'd gotten here. This trip hadn't gone at all like I expected. Aunt Erma was supposed to be here with me. Alice and her cookie shop weren't supposed to be here. 'I don't know.'

We sat in silence for a moment.

'If you stay, you can enter the snowman building competition next month,' he said with a smile.

'If that's not motivation to stay, I don't know what is,' I said.

'The prize is a gift basket that Lena puts together of stuff from around her apartment that she doesn't want anymore,' he said. 'Last year the winner got a chipped coffee mug and six bobblehead dolls.'

'Wow, I didn't realize what was on the line. I'll definitely have to try to stay,' I said. He perked up a little at that.

We finished our drinks. Henry still wanted to review the

video replay of our hockey game for fouls, but he was a good sport about it and paid the tab. We walked down the street together. We were about half a block from the pie shop when I realized I was holding Henry's arm. It was as much for stability as anything. Those drinks were strong.

Henry hadn't pulled away in disgust. Was that out of gentlemanliness or did he not mind for other reasons? My mind began to race, but I was having trouble finishing thoughts. Should I go in for the kiss? What if he was just being friendly? Then I would probably lose one of my only remaining customers. We got to the back door at the pie shop.

'Thanks for ice skating with me,' I said, suddenly aware that he was facing me. He was a little taller than me, and I couldn't help but look up through my eyelashes, a move I had seen in every romantic comedy I'd ever watched.

His hand was reaching towards my face, and I held my breath. 'Thank you for singing "Happy Birthday" to me,' he said.

'Really?' I asked, letting my breath out.

He gave me a grudging smile and brushed the hair behind my ear. Then he let out a squeal and jumped back.

'What's wrong?' I asked, wondering if my breath was really that bad.

He was looking down. I followed his gaze and saw the cat had returned and was circling around his legs. Henry sneezed. 'Sorry, I'm allergic to...' He sneezed again, pointing at the cat. 'I'll talk to you later.' Two more sneezes and he vanished around the corner.

Chapter 17

Day 13 — Monday, November 14

Dear Elodie,

I have been a dancer for as long as I can remember. Recently I suffered a severe injury to my right elbow. I have always been known within the dancing community and beyond for having superior elbow work. I'm devastated that I can't dance anymore. All of my friends are dancers and they don't seem to know how to talk to me because talking about dancing is too painful for me. My family seems to think that I should just shake it off and do something new.

I'm lost and I don't know who to turn to. Can you help me figure out what to do with myself?

Sincerely,

Dancing Dud

Dear Dancing Dud,

It can be hard when you lose something that has been such an important part of your life for so long. You

209

don't say what type of dance you practice, but you say that the problem is with your elbow. There are many different types of dance. Perhaps you could practice one that is less elbow-focused. Maybe you could become well known for your superior knee work.

If this isn't an option for you, try exploring different interests and joining some different clubs until you can find a new passion and direction for your life. Maybe some of your dancing friends can join you as you try these different things or maybe you'll meet some new friends and expand your social circle.

This may feel like you're losing something, but consider it an opportunity for new adventure.

Ask and I'll Answer,

Elodie

'Stupid cat,' I muttered, still thinking about the night before. Mitzy and I had stayed up late and gotten up early. I was full of an excited energy that I hadn't felt in a long time. I tried to channel that energy into thinking of ways to bring business back to the pie shop now that the special spices had been stolen. My mind went from advertising a happy hour at the pie shop where slices would be half off between three and four in the afternoon, to thinking about how it felt to lay on top of Henry.

I had decided to take advantage of our extra time this morning by going to the diner to pick up a couple of egg sandwiches and a cup of the special hazelnut coffee they made for breakfast. The sun felt warm and was beginning to melt some of the snow giving the sidewalks and street a nice sheen. I was trying to dodge the fat drops of water that were falling from the awnings, so I didn't spot her until it was too late. Gina was walking down the street towards me. I looked for a doorway or alley to duck into, but I didn't see anywhere to hide, and she was approaching fast.

I wracked my brain for some smooth retort to whatever snarky insult she was going to hurl at me. My brain filled with schoolyard comebacks like, 'I'm rubber you're glue,' and the ever-mature, 'I know you are, but what am I?'

She got closer. I plastered a smile on my face and hoped that I looked calm, cool, and confident. 'Hey Gina,' I said.

Her eyes stared blankly ahead. That was strange. It wasn't like her to ignore an opportunity to rip me apart.

'Gina?' I tried again. I didn't know why I was poking the bear with a stick. I was sure a therapist would trace it back to my relationship with my mother. Mitzy let out a low growl, but still Gina didn't even glance in our direction as she passed.

Wow. Gina didn't really seem like the cold shoulder type. I turned and watched her continue down the street. Her steps were quick and stiff. Was the zombie apocalypse upon us?

I saw Flora across the street skipping along. Good, someone friendly. We crossed the street to talk to her.

'Hi Flora,' I called. Her bright pink scarf was wrapped around her face, but I could tell she was smiling. 'Are you going to come into the pie shop today?'

She pulled her scarf down, 'Oh no, dear,' she said joyfully.

'I'm just coming from Alice's cookie shop.' She held up a large paper bag in her hand to show me. Mitzy let out an uncertain whine.

'What? You went to Alice's shop?' Her betrayal stung a little.

'Well, I was just walking past, and she was offering free samples. I only meant to take one because I hadn't eaten breakfast this morning, but they were so good. I had to go inside and buy a dozen.' She smiled as she told her story as though she had no idea that I would be upset about it. 'I'd share, but a dozen really isn't that many.' She clutched the bag to her chest like a child and gave me a wary look like she was afraid I would try and steal her cookies.

'OK, well, see you later.' I turned to keep walking.

'Probably not anytime soon though,' she called gleefully after me. 'I'm thinking about seeing if the others want to become the Morning Cookie Crew. Has a nice ring to it.'

My mouth fell open. What was going on today?

I froze when I got to the town square. It was packed full of people. I tried to make sense of the strange scene unfolding before me. There was a group of three women in business suits doing push-ups in unison while one of them counted out loud.

'Look, I can climb this!' A gray-haired man with a beard and glasses was trying to shimmy up the light pole.

Five people were trying to pull the bench out of the ground. I jumped out of the way as a herd of people came running down the street. Two of the women in the group were wearing tight knee-length skirts, and I saw more than one pair of high heels. My toes winced. What were they running from? I looked down the street behind them, but I didn't see a monster or a herd of elephants or a tidal wave.

'We can go faster,' I heard someone yell.

Were they running just for exercise? Wow, Gina's town weight loss challenge was really catching on. This was out of control. Maybe that was why she had been so unresponsive. Maybe that was what a happy Gina looked like. This was just nuts though. Even for Hocus Hills.

I saw Alice standing in front of her shop watching the chaos. Her brow furrowed in concern. I understood. I was concerned too. Mitzy tugged at the leash trying to pull me back towards the pie shop. I picked her up just in time to save her from being crushed by Sheriff Buddy who was doing consecutive cartwheels across the grass.

'I think we can throw her in the air.' A skinny guy with wide rimmed glasses and a poof of curly brown hair on his head grabbed my arm.

'What?' I screeched, trying to wrench my arm from his grip. Mitzy barked fiercely in my arms. For the first time ever, I wished Mitzy was the size of Willy.

'Good idea!' A young woman with a blonde ponytail and yoga pants grabbed my other elbow.

'Hey,' I said, struggling in their grip. 'There will be no throwing of anybody.' But it was like they couldn't even hear me.

A group had formed now, but instead of anyone coming to my rescue, they all began to shout bets about how high they could throw me. My heart started racing. Mitzy trembled in my arms, and I regretted that I hadn't started carrying mace with me like my mother had suggested. I yelled for help, but everyone in town seemed to have lost their minds. Hands were now grasping me and someone had initiated a count to three. They were on two when I heard a familiar voice yell, 'Move!' so loudly it made me jump even above the cacophony of the group.

'Get your hands off her.' Lena appeared by my side and glared at people until they shrank away. I was glad I wasn't on the receiving end of that look and relieved that she had come to our rescue. I often dreamt of flying as a kid, but my dreams never involved me being thrown in the air by a crazy mob. The crowd dispersed after a few terrifying threats from Lena. Her voice was deep and commanding. I set Mitzy down. She seemed grateful to be on solid ground again. I threw myself into Lena's arms.

'Thank you,' I said over and over again.

'Oh honey, it's all right,' she said in a tone much more soothing than the one she had just been using as she patted my back. 'Let me walk you two back to the shop.'

For the first time in my life, my need for coffee and food was gone. I nodded and followed her, casting furtive glances at the group that had now decided to try and lift Ralph the plumber's red van. I wondered how Ralph would feel about that until I realized he was spearheading the group. 'Lift with your legs, not with your back,' he called out to everyone as they grabbed an edge of the van.

Lena talked about what a beautiful bright November day it was on our walk back to the shop. I didn't say anything until we were safely behind the locked door of the pie shop.

'What the heck is happening out there?' I demanded.

Lena shrugged. 'People go a little stir crazy after the first snow. And you know, small towns really attract some nutty people. Did you hear about the Talbots making the whole floor of their living room a trampoline?' She stared at me with wide eyes. 'See? Nutty!'

'That was more than just a little town nuttiness,' I said. Mitzy had jumped up on the red chair and was already snoring softly.

'Here, you sit down and I'll make you some coffee.' She bustled back towards the coffee pot. I grabbed her arm.

'Do I look like I need coffee?' My eyes were wide, and I still felt a little shaky as though on caffeine overload.

'How about some Irish coffee?' she asked with a wink, and dug around in her purse for a second before producing a flask.

'No, I need answers.' I blew out a frustrated breath.

'Whoa, is that the time?' she asked, looking up at the clock. 'Sorry sweetheart, but I have a meeting to get to. You should stay closed for the rest of the day, and don't go outside again. Everything will be back to normal tomorrow, I'm sure.' She set her flask on the table. 'In case you change your mind.' She winked. She was out the door, calling a reminder to lock up behind her, before I could form another sentence.

What in the world was going on here?

Chapter 18

Day 14 — Tuesday, November 15

Dear Elodie,

I'm starting to feel like my spouse is out to get me. We've been married for a few months. Everything seemed so perfect at the beginning, but lately she has been doing so many things that are driving me crazy. She has to be doing them on purpose.

We take turns with most of the household chores. When it was her turn to do the laundry, she started folding my pants into thirds instead of fourths. Thirds! Can you imagine? Now my pants piles don't stay perfectly straight. When she mows the lawn, she does it in a diagonal pattern instead of straight across. It's so aesthetically unappealing. Then, without any discussion at all, she decided to start putting dirty dishes on the left side of the sink and clean dishes on the right. When I confronted her, she said it makes more sense to put the dirty dishes directly above the dishwasher for easier loading. I had grown accustomed to putting dirty dishes on the right. I don't like change. Shouldn't she at least have talked to me and taken my feelings into account before making such a huge life change?

I love my wife, so I hate to think that my marriage might be over, but I'm not sure if I can live like this much longer.

Sincerely,
Suffering Spouse

Dear Suffering Spouse,

First of all, take a deep breath. There is a lot of compromise involved in a successful marriage. Try to accept the way your wife does these tasks around the house. Any sort of criticism is likely to start a fight. If you find that you can't accept how she folds your pants or mows the lawn, offer to always be the one who does those particular chores.

Being married can be a major adjustment for some couples. Dig a little deeper into your soul and make sure that your desire to turn these minor issues into deal breakers doesn't stem from a deeper anxiety about marriage. Maybe your partner is feeling the same anxiety, and you two can work through it together.

Also, I'm certainly not an expert, but you might want to consider talking to a professional about your control issues.

Ask and I'll Answer,
Elodie

A Slice of Magic

The air felt different today than it had yesterday. Yesterday it felt charged, almost staticky. Today, that feeling was gone, but that didn't stop Mitzy and I from glancing over our shoulders as we stood in the grass.

The sun was shining, and the snow from a couple of days ago was almost completely erased from the earth except for a few stray melting patches in the alley.

I'd stayed closed yesterday as Lena suggested. Mitzy and I only ventured outside a few times so she could relieve herself, and on those occasions, she was a dog on a mission. No excessive sniffing. She did her business and was ready to retreat to the safety of the apartment.

Back inside, the phone rang. It was Lena telling me that everything was fine, and I should open the shop today. She assured me that she and the rest of the Morning Pie Crew would be there as usual.

I prepped the pies, making six different kinds at once. A pretty bold move on my part. The last time I tried making so many kinds of pie at the same time, I ended up putting all the sugar in the blueberry pie and none in the pumpkin or cherry pies. The result was not pleasant. Today I was making pumpkin pie, peach pie, pear pie, cherry pie, apple pie, and chocolate chip cheesecake. I was particularly excited about the cheesecake. The picture next to the recipe online was enough to make me drool on my keyboard.

Though business had been almost non-existent except for the Morning Pie Crew and Henry, I still went full speed ahead with my baking. I believed if I continued to bake a bunch of pies, the customers would eventually come to eat them.

I swung around in my euphoria to turn the oven on so it could preheat. I turned the knob. I expected to hear the familiar whoosh of the oven firing up. But there was silence. I turned the knob off and then on again. I turned it on and waited a minute before sticking my hand inside. Still there was nothing. No heat. Nada. I tried a few more times before realizing it was hopeless. The oven was broken. And yes, I did make sure it was plugged in. I gazed in dismay at my in-progress pies. What could I do?

I tried to take deep breaths as I dialed Holly. Of course, she didn't pick up. Why would she in my hour of need? I was working myself up into a nice panic attack. I had to find an oven. The small toaster oven upstairs would take days to bake all these pies. I loaded the pies into boxes. Someone in this town had to have an oven I could use. I found a dolly and carefully stacked the boxes on top of each other. I pushed them down the alley and rounded the corner onto the sidewalk. As if in slow motion, the boxes began to slide off the side. I threw myself at the stack trying to right it.

'Whoa!' All of a sudden someone was beside me, and the stack righted itself. I looked up and saw Henry. I hadn't even seen him touch the pies, but the boxes stood solidly on the dolly. I let out the breath I had been holding.

'I could hug you. Your timing is perfect!' I said. He blushed a little.

'Just the right place at the right time,' he said.

'No really, you should be wearing a superhero cape,' I said.

'I usually have it on, but it's at the dry cleaner's today.'

'Where do you live, and do you have an oven?' I asked.

He looked a little confused. 'I live a couple blocks that way—' he pointed '—and yes.'

'My oven's broken,' I wailed and started to launch into my story about how I was having a good morning with no mistakes until I discovered that the kitchen was out to get me. 'You know what? I can tell you the story while they're baking. Can I please, please, please use your oven?'

'Sure,' he said. 'Can I help you?' He reached for the dolly.

'I got it, thanks,' I said. 'Just stay close in case they tip over.'

We made it without any more pie avalanches. Henry lived in a small brick house with red shutters. I could see the remnants of a beautiful garden and a few hearty flowers still bloomed by the house.

'You garden?' I asked, surprised.

He shrugged. 'A little.'

I carefully rolled the dolly up the brick pathway to the front door. It looked like more than a little to me. There was a step up to the front door so Henry and I carried the boxes of pies inside.

Willy greeted us, his whole body wiggling as his tongue licked the air in excitement.

'Willy, sit,' Henry said, firmly.

Willy's rear hit the floor immediately. His tail thumped against the wall like a loud drum. He craned his neck towards me as though hoping I would pet him or drop the pies I was carrying.

Once we got all the pies inside, I went to scratch Willie behind the ears all while trying to dodge his giant tongue. After a minute he was satisfied by my hello and trotted off.

The inside of Henry's house was very neat and simple. He had lovely dark wood floors. His kitchen was spotless save for a dirty coffee mug and cereal bowl that sat by the sink. I was ecstatic to see that he had a double wall oven.

'What temperatures would you like them set?' he asked.

'375 and 425 please.' I unloaded the pies from their boxes.

'On it,' he said, adjusting the temperature gauge.

'Now who can I call to fix the oven?' I pulled out my cell phone.

'Probably Bob is your best bet.'

'Bob the snowplow and ice rink guy?' I asked.

'Yes, he's also the appliance repair guy,' he said, 'but I wouldn't call him before noon.'

'Why?' I was still poised to dial.

'He is not a morning person, and if you wake him up, he'll charge you three times his normal rate,' Henry said.

'Is there anyone else I can call? With everything that's been going on, the last thing I need is to give customers another excuse to go get cookies instead of pies,' I said.

'I'd wait for Bob. He's the best. If he can't make it today, you can always come over again tomorrow and use my oven,' he offered.

While the pies baked, Henry and I chatted and drank coffee sitting at a little table just off the kitchen. Henry told me about his mom who had passed away ten years ago, and his dad who lived in a condo in Florida. He had three brothers who were now scattered across the country. With just a few minutes left on the timer, I got up to check on the pies. On the way back to the table, I saw a framed picture of him and all the residents from the nursing home on the wall.

'Nice picture,' I said.

'Oh yeah.' He looked over at it. 'They gave that to me for my birthday a couple years ago. Mrs B told me that I should display it prominently in my house because, and I quote, "the chicks will dig it,"' he laughed.

'How's that working for you?' I asked.

'Well, so far you're the only "chick" who's seen it,' he said. 'If you don't mind me asking, are you "digging it?"'

Before I could answer, Henry's cell phone rang.

'Excuse me, I have to get this.' He walked towards the front door, and his landline rang. 'Wow, I'm popular today. I'll let the answering machine get that one.' He stepped outside with his cell phone and the answering machine picked up the landline.

I could hear Henry's voice coming out of the answering machine. 'Hi. You've reached Henry Doyle. Please leave your name and telephone number after the beep and I will get back to you as quickly as possible.' He sounded so official.

I knew it was rude to listen, but I was standing right there. What was I supposed to do? Plug my ears?

A male voice began to speak urgently. 'Henry, call me

immediately. We need to discuss the developing situation around that new woman in town. I think I found something else out. Call me.' Click.

My heart raced. Who was that man on the phone? He had to be talking about me. Or Alice. There really weren't many new people in town to choose from. Maybe Henry would have a perfectly logical explanation for the message when he came back inside.

As my mind wandered, I began to wander too. Just off the eat-in kitchen, there was a cozy living room with a couple of brown corduroy overstuffed chairs that matched the sofa and a big screen TV. There was a giant dog bed by one of the chairs. Just to the left of the living room was a small hallway where there was a bathroom with dark blue walls and a claw foot tub. Next to that was a bedroom with a perfectly made bed. Willy was sprawled across the navy bedspread. He stretched from corner to corner and his legs twitched in his sleep. Across from the bedroom was an office. The office was the only cluttered room in the house. There were bookshelves filled with books and one bookshelf held several knick knacks. It almost seemed out of place for Henry's bare-boned style. I picked up a small bird figurine and saw 'To Henry, Thanks for everything, Love Maisy.' I picked up a tiny accordion and jumped a little when noise came out. On the bottom of that was written 'To Henry, Keep polka-ing, Love Ginger.' These must all be gifts from people at the nursing home. I smiled a little. I couldn't help but think chicks would definitely dig this.

I went over to his desk. It was piled high with papers. My eyes widened as I read the words in the notebook. 'Susanna Penelope Maxine Bennett Daniels,' was written at the top of the page. How did he know my full name? Underneath it he had written little bullet points. 'Erma left on the second of November. S claims no contact. Pies are different. Break-in: Innocent or set-up? Spells are spreading.' Spells are spreading? What did that mean? I felt a strange tingling feeling on the back of my neck.

'Susanna?' I heard Henry's front door bang as he came back inside.

I rushed out of the office.

'Sorry, I was just using your bathroom,' I called. 'I hope you don't mind.'

'Of course not.' He appeared in the living room. Then he slid past me and closed the door to his office. 'Sorry, this room is so messy. Would you like any more coffee?'

'No, thanks,' I said. All I really wanted right now was to get out of there. The timer beeped and I rushed to the kitchen to pull the pies out of the oven.

It wasn't like he had a picture of me with a target drawn over my face or anything. I was probably just overreacting. Maybe the phone message wasn't about me. I couldn't figure out how to explain the notebook away though. If this was how he romantically pursued women, his technique could use a little revising. This felt more like stalking than innocently flirting.

'I don't mean to keep you from whatever you were doing today,' I said. I set the last couple of pies on the counter and willed them to cool off enough for me to put back in the boxes.

'It's no problem at all,' he said. 'Today's my day off. I don't have anything special to do until it's time to meet the Morning Pie Crew. And I can't do that if there's no pie to eat,' he said with a smile.

'You're meeting the Morning Pie Crew?'

'Yes, I sometimes catch up with them on my days off,' he said. 'I know, I should get some friends my own age, but I get along so well with the older generation. Always have.' He shrugged with a little smile.

Maybe because you keep creepy notebooks about people your own age, I thought, but I just gave him a little smile back.

After a couple minutes, I began to pack up the pies.

'Don't you need to let them cool more first?' Henry asked as I boxed them up.

'No,' I said even though they were burning me through the oven mitts I was wearing, 'I need to get going. I've already taken up too much of your time.'

'I can bring some of them when I come by. Then they can cool a little more,' he offered.

I hesitated, worried they would turn into messy globs in transit, but I decided to risk it and turned down his offer.

Henry helped me load up the dolly with all the pies.

'Thanks for the oven. See you later,' I called as I wheeled them down the street. When I glanced back Henry was standing on his front step watching me go.

Chapter 19

Day 14 — Tuesday

Flora looked sheepish when she walked through the door later that day. 'I just wanted to apologize for my terrible behavior yesterday,' she said, not quite able to meet my eyes. 'I'm on this new medication, and it makes me say the silliest things.'

I forgave her, of course. What was the rest of the town's excuse though? Was everyone on new medication?

Lena and Mr Barnes came through the door loudly singing songs from 'The Sound of Music'. Flora still looked worried, so I patted her on the shoulder and smiled. She gave me a small smile back, and they all ordered their pie.

'I think I finally figured it out,' Lena was saying when I got back to the table with their pie.

'What?' Mr Barnes and Flora chorused.

'I think I know who Elodie is,' she said. We all leaned forward. I'd be lying if I said I had forgiven Elodie for the articles she'd written about me. Lena let the dramatic pause grow until Flora motioned impatiently. 'I think it's Gina.'

She paused to let that sink in. It actually made a lot of sense to me. Gina certainly wasn't a fan of mine, so it wouldn't surprise me if she wrote articles bad mouthing me.

'Think about it,' Lena said. 'She gets a lot of dish at the gym so she can write those gossipy articles like the ones she wrote about Susie, and whenever I see her at the diner, she's huddled over her computer. Maybe writing her secret advice column?'

'I've seen her at the diner,' Mr Barnes said. 'She's watching workout videos. I overheard her saying that even watching exercise helped burn calories.'

'Oh.' Lena looked deflated. 'That doesn't mean it's not her.'

I nodded supportively. I was willing to blame Gina for the articles.

That conversation only temporarily distracted me from the questions I had. I wanted to ask more about what happened yesterday. I tried to wait for a lull in the conversation. But there was no lull. It was almost as though they were trying to make sure there was no break in the conversation. They talked about the weather, about Mr Barnes's new shoes, about the upcoming holidays, and about what each of them had for dinner every night this week.

Finally, I couldn't take it any longer. 'Why was everyone acting so strangely yesterday?' I cried out over their voices. They all stopped talking and turned to stare at me.

'I already explained—' Flora began.

228

'Not just you,' I cut her off. 'The whole town was nuts.'

'Here, let me refill your coffee.' Mr Barnes got up and grabbed the half empty cup that was in front of me.

'You don't have to do that.' I waved him off.

'It's no problem.' He was already halfway to the pot. Lena and Flora exchanged glances, and I waited for them to answer my question.

Mr Barnes handed the steaming cup back to me. I took a sip. A strange feeling washed over me. Suddenly that question didn't seem so important. So I moved on to my next question, 'Have you guys ever noticed anything strange about Henry?' I tried to keep my tone light.

'Strange how?' Flora asked.

'He's such a good boy,' Lena said.

'I got a weird vibe from him,' I said, treading carefully.

'Like a "he likes you" kind of vibe?' Flora asked wiggling her eyebrows.

'No,' I said, feeling a little embarrassed. I really should have prepared my line of questioning more carefully. 'Like what's his story?'

'His whole life story?' Mr Barnes chimed in. 'How much time do you have?'

'He's lived here his whole life, so we know everything,' Lena said.

I sighed, this was getting me nowhere.

'He was the politest child,' Flora started. 'He would help me unload the new shipments of books and then he would thank me for the opportunity to work. I would have to push him to accept a couple dollars as payment.'

'He's such a sweetheart working those long hours at the nursing home taking care of everyone,' Lena said.

'Really a stand-up citizen,' Mr Barnes said with a firm nod.

They continued to eat their pie and gossip, but I was having trouble focusing. They gave such a glowing review of him, but I couldn't help but wonder if they knew the real Henry. Maybe it was possible to have secrets in a small town after all.

I cleared the plates while the other three continued to chatter. Henry and Bernie walked through the door. I tried to smile, but I felt like too many of my teeth were showing.

'Sorry, I'm late. They needed me at the nursing home for a bit, and then with some persuading, I convinced Ms Bernie to join me for pie,' he said, taking Bernie's purse from her and setting it on a chair.

'We're glad you both came,' Flora said.

'Don't worry, I was thinking about ordering another slice.' Mr Barnes turned and looked at the display case.

I served up a cherry for Henry, and two pumpkins for Mr Barnes and Bernie. After I set down the slices in front of everyone, Bernie got up and followed me back to the counter.

'You haven't listened to me,' she said in a low voice as she leaned across the display case.

'Of course I have.' I nodded enthusiastically. 'I've dusted the heck out of that cat.'

She shook her head slowly. 'No, you haven't.'

'Well, I will. Soon,' I promised.

'Yes, you will. Soon,' she repeated. I nodded. She looked satisfied and headed back to her chair.

'I have been thinking about this pie ever since I smelled it baking earlier,' Henry said taking a bite.

'You were here this morning?' Lena asked, a naughty smile playing on her lips.

Henry blushed. 'No, I just ... Susanna needed my oven this morning.' He looked at me for help.

'Henry was a life saver when the oven here broke this morning.' I wasn't quite able to meet Henry's eyes when I spoke.

'Come, sit with us again.' Lena pulled up a chair from a neighboring table next to Henry.

'I should really get back to work,' I said, backing towards the kitchen.

'Nonsense,' Lena said patting the chair. 'You deserve a longer break.' I stiffly sat down.

'Do they have any suspects in the break-in yet?' Flora asked.

I shook my head. 'Not that I've heard. Who would break in just to steal a box of spices anyway?'

'Once, on one of those cooking competition shows, a woman stole the baking soda from all of her competitors so they ended up making flat cakes,' Flora said. 'In the end, she almost won too. Terrible shows spreading the message that cheating is acceptable behavior.'

'Don't you still watch that show every week?' Lena asked.

'Well, yes, but I just watch it for the recipes,' Flora said indignantly.

I don't know why I hadn't thought of it before. Alice has been out to get me. She had motive and opportunity to steal the spices. How would I prove it though? She seemed to have the whole town in the palm of her hand. I would need some hard evidence to get any of them to listen to me. While the others talked about various reality shows, I planned my evening. There was only one way I could think of to get the answers I needed.

Before Henry and Bernie left, he turned to me and said, 'Give me a call if the oven isn't fixed by tomorrow. I can help you bring the pies over to my house.'

'I'm sure that won't be necessary, but thanks.' My voice sounded weird. I forced a bright smile on my face. I could tell he was wounded when he glanced back at me as he held the door open for Bernie. I focused on stacking the dirty plates.

I considered trying to fix the oven myself, but with everything that was going on, I couldn't risk making any more mistakes. I called Bob after noon.

He answered with a curt, 'Yeah?' I hoped I hadn't woken him up. He told me that he was booked today, but could come look at the oven tomorrow. I shuddered at the thought of going back to Henry's tomorrow.

'Bob, please, you have to help me out,' I pleaded. 'I'll give you a whole pie if you come out today.'

'The pie that lost the baking contest?'

I let out a frustrated groan. 'That was a misunderstanding.'

He paused. 'Throw in a sandwich, and I'll try to come later

this afternoon.' I thanked him and promised a delicious sandwich would be waiting for him. I made a tomato, cucumber, and cheese sandwich and put it in the fridge for Bob.

Since everyone was still talking about the baking contest, I only had a couple of customers, both passing through from out of town.

Bob lumbered through the door carrying a rusty red toolbox a little after four-thirty. He had greasy gray hair and a bottom lip that protruded out giving him a permanent scowl.

'Hi, you must be Bob.' I walked towards him with my hand extended.

'Where's my sandwich?' he asked, giving my hand a quick shake. I led him back to the kitchen and gave him his sandwich.

'How is it?' I asked, after he took a bite. He grunted a noncommittal response and then went and stood in front of the oven.

'Do you need some help?' I offered. 'I worked for a handyman company back home. Not a lot of experience with ovens, but I'm willing to try.'

'Nope, I work alone,' he said, his mouth full of sandwich.

'OK,' I said. I lingered by the island and babbled about what a great job he did on the ice rink while he opened the door and looked inside.

'I'd prefer to be left alone,' he said, shooting a glance back at me.

'Sure, right. Let me know if you need anything.' I hurried back out front.

I heard some grumbling and resisted the temptation to go back there. After a few minutes, he came around the corner.

'Fixed,' he said.

'Already? What was wrong?'

'It was broken.' He slapped a bill down on the counter in front of me. I wrote a check out and handed it to him.

'Pie,' he said.

'Oh, right,' I said. Despite his gruff personality, I was glad he still wanted pie. Maybe he could help me repair my reputation, though I had a feeling he didn't go around singing many praises.

He picked a cheesecake, and I boxed it up. With a head nod, he was gone.

The rest of the day was quiet. I kept checking that the oven was working, turning it on and off, until I worried that I would break it again. I was pretty sure Bob wouldn't skip right back over to fix it a second time.

I had to focus on tonight anyway. I needed a plan.

It was ironic. The town had accused me of being a burglar during the Fall Festival, and here I was on my way to break into Alice's shop.

I slinked down the sidewalk, keeping close to the buildings and trying not to look suspicious. My pockets were filled with bobby pins. I had found a flashlight in Aunt Erma's closet. It was one of those long metal ones that police officers carried. I wondered where she got it as I tucked it up my sleeve.

I desperately wanted a disguise. I didn't have time to order a mask online, and I didn't dare go to the store to pick one up. Even stores in surrounding towns weren't safe. Serena Leeks who ran the clothing store in Mavisville, the next town over, played pickleball with Lena's cousin's son who also happened to be Mrs Lanigan's doctor. Gossip would spread, and I couldn't take that risk.

So in all my brilliance I decided to take one of Aunt Erma's old stocking hats and cut a couple of holes in it. Unfortunately, it was zebra stripe and not exactly in keeping with the low profile I had hoped for. However, it did cover the top half of my face, and I prayed that would be enough to keep anyone from recognizing me if anyone saw me going in or out of the shop.

I spent some time on the internet looking up how to break in. There were way too many how-to guides out there for comfort. After spending an hour researching, I spent another hour looking up different alarm systems I now felt I should install. I just hoped that the sheriff wasn't high-tech enough to search my internet history.

First, I tested the door to make sure it was locked. This was a small town, maybe people trusted their neighbors. The door was locked so I pulled a bobby pin out of my pocket and began twisting it around inside the lock. Nothing happened other than I mangled my bobby pin.

Next, I pulled out a gift card I had found in my wallet for a butcher shop. It was a gift from my old boss, Hal. A less than thoughtful gift considering I'm vegetarian and had been the entire time I'd worked there – a fact we had discussed on many occasions. I slid the card between the door and the door frame, and the card cracked in half.

My nerves were dancing and my frustration growing. I grabbed the doorknob with both hands and shook it. The lock just popped open. I stood in shock for a minute in the open doorway. That was not one of the ways I had researched.

I quickly stepped inside and pulled my flashlight out of my sleeve and began shining it along the countertops, careful not to let it shine out any of the windows. Alice was no dummy, she probably wouldn't have left stolen goods out in the open.

I found the door to the pantry and stepped inside. It was packed with flour and sugar. I shined my flashlight up and down the shelves. I reached behind one of the bags of flour where I thought I could see a small bottle. As I pulled it out, two bags fell off the shelves and fell with a poof to the ground. One broke open and flour swirled around my feet. I froze for a minute, but there was still silence. I breathed a sigh of relief, shoved the bottle in my pocket, and continued my search.

My foot made contact with something and the air filled with a clattering noise that was deafening against the silence. I turned my flashlight down. I had kicked a stain-less-steel mixing bowl. Who in the world would leave a mixing bowl on the ground. I didn't have long to ponder that.

'Hey, who's there,' a voice called through the darkness. The voice was familiar, but it wasn't Alice.

I turned and ran as fast as I could out the back door. I could sense someone following me, but I had seen enough movies to know that if you turn around to see who it is, you'll probably fall or run into something, so I just kept going. I gripped the flashlight tightly in my hand. If whoever was following me got too close, I would be ready to turn around and knock them in the head with it. I kept turning corners. Every corner I could, I would turn one way then another. I hoped my mask was enough to maintain my anonymity. The last thing I needed was to be accused of breaking into Alice's shop when I had in fact broken into Alice's shop.

I saw the nursing home ahead and ran through the door. No one was at the front desk. I bent over for a second to catch my breath. I heard singing. I took a few steps back towards the dining room and peeked inside. Henry sat there with a guitar on his lap. Several of the residents in the room were crowded around him. Some of them were humming and some were singing along. Many of them swayed to the tune. His voice gave me goose bumps, and I wanted to keep listening. I had always been a sucker for a man who could sing. I had to keep moving so I rushed down the hall, out the back door, and down the street.

Finally, I'd zig-zagged enough that I thought I'd lost my pursuer. I stopped in a doorway so I could look behind me. The coast was clear. I hurried back to the pie shop. I tried to walk a normal clip just in case anyone was looking out their windows.

I finally let myself breathe when I closed the door of the

pie shop and locked it. The climb upstairs seemed long after that run. My legs were burning. Mitzy looked concerned from her spot where she was laying on the only clean pair of underwear I had left.

I glanced out the window in the kitchen and saw a figure disappearing around the corner of the alley. I didn't get a good look at who it was, but the sight made my heart pound in my chest.

I had a bad feeling that whoever was at the cookie shop knew where I was now.

Chapter 20

Day 15 — Wednesday, November 16th

Dear Elodie,

I just found out a huge family secret. I mean huge. I don't know what to do next. I'm an adult and this secret has been kept from me my whole life. Even now, I only found out by accident. I'm questioning everything. How do I forgive my family for keeping this from me all these years? I want to move forward, but I just keep thinking about how they lied to me. It was a lie of omission, but it was a pretty big omission. Help me get past this, please.

Sincerely,

Stumbling on Secrets

Dear Stumbling on Secrets,

Finding out a family secret can be shocking. Especially if it makes you question your whole life up until now. There are many reasons people keep secrets. Talk to your family and try to understand why they did what they did. It might be hard, but take a step back and really try to see it from their side. That's the first step to being able to forgive them. Most often secrets are kept out of fear or to protect someone. Remember that holding on to this resentment will only hurt you further.

Ask and I'll Answer,
Elodie

I couldn't sit still for the rest of the night. I was filled with a nervous energy. Mitzy seemed to pick up on it, and she followed me everywhere, including the bathroom, with anxious eyes. Every now and then she would catch my eye and give me a low, uncertain tail wag.

The bottle I had swiped from Alice's was, in fact, Spice #7. This one bottle wasn't enough though. I had to get them all back.

I couldn't quite figure out why she had stolen them in the first place. They were really great spices, but it seemed like an awful lot of trouble to go through. Was she really just trying to destroy my business that badly? Was she a complete nut job? I was pacing faster and faster. I had to stop myself and find something else to do before I wore a hole in the floor.

After all this time trying to respect Aunt Erma's privacy, curiosity was getting the best of me. I opened the front closet and pulled out a box. My mother had taught me well, so at least I felt guilty about snooping. The front closet seemed like the safest place. I didn't want to accidentally discover that on the side Aunt Erma was a dominatrix or something, and I figured those things would be kept in her bedroom closet.

The first box I pulled out was full of gloves. Fancy gloves with lace and ribbons and sequins. The box smelled a bit like Aunt Erma's ever-present cinnamon scent. I held up each pair, oohing and aahing a bit. I wondered why she needed so many pairs of fancy gloves. I imaged Aunt Erma at fancy balls dancing minuets while violins played in the background.

I ran my fingers along a red velvet one before sticking my hand inside. It fit perfectly. A strange rushing feeling ran through my hand. I pulled the glove off, and it stopped. I put it on, and again I felt a strange surging feeling through my hand and up my arm. I pulled it off. It must be some strange static electricity thing or maybe I was having an allergic reaction.

I moved on to the next box which was filled with pictures of Mitzy. Lots of pictures of Mitzy.

'Really, you put up with this?' I asked Mitzy, holding up a picture of her in a frilly tutu with hearts for what I could only assume was Valentine's Day. Mitzy glared at me, clearly not happy that I had discovered her box of shame. 'The things we do for treats,' she seemed to be saying.

The next box I grabbed was packed full of envelopes. I pulled the first one out of the box. It was addressed to me in Aunt Erma's handwriting. The envelope wasn't sealed, and I took out the letter. It was dated twenty-one years ago, when I was nine years old. It must have been shortly after she left. In the letter she apologized for leaving and said she would explain it all to me one day. She said no matter what my mother said, I should never forget who I am.

What did that even mean?

I pulled out a handful of envelopes and leafed through them. They were all addressed to me. They were detailed accounts of Aunt Erma's life but also filled with questions about my life.

'Did you ever conquer your fear of horses?' she wrote in one. *'I'm still working on mine. I signed up for riding classes at a ranch out here, but at the last minute I opted to join a book club instead.'*

The next letter changed everything.

Dear Susie,
 I wanted to tell you this in person, but I worry that I won't see you again. Our family descends from fairies.

I stopped reading at this point and flipped the page over to see if it ended with a 'just kidding,' but it didn't. I kept reading.

Your mother and I grew up learning about magic and how to use it. She began to drift away from it when you were little, after your dad got sick. She struggled with magic's limits, but I want you to know who you are if your mother doesn't tell you.
 I think you have the power in you. I saw evidence

of it several times when you'd make things happen or fix things that were broken with such ease at a young age. Your mother forbade me from telling you about it. She wasn't sure she wanted this life for you. It can be dangerous. Especially if people find out you practice magic.

I moved to this town when I found out they were like us – people who shared our magical abilities. It's a wonderful and safe place to live where I can be who I am. I hope you can visit me here someday. I'll teach you about all the different spells and how to use them.

Some people who live here are part-fairy, some are part-elf, and a few are part-giant. Everyone here was born with a particular natural ability. Mine is making magical spices. Flora is good at knowing exactly which book people need in their life. Mr Barnes can effortlessly put people at ease. Lena is a whiz at fixing things. I suspect you share her ability.

Everyone still has to practice their magic to hone their skills, and you can learn different skills. Mr Barnes is trying to teach me to put people at ease, but it's been a bit hit or miss. I would like to teach you how to make the magic spices. Maybe you and Lena can teach me how to fix things.

I love you.

Love and Sparkles,

Aunt Erma

I slammed the letter down against the coffee table. I felt like my brain was going to explode. Aunt Erma had always been a little kooky, but this was a whole new level. I didn't know what to do with this information or how to process it. I assessed my body. I didn't feel magical. My active imagination wanted to believe it was real, but the logical side of my brain wondered what kind of crazy fantasy world Aunt Erma lived in.

Mitzy watched me, perfectly still from her perch on the back of the sofa. It was as though she couldn't decide if she should hop down and comfort me or if she should stay safely in her spot. I sat frozen too, staring straight back at her. I let it all sink in for a minute. The thought of magic being real was both perfectly insane and made complete sense all at the same time. It would explain so much, including why the spices were so important.

I read the letter and read it again. I got up to make a pot of coffee because with my brain moving at a hundred miles an hour, my body needed something more to do. I paused as I was reaching up to grab the bag of beans out of the cupboard.

'Come here coffee beans,' I said in an authoritative voice. I waited for the bag to fly through the air. 'Come,' I said more forcefully. Mitzy came trotting over and sat attentively at my feet. I gave up and grabbed the coffee out of the cupboard.

Mitzy's tail wagged harder. She wanted a reward for her obedience so I gave her a treat.

Coffee was clearly a mistake. All of the emotions and

thoughts that I was having before, I was still having only even faster and more confusing. The questions in my head were all fighting for top billing at once. So I switched to wine. Wine would help me relax and then maybe I could finish a thought. I poured a big glass and drank it far too quickly. I lay down on the sofa and wondered if there was a spell to get rid of a stomachache.

I thought back to my childhood. All those fairy tales Aunt Erma had told me. Were they real? I squeezed my eyes tightly shut. No, that would be impossible. This was all impossible. I grabbed the next letter out of the box.

Dear Susie,

If your mother hasn't told you about it, I'm sure learning that magic is real would be quite a shock. Your grandparents taught your mother and I magic as soon as we learned how to talk. I thought everyone knew about magic. It wasn't until I went to school that I learned that not everyone knew, and we weren't supposed to talk about it. As a child, that was hard for me to wrap my mind around. Magic was so wonderful, I thought everyone should know about it. My parents were firm, and I obeyed them. I learned as I got older that magic could be dangerous in the wrong hands.

I was thinking about you a lot the other day when Lena helped me build a dog house for Mitzy. Watching her work reminded me of the time we built that fort in your parent's living room. Well, really you did most of the work. You got this look in your eyes as you built the

*most intricate, beautiful blanket and pillow fort I have
ever seen. Lena got that same look in her eye as she
built Mitzy a two-story dog house. You probably didn't
realize at the time that magic was at work, but I could
tell it was.*

*I hope I get to show you all the wonderful things
about magic! Flora has some amazing books. They have
stories and spells in them. Even I still have so much to
learn.*

*Susie, I hope we can find our way back to each other
one day. I hope your mother and I can heal and reunite
too. I miss you both more than I can even put into
words.*

Love and Sparkles,
Aunt Erma

Why didn't she ever send these letters to me? If she really
was magical, couldn't she have found a way? She'd essentially
been lying to me my whole life. Was she off having some
magical adventure while I floundered here, trying to run
her shop?

I didn't sleep a wink. I stayed up all night reading and
re-reading the letters and occasionally trying to make something magical happen. I checked all the books on the
bookshelf again to see if any of them were spell books.
They weren't. So I tried making up my own incantations.
I felt a little silly waving my hands around trying to move
things across the room or make pages in a book turn, but
I had no one there to judge me besides Mitzy.

Did everyone in town really know about this? Holly would have told me, wouldn't she? What about Henry? And the Morning Pie Crew? This would be a pretty big secret to keep.

My emotions ranged from anger towards my mother and Aunt Erma for keeping this a secret, to fear over what magic could do, to excitement at the prospect of being magical.

I was a jittery mess the next morning when I heard Stan crash into the kitchen. Maybe that fifth cup of coffee had been a bad idea. I cautiously went downstairs to see what he'd brought me today.

I pushed open the door to the kitchen, and he jumped up quickly from the spot he was crouched down at looking in a cupboard. He looked even more nervous than usual.

'I was checking to see if I brought the powdered sugar last time.' He answered the question I hadn't asked.

'OK,' I said. 'But I keep the sugar in the pantry. Like my aunt always did and yes, you brought the powdered sugar.' In fact, I think that was the only correct thing he brought me last time.

I sized Stan up. Why was he snooping through the cupboards? Was he magical? What was his ability? Clearly it wasn't making deliveries.

'Right.' He nodded. 'Well, here's today's delivery.' He presented it with a flourish of his arm, and he was out the door. I heard the truck pull out of the alley before I realized he had left his dolly in the middle of the kitchen.

I unpacked the delivery. Everything felt different this

morning, even the clean kitchen. How did all the dishes get done? Was it actually through magic? I eyed the sparkling countertop suspiciously. I couldn't get the unsettled feeling out of my head.

It was my need for ice cream that drove me out of the shop that morning. We only served vanilla at the pie shop, and it was not a vanilla kind of day.

I needed something with chocolate, and maybe peanut butter, or mint, or cookie dough. The cravings were coming fast and strong. I headed to the grocery store while the pies I'd baked cooled on the counter. The oven had worked perfectly, and I was glad I didn't have to see Henry. Before I left, I checked the freezer to make sure there was plenty of room for ice cream in case impulse won out over discipline.

Everyone and everything looked peculiar today. More magical. Did the buildings have a little sparkle to them? Was that a stain on that brick wall or a magical doorway to a secret land? I sized up every person I passed trying to gauge if they had magical abilities. I saw Mr Lanigan, the mailman, walking down the street. His mailbag was stuffed full, but he effortlessly switched it from one shoulder to the other as though it was light as air. Without looking he reached into the bag and pulled out a stack of mail and put it in a mailbox. At the next building he did the same. It was almost too much for my brain to handle. I considered turning back, but I convinced myself to continue my quest because I wanted the ice cream.

The grocery store was quiet. I must have beaten the

midmorning rush. I let out a sigh of relief when I saw Luanne wasn't at the register. I wasn't sure I could handle a lecture on the importance of getting enough fiber in my diet right now. I went straight back to the freezer section and stared through the glass doors debating between triple chocolate fudge and the chocolate peanut butter swirl. I was just deciding that I should get them both and maybe the mint chocolate chip too, when I saw Henry turn the corner from the canned soup aisle.

I leapt behind a display of granola bars. I wanted nothing more than to avoid him. I still hadn't come up with a non-creepy reason for his notebook about me. Even magic couldn't explain it away. Henry was slowly pushing his cart towards me with his elbows as he looked down at his phone. I didn't think he'd seen me.

I watched him put his phone in his pocket and then study the freezer case for a minute.

'What are you doing?' a voice whispered in my ear and I jumped out of my skin. I turned to see Holly. She crouched down next to me and peered around the display until she spotted Henry. 'Do you want to talk about it?' She gestured at Henry, still keeping her voice low.

I shook my head then peered around the display again. Henry was pulling boxes of something out of the freezer and setting them in the cart. What were they?

I leaned a little closer and my mouth fell open when I saw them. He was buying several boxes of frozen pies. Even after everything that had happened the last few days, I still felt a little wounded by his actions.

'Oh no he didn't,' Holly whispered and then jumped to her feet.

I tried to grab her arm, but she moved too quickly. 'Hey, Henry!' Holly greeted him with a wide smile.

Henry froze with one box of pies still in his hand, his eyes wide.

'Ew, gross! Why on earth would you buy frozen pies instead of Susie's pies?' she spoke loudly, and Henry flinched a little. I reminded myself again to never get on Holly's bad side.

'Look at the time.' Henry pointed to his wrist, but he wasn't wearing a watch. 'My break is almost over. I have to get back. Great to see you, Holly.' He practically flew out of there. Luckily he didn't look back or he might have seen me crouching down clutching two tubs of ice cream.

'Well, at least he's ashamed now.' Holly looked pretty proud of herself as she marched back over to me. 'Um, honey, I think you're melting.' She pointed to my shirt. I looked down and saw streaks of chocolate running down the front of my white shirt underneath the containers of ice cream I was closely holding.

I muttered a few choice words and then grabbed the mint chocolate chip and cookie dough out of the freezer, stacking them on top of the melting peanut butter and triple chocolate. Today was not a day to limit myself.

When I got back to the shop, I put away the ice cream and ran upstairs to change my shirt. I jumped back. Mitzy was standing on top of the bookshelf just inside the door.

Her tongue was already licking before she even made contact with my shirt.

'Ah, no,' I said nudging her away, much to her dismay. How did she know I would be covered in ice cream? I changed, running the chocolate covered shirt under cold water for a few minutes before throwing it in the washing machine. I was both hoping to keep the stain from setting and trying to deter Mitzy from licking my shirt clean. Knowing that dog, she would be able to find it no matter where I hid it.

I headed back down to the pie shop still muttering angrily at Henry and his frozen pies.

The Morning Pie Crew came bursting through the door in the afternoon.

'You guys are late today,' I said as they all sat down at their usual table. I wanted to ask them questions about magic, but I had no idea how to broach the subject. What if Aunt Erma just wrote those letters for fun? Maybe she was just getting in a little creative writing. Maybe my sleep-deprived mind was twisting everything that was happening up into some fairy tale, when it all had a perfectly mundane explanation. If they were true, they would explain a lot about what had been going on though.

I looked at Mr Barnes. Did I feel extra at ease around him? I wasn't sure.

'We're celebrating.' Lena threw her arms out wide.

'What are you celebrating?' I asked.

'Flora's bookstore was named one of the top ten small

town bookstores in *Town and Travel* magazine,' Mr Barnes told me as he patted her shoulder proudly

Flora flushed. 'It's no big deal, really.'

'Of course it is,' Lena cried. 'And we're going to celebrate all week!'

'Oh Lena, you'll use any excuse to celebrate,' Flora laughed.

'That's true, but this is still a big deal.' She hit her fist on the table. 'You're going to bring so much tourism into town.'

'That would be nice,' Flora said.

'Congratulations, Flora,' I said. 'Pie is on the house today.'

'No, no.' She wagged her finger at me. 'I won't let you do that.'

They ordered their pie and while I was serving them, Lena reached into her bag and pulled out a bottle of champagne.

'Come on, Susie, join the celebration.' She popped the top off.

I laughed. 'Do you need glasses?'

'Oh no, I have those in here somewhere too.' She rooted around in her large purse before producing four champagne flutes. 'Always be prepared to party, that's my motto.' I wondered how she managed to lift that purse that seemed to hold everything. Was it magic? I was afraid to ask.

'I noticed you were up kind of late last night. The lights were on in the apartment well after midnight. That's not healthy. You need to get eight hours of sleep. I'll be watching,'

Flora said with the lack of social boundaries I had come to accept as normal in this town.

I assured her I would go to sleep earlier tonight, and she seemed happy. I should really get thicker curtains for the windows.

We drank champagne and ate pie. A little unorthodox, but a very satisfying experience. We were all suffering from a severe case of the giggles when my mother strode into the pie shop.

Chapter 21

Day 15 — Wednesday

It was strange having her in the kitchen. My mother stood next to the island in a crisp red suit. Her hair was dark, short, and straight, all the result of a lot of time at the salon. If she left it untouched, it would be the same curly brown mess that mine was. All of her features were like mine, but sharper – including her blue eyes which darted around critically studying everything. She kept fumbling with her hands as if she didn't know where to put them.

The Morning Pie Crew had discreetly slipped out and moved the celebration to the bookstore after being introduced to my mother. I invited my mother back to the kitchen to visit with me while I prepared a special order. Henry had called and ordered three caramel apple pies for Penelope's birthday. Apparently, they didn't have caramel apple in the frozen section of the grocery store. I wasn't thrilled at the prospect of him coming in, but I couldn't afford to lose the business.

'You could sit,' I offered, walking to the back to pull out the desk chair.

'Oh, no, that's not necessary,' she said, waving me off.

We talked about the weather – crisp, cold, and sunny. We talked about the best gift shops in town. Mom wanted to buy something for her friend Nina. We talked about what's been happening on our favorite television show. Mom and I used to watch this historical drama together on television, and we both kept up with it. I don't know if either of us really loved it that much, but it was the one thing we could connect over. It's amazing the things people will do to stay connected. Usually I had to record it and watch it twice because I would fall asleep the first time, but I always made sure to watch it all. Otherwise, by some miracle, she would know which parts I had missed, and she'd only want to talk about the parts I had slept through. Sometimes it felt like a test, and she was trying to keep me from using the cliff notes. This time, however, I managed to discuss it in a satisfactory manner.

I began hand mixing the crusts in a bowl, not bothering with the large mixer since I was only making a few pies. I took out the ingredients while my mother recounted her favorite scene between the duke and duchess where the duchess had found out that the duke was lying to her and she was making very graphic threats to him. My mother loved drama, even though she tried to pretend she didn't. If she were to talk about the show with one of her friends, she would probably focus on the outfits and the lovely scenery.

As I mixed the flour, butter, and water in the bowl, I saw my mother purse her lips out of the corner of my eye. I knew that look. I had seen it so many times before. She was dying to tell me what I was doing wrong. In fact, despite her effort to keep it inside, I had a feeling she wouldn't be able to hold in her criticism for longer than five seconds. I began mentally counting. Five, four, three, two...

'You're adding too much water,' she said.

Bingo. I knew it. 'It's fine, Mom,' I said. 'People haven't been complaining.'

'Well, then, people here are just too polite.' She sniffed. 'Too much water will make the crust tough instead of light and flakey.'

I wanted to bang my head against the table, but instead I plastered a smile on my face.

'Will you show me?' I asked, pushing the ingredients towards her.

She narrowed her eyes at me. 'I am not really dressed to bake.'

'Don't worry, I have an apron for you to wear,' I said sweetly.

My mother usually preferred to critique and oversee, not to participate. Participating opened her up to being judged by others and that was unacceptable. I gave her an apron covered in little yellow ducklings. She held it out between two fingers.

'Is this the only one you have?' she asked.

'I could get you the one with dancing fairies on it or the one that says, "Will bake for Wine," or the one that's purple and sparkly.' I listed them off as I headed back to the hook where the aprons were hanging.

'Never mind,' she said putting this one on over her head carefully so as not to mess up her hair. 'This one is fine.'

'Oh, I'm going to need you to wear either a hat or a hairnet too,' I said apologetically. At least I hope it sounded apologetic; inside I was dancing with joy.

'What?' She froze, looking horrified.

'Yes, the health inspector keeps stopping in, and I have to make sure I maintain the utmost standard of cleanliness.' I was starting to enjoy myself now and wondered if I could snap a picture of my mom without her noticing. 'The fact that you've even been in the kitchen without a hairnet or hat is probably enough to get me in trouble.'

'Why has the health inspector been coming in?' my mother asked.

'I don't know.' I realized I had just given my mother ammo to further attack me. 'She seems very intent on talking to Aunt Erma.' At the mention of her name, my mother flinched a little. 'I keep trying to show her the kitchen because it's always spotless.' I decided not to mention that it was spotless because mystery cleaners cleaned every night, not because I was particularly adept at keeping the place tidy.

'Hmm,' was all my mother said to me.

I offered her a hat and a hairnet. I could sense her inner struggle. A hat was more stylish, but a hairnet was necessary for not smashing her hair. Heaven forbid she end up with hat hair. I don't know how my mother kept her hair so perfect. It was a skill I had always tried to master, but no matter how much I worked on it, I could not seem to maintain the same amount of perfection that she could.

She finally landed on the hairnet and put it carefully on her head. Seriously, I don't think in the history of hairnets that one has ever been placed that carefully on anyone's head – ever. She went over to the sink and washed her hands.

'Mom,' I said softly when her back was turned towards me as she dried her hands off. 'What really happened between you and Aunt Erma?' She froze for a moment, still clutching the paper towel.

'Oh Susie,' she began in the voice she always used when she was about to brush me off.

'I know about the magic,' I said. She was still facing the wall, and I could see her whole body tense. I thought for a minute she might storm out of the kitchen.

She turned towards me, and our eyes met. She seemed to be sizing me up as though deciding whether or not to tell me something. I held her eye contact and hoped that my face didn't look too confrontational.

'There's a lot to explain,' she said slowly. It was vague, but not a total shut down.

'I have time to listen while we bake,' I said. 'Or while you bake since I'm not fit to make the crusts.' I shrugged a little with a tiny smile on my lips.

A smile flashed across her face. Whoa. Usually my mother would tell me to stop being ridiculous and dramatic after a comment like that, but this time I just got a smile? I watched my mother surround herself with all the ingredients. She took the bowl I had been working in and went over to the garbage and dumped the contents out. That seemed more like it.

It was strange seeing her measure out the flour with such ease. As far as I knew, she hadn't baked since before my dad died.

'We have to start fresh,' she explained. 'There's no going back once there's too much water in the crust.' It took all my willpower to make sure I didn't roll my eyes.

'So what happened with you and Aunt Erma,' I prompted again. I washed and peeled the apples while my mother measured flour, salt, shortening, and just a smidge of water into the bowl.

'Well, when your father died...' She stopped to take a deep breath. I knew this was a hard topic for her. 'You know he'd been sick for a while. I'd been trying to make him better with all the spells I knew, but they weren't working.'

My mind was spinning. Hearing my mother say things like 'spells,' was bizarre and unexpected. I just quietly listened though because I was afraid of stopping the topic of conversation when I needed to hear more. I didn't want to scare her out of telling me the whole story.

'I tried to get Erma to help me, but she wouldn't. Erma's always been the more powerful one in the family. No matter how hard I tried, how much I practiced, she was always more powerful.' My mother sounded a little bitter now. 'She didn't even have to try.'

I wondered how far back this magic thing went in my

family. Generations? Questions raced around in my head, but I continued to peel the apple in my hand slowly. It felt significant, like I was finally peeling back the layers of my mother. I tried to picture her, younger and performing magic. It must have been so difficult for her to believe that she should be able to save my father, but he died anyway.

'I tried to get Erma to help. Begged her,' she continued, 'but she refused. She said that wasn't what magic was for. That we couldn't mess with mortality because it's such a dangerous road to go down.' My mother's voice cracked. 'I just wanted my husband for a little while longer. I wanted him to be there for me and help me raise our little girl.' She looked at me, tears glistening in her eyes. I felt tears prickle at my eyes too. I fought them back. If we started crying now, we might never stop.

'When he died, I lost it,' my mother continued, blinking back her tears and looking down into the bowl. 'I blamed Erma for not helping me. She moved away, and that was that.' She squeezed the dough tightly in her hands.

'You didn't ever try to talk to her again?' I asked. 'I mean, it has been over twenty years.'

My mother shook her head. 'She let your father die. She just stood by and watched, and then tried to comfort me. I wouldn't have needed comforting if she had just helped.' Her voice was rising, and she had a wild look in her eye.

I just stared at her silently. I wasn't really sure what to say. We both stood there, frozen, looking at each other. After a minute I spoke. 'Mom?'

'What?' Her voice had an edge to it.

'I love you,' I said.

She looked surprised for a moment. This was not exactly how my family behaved. We were more about implied love, not overt expressions of it. After a minute of silence, her face softened.

'I love you too, Susie,' she said, looking back down into her bowl of pie crust dough.

Chapter 22

Day 15 — Wednesday

Dinner with my mother. Why on earth was I having dinner with my mother? She was spending the night at the one inn in town. She said it was because she didn't want to put me out, but I had a feeling she didn't want to set foot in Aunt Erma's apartment.

Henry had stopped by to get his special order. I grabbed his money and practically threw his pies at him before ushering him out. I saw him hesitate at the door for a moment, but I disappeared back into the kitchen.

I called Holly and told her to call me in exactly one hour with some emergency that would require me to leave dinner immediately and come to her aid.

'But your mom came all this way to see you,' she said. 'Don't you want to have dinner with her? One meal with your only mother?'

'I don't have the stellar relationship with my mom that you have,' I told her.

'Stellar relationship?' she laughed. 'My mother just told me that my underwear is too grandma-ish and if I'm ever going to reel in a woman, I need to spice it up with a little lace and maybe a thong or two.'

'I've been meaning to talk to you about that,' I teased. 'How does she know what your underwear looks like?'

'I have been struggling with the very same question, but I'm afraid to ask,' she said with a sigh.

'One hour, please,' I begged.

'Fine,' she said, 'but if when I call everything is going really well, you should just say, "I'll pick up the donuts tomorrow," and I'll know that everything is OK, and you don't need rescuing.'

'I'll pick up the donuts tomorrow? That's the code?' I asked.

'Well, you come up with something better.'

'Donuts is fine,' I said. 'Thank you for your help. I'll owe you one.'

'I think you already owe me two or three,' she said.

'I'll help you buy some sexy underwear. Maybe your mom and I can go shopping together.'

'I'm hanging up now,' she said, and with a click she was gone.

So there I was at dinner with my mother. She had been waiting for me at a table near the front when I got there 'I got here early,' my mom explained. 'I wasn't sure if we'd have to wait for a table.'

'I don't think anyone has waited for a table here since Eisenhower was president,' I said. She was drinking water.

The waitress came by. 'Margaritas for both of us,' I said. 'The biggest ones you have.'

'Oh Susie, I don't know if that's a good idea,' my mom said.

'Sure it is. They're the best margaritas you'll ever have,' I announced as the server left.

'I think you should come back to the city with me,' my mom said abruptly.

'Don't start,' I groaned.

'I know you've always had a special connection with your aunt, but you don't belong here,' she said.

'I don't have a job to go back to. I'm at least going to stay until Aunt Erma gets back,' I said.

'There are still a lot of opportunities for you back home. Nina said she could get you a job as an office assistant.'

This was not the first time my mother and I had had this conversation.

'No, Mom. I'm staying. At least for a while longer,' I said firmly.

My mom got quiet and looked down at her menu as though she had never seen a menu before.

I pulled my phone out of my sweater pocket and glanced at the time. I had been here for three minutes. Fifty-seven more to go before Holly called. I had so many more questions for my mom. About magic. About Aunt Erma. I didn't know where to begin. I wanted answers, but I knew my mom. If I didn't broach the topic carefully, she would just shut down. We sipped our drinks and got warmed up with small talk.

The margaritas were magic. Hey, maybe they really *were* magic. I wondered if there was a spell they put on alcohol. Or maybe just alcohol was magic. My mother was halfway through hers and had actually begun to make eye contact with me again.

'Hello ladies.' Mr Barnes appeared behind me.

'What are you doing here? You should join us,' I said. I pulled out a chair.

'I don't want to intrude,' he said. 'I'm just waiting for my to-go order.'

'Nonsense, we'd love to have you,' my mother said, using the same bright voice she used when a cashier asked how her day was going.

'So you just came up from the city?' Mr Barnes asked my mom.

'Yes, I just wanted to check on my only child.'

'Alice, the woman who runs the cookie shop in town,' he clarified for my mother, 'was heading to the city for some family thing tonight. I think she's originally from there. I don't get down there much myself anymore.'

'Yes, it's fabulous. Full of so many wonderful opportunities.' My mom was talking to him but looking at me.

Luckily the conversation moved on to happier topics like where my mother could buy a snow globe for her friend Nina. After that burning question was answered, Mr Barnes got his bag of food and left.

'I wonder how early the shops open,' my mother said. 'I certainly hope that place he mentioned doesn't stay closed on Thursdays or something crazy like that. I hate how small-town stores always close on some random day during the week, usually the day you want to go there.'

'Mom.' I let out an exasperated sigh.

'What?' she took a sip of her margarita.

'Why didn't you ever tell me about magic?'

'I wanted to raise you to be practical,' she said. 'Believing in magic just sets you up for disappointment. Your father and I decided to wait until you were eighteen to tell you, but then he died, and I didn't want to shake up your world again. Or mine.'

'How does magic work? Could you teach me?' I asked.

My mother looked like I'd asked her to teach me how to do a keg stand.

'I told you, I don't do that anymore.'

I wasn't going to let her off the hook that easily, but just then Holly rushed over to our table looking panicked. Wow, she was really committing to this get-me-out-of-dinner thing.

'It's OK, Holly. I'll eat the cupcakes. Or get the donuts?' I really needed to write these secret codes down in the future.

'I need to talk to you.' She sounded as panicked as she looked. Her acting was superb. She must be going for extra friend points.

'Can we talk tomorrow?' I nodded towards my mother meaningfully.

'Flora got arrested!' she said, ignoring me.

'What?' I leapt out of my seat and a few heads turned. 'Why?'

'Let's talk about this outside.' My mother threw some money down on the table and took the last swig of her drink before ushering us to the door.

'Mom, this is Holly. Holly, this is my mother, Corinne,' I said, remembering my manners before turning my full attention on Holly.

'Why was Flora arrested?' I asked again.

'They think she did something. She didn't do it, of course. She must have been set up.' Her words tumbled out.

'Holly.' I put my hands on her shoulders and looked her squarely in the eye. 'Does it have something to do with magic?'

Her eyes widened in shock for a second, and she looked from my mother to me.

'Yes. They think she's trying to alter Erma's spices to control people. They found a spice bottle stashed in the back of one of the shelves in her shop. There's no way it was her though. There's just no way.' Holly almost sounded like she was trying to convince herself just as much as us.

'We have to go see her,' I said.

With no plan beyond that, we all piled into my car.

'Where are Mr Barnes and Lena?' I asked.

'They're already at the station,' Holly said. She squeaked the first time I hit the brakes and the car shook, but she recovered quickly and gave directions to the police station in between criticisms from my mother about my car.

'This is really a hazard on the road,' my mother said.

'Turn left,' Holly said.

'Yes, you're right,' I said, making the turn. I figured the

best way to get her to back off was to agree with her. Luckily the drive was short and as we pulled into the parking lot, my mother was informing me that there probably wasn't even a junkyard that would accept my car because it was such an abomination.

'Wait.' I grabbed Holly's arm to stop her before we got to the door. 'Is a magical jail different from a regular jail?' I asked. I wanted to know what I was getting myself into. I had visions of us finding Flora in a dungeon guarded by goblins and dragons.

'It will look like any other jail, but there are some spells in place to make it more secure,' Holly said. That made me feel ever so slightly better.

When we walked through the door, Mr Barnes and Lena were out front. It was a small dingy room with tan walls. A few brown chairs were lined up on one side. They were covered in mystery stains and I took a step away from them. There was a window at the back that looked over an empty desk. The door next to it was dented and scratched as though it had been through a few scuffles.

Lena was towering over a small rather nervous looking officer.

'Now listen here, little Donnie Walsh,' she roared in a voice that made us all shrink back. I noticed Mr Barnes appeared to be taking deep calming breaths. 'I used to babysit you. You spit up on my favorite jacket, so you owe me. You are going to let us see her, now. I don't care what Buddy said. Don't make me call your mother.'

'Let me make some calls,' he said before he quickly

disappeared through a door at the side of the room. I had a feeling we weren't going to see him again. Lena glared after him for a minute before she noticed us standing there.

'Oh good, you're here,' she said. She somehow managed to wrap all three of us in her arms for a bone crushing hug.

'What's happening?' Holly asked, once Lena had released us and we could breathe again.

'They aren't telling us much,' Mr Barnes said. He glanced towards me and my mother.

'It's OK, they know about the magic,' Holly said.

A look of surprise flashed across his face before he continued. 'They found a bottle of the magic spice in the back of her bookshop, and they think she's the one who broke into the pie shop and stole the spices.'

'That's ridiculous,' I said.

'Why were they even looking in her shop anyway?' Holly asked.

Mr Barnes shrugged. 'We're not sure.'

My mother pulled me aside while the three of them talked.

'Are you sure she's innocent?' she asked me in a low voice.

'Of course I'm sure,' I said, stomping my foot in frustration like a child.

Sheriff Buddy walked through the door and Lena was on him before the door swung all the way closed.

'What's going on here, Buddy? You know Flora. You know she's not a thief,' Lena said.

'Now, Lena,' he began rubbing his hand through his thinning hair, 'you know I'm just doing my job.'

'Doing your job, my foot,' Lena said.

Violet came through the door.

'What's she doing here?' I asked. Why was a health inspector at the police station?

'Violet's a Magic Inspector,' Holly said. I blinked at her as I tried to process that.

'A Magic Inspector,' I repeated back slowly. Holly didn't have a chance to explain further because Violet started talking.

'We got an anonymous tip that Flora might be in possession of the stolen spices. You know we can't let those fall into the wrong hands. The tip was enough to get a search warrant, and we searched her place, and found one of the bottles,' Violet said.

We all spoke at once.

'Why would she break in?' Mr Barnes asked.

'Obviously it was planted,' Lena said.

'I'm sure if that's the case, it will all come out in the trial,' Violet said. She remained prim and business like even as we became more like an angry mob.

'Bail has been set at ten thousand dollars,' Sheriff Buddy said. My mouth dropped open. I had never in my life had ten thousand dollars in my bank account at one time.

'Would you take an IOU?' Lena asked feebly.

Sheriff Buddy looked tired as he shook his head no.

'I'll take care of it,' my mother said briskly as she fished around in her purse for her checkbook. We all watched in awe as she wrote out the check without hesitation and handed it over to Sheriff Buddy. He looked from my mother to the check and back to my mother, then shrugged.

'I'll go get her,' he said.

'She'll be on magical restriction until after the trial,' Violet said, sizing us all up as though she dared us to challenge her before she also disappeared behind the door.

'Magical restriction means she won't be able to do any magic, and no one will be able to perform any magic on her,' Mr Barnes explained as we waited. 'It makes it easier for them to keep tabs on her until she's cleared.'

The door swung open and Flora stepped through it. We stared at her, stunned for a moment. Her usually perfectly combed low ponytail had come loose and some stuck straight up while other bits hung in her face. Her eyes looked empty and exhausted, though she forced a smile once she saw us all there.

Mr Barnes was closest, so he hugged her first, but we all followed suit.

'Are you OK?' we all kept asking.

'Yes,' she said every time, but her voice sounded flat.

We surrounded her and walked her to Lena's car.

We agreed to all meet back at the bookshop to get Flora settled in.

None of us spoke on the drive. I turned the radio on and half listened to the oldies that played. We pulled in right behind Lena's car and all got out.

I gasped when we stepped inside the bookstore. The place was a disaster. The floor was covered with books.

They had really searched the place thoroughly. Flora stayed quiet, but I saw a tear slip out of the corner of her eye. Mr Barnes, Holly, and my mother began to pick up books while Lena went off on a tirade about how they wouldn't get away with this. I joined the efforts to pick up the shop. I knew we weren't stacking them right and that Flora would redo everything we were doing, but it made us feel better to be productive for a bit.

'Where is Erma?' my mother asked me in a low voice. 'Something isn't adding up.' I agreed, but I didn't want to get her involved in what I had planned. Before I could answer, we heard a yell come from the back of the shop and went running. Flora stood in the doorway I had seen the first time I had been in the shop. The one she had ushered me away from when I got close to it. I peered around her and saw a small room with a table and chair in the middle. The walls were lined with empty bookshelves.

'They took them. They took them all,' she wailed.

'What did they take?' I asked.

'Her magic books,' Mr Barnes said. 'They must have confiscated them until after the trial.'

At that moment I knew what I had to do, but I didn't tell anyone because I was afraid they would try to stop me.

'I'll stay with her tonight,' Lena said with her arm around a distraught Flora.

'You call me if you need anything,' I told them. 'I can be over in no time.' Lena nodded, but Flora just stared at me blankly as though she wasn't sure she'd understood what I just said.

We went outside, and Mr Barnes gave us a slightly forced 'Everything will be OK,' speech before disappearing into the night. Holly left next promising to check in later.

'I should get going too,' my mother said. 'Unless you want me to stay with you?' The offer was sweet, but I was working on a plan and needed to be alone.

'I'm fine, thanks. Mitzy and I will walk you to the inn.' I ran into the pie shop and got Mitzy.

We walked mostly in silence. Occasionally my mother would comment on a cute looking store.

At the door of the Hocus Hills Inn, my mother turned to me and studied my face. I shifted uncomfortably. 'Be careful,' she said firmly. What a strange thing to say. Did she know what I was planning?

'OK,' I said and gave her a hug. She squeezed me tightly and my muscles relaxed for a second.

'Everything will work out,' she said, and I tried to believe her.

Henry was standing in the alley by the back door when I got to the pie shop. I wished I had gone in the front door.

'Hey,' I said, digging around in my pockets trying to find my keys.

'Can we talk?' he asked. His brow was furrowed which made me feel nervous.

'It's been a crazy night. I just need to get to bed.' I dropped my keys on the asphalt.

'Please?' He bent down to pick up my keys.

'I got them,' I said, waving him away and grabbing them myself.

After the night I'd had, I wanted to watch some mindless television and eat a giant bowl of popcorn, but I knew what had to be done. Henry followed me inside.

'Are you mad at me about something?' he asked.

'No,' I said a little more harshly than I intended. I picked up a piece of paper and a pen and began to move around the kitchen making notes of things I would need Stan to deliver next time. I pushed the pen too hard into the paper when I wrote 'butter' in bold letters.

'Is it because I didn't call the day after we went ice skating? I meant to...' His voice trailed off, and I rolled my eyes at the eggs in the fridge before pulling my head out.

'Look Henry, I have a lot of stuff to get done tonight. Could we talk about this some other time?'

He looked a little taken aback. 'No, talk to me now. Please.'

'I don't think this is going to work out, me and you.' I pictured the notebook on his desk.

'Why not?' he asked, gripping the edge of the kitchen island.

I sized him up for a minute. 'Why did you have a notebook with information about me written inside?'

He froze. His face turned red.

'I ... I...' he stuttered. 'Look, I promise there is a good explanation, I just can't tell you what it is.'

'Wow, does anyone really fall for that line?' I asked. 'I think maybe you should leave.' I tried to look firm. I wanted to just ignore the warning signs, the red lights, the ones that told me to stop and run the other way. I wanted to invite him to come upstairs and watch a movie with me, but I had ignored the warning signs too many times in my life, and now I had to know better, be better.

He looked like he wanted to say something, but then he turned and left.

I stood in the middle of the empty kitchen and let the pen fall out of my hand and roll across the floor.

Chapter 23

Day 15 — Wednesday

I jiggled the door, and I was a little surprised that the lock popped open again. I thought after last time, Alice would have gotten it fixed. I guess people in small towns really did trust their neighbors.

I slid through the door. I paused for a second in the darkness and listened. My skin prickled and my muscles tensed ready to run if I heard anything, but it was silent. I felt a little silly in my black leggings, black tunic, and black stocking hat. I found the black hat in the back of Aunt Erma's closet, so I left the zebra striped one behind. How had I convinced myself I needed a special break-in outfit this time? Now if someone caught me, they would definitely know what I was up to. I should have just worn a law-abiding citizen outfit. Something with flowers on it. Flowers screamed innocence. Plus, the black was much less effective now that it had begun to snow again. There was no time for all this second guessing. I pulled out my flashlight, turned it on, and began digging through the first cupboard I came to.

'Focus,' I whispered to myself.

'You'll never find them,' a voice said, and I jumped up hitting my head on the cupboard door dropping the flash-light.

A lamp turned on in the corner, and I saw Alice sitting at her desk.

'What are you doing here?' I demanded even though I was the one breaking into her store. I rubbed my sore head. 'You told Mr Barnes you were going to be out of town.'

She let out an evil cackle. 'Yes, and of course he ran right over and told you. It wasn't hard to figure out it was you who broke in last time. I knew you'd be back.'

'Why did you steal them in the first place?' I asked.

'Oh honey, your aunt is very powerful, but she's not using her powers to their full potential, so I stepped in to use them.' She seemed to relish the sound of her own voice. She looked at the ceiling as she spoke.

I began to inch towards the door.

'I needed the original product so I could study the spells she used on the spices and alter them to do more than just make people happy.' She made 'happy' sound like such a terrible thing.

I could almost reach the door knob.

'Ha, I'm not going to let you just walk out of here.' She swiftly moved to block the door.

'What do you have against me?' I asked innocently. I had to keep her talking while I figured out how to get out of this situation.

'You're just a pebble in my path,' she said, motioning

towards the door. My stomach sank as I heard the sound of popcorn popping. She must be locking the door with a spell. I tried not to cringe as she took a couple of steps towards me.

My fingers reached around on the counter behind me. I grasped something. Please be a knife, I thought as my fingers curled around a handle and I whipped it out in front of me. Why didn't my wishes ever come true? I was brandishing a wooden spoon at Alice.

She shook her head and looked sorry for me.

I felt a little sorry for myself to be quite honest.

'It was my sister, Nellie, who first taught me about magic,' she began, circling around me, easily disarming me of my wooden spoon weapon. 'Both of our parents died when we were young, and we were shuffled from foster home to foster home.'

I saw Alice's cat peering at me from under the desk. If I got out of here, I could report her to a health inspector for having an animal in the kitchen area. When, not if, I corrected myself with a shudder.

'At one of the homes we were placed in, my sister made friends with a woman named Dolores who lived down the street. There were rumors in the neighborhood that Dolores was a witch. She had one of those houses that no one ever stopped to trick-or-treat at. Thick prickly bushes lined a long winding path to her front door, and she hung plastic skulls along her fence at Christmas. My sister's whole demeanor changed after a few weeks of spending time with Dolores.' Alice continued to pace around the kitchen. I wondered if she would turn her back long enough for me to leap out the window.

'Nellie became more secretive and more confident. She was no longer the mousy go-along-with-anything girl. She began to stand up to our foster parents who grew more and more afraid of her as strange things happened around the house. It started small – things went missing or moved from one end of the house to the other. Then she would make doors upstairs slam when we were all downstairs in the living room together. One day when our foster mother was yelling at her, Nellie murmured something and threw her hands into the air. All the glasses in the kitchen exploded. No one was hurt, but everyone steered clear of her after that. She would tell me that we deserved better. Finally, one night she taught me about the magic that she was learning from Dolores.'

Alice seemed lost in her own memories, and I noticed the cat was still watching me with her bright blue eyes from under the desk. The cat stuck out her left paw and then pulled it back in before sticking it out and shaking it. Was the cat doing the hokey pokey? Maybe my panic was causing me to hallucinate.

Alice talked about how her sister had been killed in a car accident a year ago. I felt a twinge of pity for her. I knew what it was like to lose a family member. 'My sister taught me that many people in this world are too ignorant to be useful. They need someone like me to lead them. To make them productive members of society. I met Dolores's family at Nellie's funeral. They told me they were helping

Nellie with her plans to manipulate the weak through a widespread use of magic spices.' The cat repeated the movements with the other paw. 'Dolores's family knew of a woman in a small town who was very powerful, and Nellie was on her way to meet her when she was killed. Nellie never told me about this plan, but I'm sure she would have shared her success.' Alice pursed her lips. 'She always tried to protect me even though I'm the older sister. She was braver and stronger. We could have ruled the world together. When she died, I decided to pursue the mission in her honor.'

The cat put her right paw out in front of her, then pulled it towards her before sticking it back out and shaking it. Aunt Erma and I used to do the hokey pokey in the kitchen while we waited for pies to bake. She would play the song on her old record player.

'We've been testing spells on nearby towns, but without the spices, we couldn't make anything with strong enough magic,' Alice continued. 'Stan has really been invaluable to me.'

'Stan?' I asked. 'What does he have to do with any of this?'

'Oh, didn't I mention Stan is Dolores's grandson? Kind of a whiny kid. He complained a lot about having to do your delivery without magic.' That explained Stan's clumsiness. 'But I really couldn't have done it without his spying skills. No one ever suspects the delivery guy.' Alice recounted her so-called triumphs from when she used stolen spices. 'At first I just reeled people in because I was offering something different. Something other than tired old pie. But once I got the spices, I knew I'd have customers forever. I'd sell out of cookies, and they'd beg for more, offering to pay top dollar. I had half of the town ready to build me a castle if I wanted them to. But the effects are still short-lived and hard to control. I need to figure out Erma's secret.' Alice was quiet for a moment, lost in her own thoughts.

'So that day everyone in town was acting crazy and trying to lift everything up, that was you?' I asked.

She rolled her eyes. 'A minor setback in an otherwise glorious tale.'

The cat shrank back under the desk as Alice got closer. I heard Bernie's voice in my head. 'Dust the cat,' she had told me. At the time, I had dismissed it as the ramblings of a woman slipping into dementia, but now her words came to me so clearly. It was almost as though she was in the room saying them. I could feel the small bottle Aunt Erma had left for me dangling on its chain against my chest.

'I'm too close to a breakthrough, and I can't have you getting in my way. No one will really miss you. They'll just assume you couldn't hack it here and went back home.' She had a little smile on her lips as though she was saying something perfectly pleasant.

'The Morning Pie Crew will look for me,' I said confidently.

'Not after they have some of my cookies,' she said. 'I have a new recipe to test out. They'll either forget about you, or forget everything they ever knew. Either way it's a win.'

Alice looked out the windows and continued to work through her plan, none of which sounded good for me. I slowly reached under my shirt and grasped the small bottle. I carefully pulled it down until the stopper that was attached to the chain popped out. The cat began to slink towards me.

Alice turned around. 'Hey, what are you...?'

I turned the bottle upside down and the white glitter fell on the cat as Alice charged at me. I jumped out of the way as I heard a popping noise and glitter swirled through the air as Aunt Erma appeared where the cat had been. Her curly hair was grayer than I remembered and her face had a few more wrinkles, but there was no doubt it was her. She sat on the floor blinking her large blue eyes. Alice and I both froze for a second before she lunged for my hand that held the bottle again. Aunt Erma jumped up and pulled Alice off me. She was pretty strong for such a small lady.

'Give me the bottle, Susie,' Aunt Erma cried, and I pressed it into her hand.

She threw a pinch of the dust at Alice. The air sparkled and popped and a dark gray cat appeared where Alice had been. Aunt Erma threw a large wire basket over the cat. We both breathed heavily as we watched the cat hiss and growl at us.

'I'll call Violet to come pick her up,' Aunt Erma said, breaking the silence.

I nodded because I couldn't speak yet. Aunt Erma had been a cat. The cat had been Aunt Erma. Now Alice was a cat. The room began to spin a little. My heart was pounding so hard it was almost deafening and my knees felt weak.

'Sit down,' Aunt Erma commanded, leading me over to the chair at the desk. The cat hissed and growled. 'Oh hush.' Aunt Erma threw another pinch of the glittery dust at the cat, and it was silenced. The cat's eyes turned wild with anger. If looks could kill, we'd be dead now.

While Aunt Erma called Violet, I tried to wrap my head around what was happening. I would never look at a cat the same way again. How many animals were actually humans?

Violet appeared at the door quickly, and Aunt Erma explained how Alice had turned her into a cat and tried to make her recreate the spells she put on the spices. When she wouldn't, Alice broke into the pie shop and stole the spices to study the spells she had used. Alice was working with Stan and his parents. They altered the spells to control people.

'I knew it couldn't be you,' Violet said. 'The higher ups kept pressuring me to look into you because it appeared so suspicious. You disappeared right when those spells started popping up in surrounding cities. They were like yours, but they had been modified so the magic was darker. You're not the dark magic type.'

'That's right. I'd rather have a world full of happy people, not zombie drones,' Aunt Erma said.

Aunt Erma went on to explain how Alice had changed and produced the spices. She used a lot of magical terms that I didn't understand.

Violet listened carefully, every now and then taking notes on her small notepad. Occasionally she would glance in my direction. I just watched on, still wide-eyed.

'Where are the spices now?' Violet asked when Aunt Erma had finished her story.

'She kept them in here.' Aunt Erma went over to a small lidded trash can that sat under the desk. Of course, the trash can. I would have never thought to look there. She pulled out the box and opened it. Three of the slots were empty.

'I have one of the bottles. Number seven,' I offered.

'Number eleven is the one we found planted at Flora's,' Violet said. 'So where's the other one?' she demanded, looking back and forth between Aunt Erma and me. 'Number three is missing.'

We both shrugged. Aunt Erma went over to the basket and peered in at the cat.

'What did you do with the other bottle?' she demanded. The cat curled up and looked sweetly at Aunt Erma before closing her eyes. For a minute, I thought Aunt Erma was going to kick the basket, but she thought better of it. 'I don't know where the other bottle is. I never saw her take it,' she told Violet.

Violet took the box of spices to be used as evidence, and took Alice the cat to be detained until she could stand trial at the magical courthouse. When I asked where the magical courthouse was, Violet said I would find out when I was called as a witness to testify. The idea of testifying against Alice sent a nervous shiver through me, but Aunt Erma assured me she would be right by my side, and I didn't need to worry about it tonight anyway.

Chapter 24

Day 15 — Wednesday

Aunt Erma and I walked back to the pie shop in silence, fresh snow crunching under our feet. I had so many questions, but I didn't even know where to begin. I cast a sidelong glance at her, and she looked like she was going to say something, but then stopped herself.

When we got back to the pie shop, my mother was waiting out front. When she saw Aunt Erma, her eyes got wide, and she froze. The women stared at each other and then Aunt Erma threw herself into my mother's arms. They embraced for a minute and when they pulled away, both of them had tears in their eyes.

'I'm...' my mother began and then her voice trailed off.

'Me too,' Aunt Erma said. Then more briskly, 'It's cold out here. Let's go inside and warm up.'

I unlocked the door, and we went inside. It's funny how sometimes when there's so much to say, no one can say anything. We didn't have to struggle for words for long before the Morning Pie Crew burst through the door. They surrounded Aunt Erma and hugged her.

Even though it had only been a few hours since I'd seen Flora looking like she needed a hundred hours of sleep, she already looked like her old self again.

'You look great,' I said, joining in the hugging spree to hug her.

'Because you caught Alice, I got my magic back,' she said. Her smile stretched across her face.

'That was fast!' I said, and she nodded in agreement. 'And the books?' I asked.

'Yes, I got the books back too.'

'What exactly are magic books?' I asked.

'Ah, that's a story for another time,' she said with a twinkle in her eye.

'Where have you been?' Lena demanded, crushing Aunt Erma with another hug.

'It's a long story,' Aunt Erma said.

'That must mean we need coffee.' Mr Barnes went behind the counter and started making a pot. The rest of us all sank into chairs. It felt like it was the middle of the night, but the clock said it was only 9.30 p.m.

Aunt Erma began to tell us her story. 'A couple of weeks ago, I noticed my notebook was missing.' Flora gasped, and I waited for someone to explain the significance. 'Don't worry. I don't keep the most powerful spells in there,' she said, tapping her head. Alice had gotten ahold of her spell notebook, probably through Stan. That same day she got a warning from Bernie that danger was coming. She called me right away and asked me to come and help her at the pie shop. She was going to leave town for a few days because she was hoping to get her notebook back and find out who was after her spells and why.

'I didn't know who it was, but I thought I'd be able to handle it, and I could come back and all would be well,' Aunt Erma said.

'You should have come to us for help,' Lena said.

'I know, I'm sorry.' She picked at a piece of lint on her pants. 'I was on my way back from leaving the notes for Susie and Flora at the bookshop when Alice attacked me like a coward from behind with a spell. She realized I hadn't written all the spells down. Suddenly I was a cat.' Aunt Erma shuddered. 'Cats are the worst.' Mitzy yipped in agreement. 'She made me eat nothing but tuna. But a few times I snuck some licks out of the bowl full of cookie dough.'

'Oh, gross. I ate some of those cookies.' Flora wrinkled her nose.

'Thanks, Bumfuzzle,' Aunt Erma said, taking a mug of coffee from Mr Barnes. We all stared at her.

'Erma!' Mr Barnes exclaimed, his voice a few octaves above its normal register.

'Sorry.' she grimaced.

'Wait, Bumfuzzle is your real name?' Lena shrieked.

'Don't make fun.' Flora swatted Lena's arm. Then she turned to Mr Barnes. 'Can we call you Fuzzy?' she asked. Her face was perfectly serious, but her eyes twinkled.

'Or how about Bum?' Lena almost fell out of her chair. My mother snorted, then looked down at the table guiltily.

I saw Mr Barnes take one of his deep yoga cleansing breaths before sticking his tongue out at Aunt Erma. She gave him an innocent shrug.

After a little more teasing, everyone settled down and Aunt Erma went on to tell us how every now and then Alice would lock her up before turning her back into a person and trying to make her reveal the spells she used on her spices.

'But I'm tougher than I look, and she couldn't make me talk,' she said a little proudly. With her brow wrinkled, Flora patted her on the arm. 'Thank you, but I'm just fine. Her weak spells barely worked on me,' Aunt Erma said, dismissing her concern.

Mr Barnes finished handing out the coffee. Aunt Erma leaned down towards her cup and began lapping it up. She paused when she realized we were all staring at her.

'Old habits.' She shrugged and picked up the mug with both hands.

Just then, Violet peeked in through the door. 'Can I come in?' she asked, looking pleasant for the first time since I'd known her.

'Of course.' Erma waved her in warmly.

'The Magical Law Enforcers came and took Alice away,' she informed us.

'What's going to happen to her?' I asked, wondering if everyone else already knew.

'She'll stand trial and probably be stripped of her magical powers,' Violet said grimly.

Flora turned to me. 'It's a very strong spell, and it's very permanent.'

'Will she just go back out into the world?' I asked. Even without magic, a person could do some damage.

'She'll be closely monitored,' Violet assured me. 'Also, Stan and his parents are missing.' Aunt Erma's brow wrinkled.

'I'm sure you'll find them soon,' Flora said, but she looked worried too.

Violet looked at her apologetically. 'I'm sorry,' she said. 'The higher ups were breathing down my neck and all signs pointed to you and Erma as the guilty ones. We thought Erma was trying to change her spices to do evil instead of good, and we thought you were helping her research different spells because you have all sorts of information in those books in the back room of your shop. Then we found the spice bottle there.'

'But I would never—' Flora began.

'I know,' Violet said. 'Alice admitted giving the anonymous tip that led to your arrest. I can't believe I let her trick me.' She looked truly disgusted with herself.

The bell tinkled as Henry peeked his head through the door. 'Erma, it's so wonderful to see you. I heard you were back,' he said, still standing behind the door. How had people heard about this already? Was there a magic news channel on television? Was everyone in town able to pass telepathic messages back and forth?

'Come in, Henry.' Aunt Erma enthusiastically waved him in. 'We have coffee and pie.'

'That sounds great. Maybe in a minute.' He turned his head to me. 'Can I talk to you?'

I wanted to say no, but everyone's face had turned towards

291

me and several eyebrows were raised. I didn't feel like saying no was an option.

'Sure.' I reluctantly pulled myself to my feet and grabbed my coat. I planned on staying close to the pie shop in case it turned out Henry was indeed a serial killer. I wanted to make sure everyone could hear me scream. I followed him out, and we stood under a streetlight in front of Flora's bookshop. Still screaming distance to the pie shop, I thought.

Henry fidgeted nervously from one foot to the other.

'What do you want to talk about?' I asked with a little edge to my voice. I wasn't in the mood to mess around trying to gently pull information out of him.

'I wanted to explain about the notebook,' he said.

'OK,' I said slowly. This was going to be good. I couldn't come up with any explanation for the notebook that didn't make Henry look like a nut job.

'I know it probably looked weird, maybe even creepy,' he said.

'Yeah, a little,' I said as I backed up a couple more steps towards the pie shop. 'There are many ways to get to know someone, but keeping notes on them isn't one I've heard of outside of a good crime show.'

'I'm not a criminal,' he said. 'Well, as long as you don't count the one time I stole a bone for my dog, Victor, but I was four and have since learned my lesson.'

'So why are you keeping a notebook about me?' I demanded. I didn't want to be sucked in by his cute story about his dog. I tried desperately not to think about how adorable Henry would have been when he was four.

'I'm Elodie,' he said.

'What?' I asked, not sure what he was saying. It definitely wasn't what I expected to hear from him.

'I write the column "Ask Elodie" and sometimes other pieces for the newspaper,' he said, watching my reaction. 'Those notes were for the pieces I wrote about you. My editor demanded that I do it, and then he "spiced it up a little." His words not mine. I didn't write all those things that they printed. At least not the way they spun them. I'll show you the original articles.'

'Why would you even write about me in the first place? I thought we were ... friends,' I said.

'At first, I thought you might be wrapped up in the magic spices, and I was trying to get to the bottom of the story. Once I got to know you, I knew that couldn't be the case. Willard was after a good story, and you being a brave and persistent person wasn't enough of a story for him. After the second article, I threatened to quit, and Willard promised he wouldn't do it again. Plus he said I could write another article about you, and he would publish it without changing it.'

I wrinkled my nose. 'I don't think that's necessary.'

'OK, it's totally up to you. But I could let you read it first,' he offered. 'Imagine this headline, "Susanna Daniels – Hocus Hills Hero."'

'That does have a nice ring to it,' I admitted with a smile. 'So wait, when we're all in the pie shop gossiping about "Ask Elodie" and arguing about the responses, you're the one who wrote them?'

293

He nodded, looking down.

'I know you don't owe me anything, but could you keep my secret?' he asked, meeting my eyes with a hopeful smile. 'It's a mystery best kept. Plus can you imagine what it would be like when people don't agree with me? I'd never hear the end of it.'

He was right. They would hound him until their dying breaths if he didn't print a retraction every time they disagreed with his advice.

'Will you forgive me?' He looked at me with big hopeful eyes. 'Both for writing about you without your permission and for scaring you with my very thorough note keeping?'

It was hard to stay mad at him. Then again, if he was able to keep the fact that he was Elodie a secret, who knows what else he might be keeping a secret.

He seemed to sense my hesitation. 'We can take things as slowly as you want,' he said. I don't think he intended for the words to be sensual, but I felt a tingle run down my spine. 'Is that a deal?' He extended his hand. His face was full of concern and hope.

I grabbed it and pulled him closer to me. I saw a hint of surprise in his eyes and then he smiled as I leaned in and kissed him. The tingling sensation extended throughout my whole body, and he reached up and brushed his hand through my hair. His eyes were sparkling and his face was flushed when I finally stepped away from him. I was pretty sure I had the same stupid grin on my face.

'We should probably get back,' I said, after a minute of us staring into each other's eyes.

When we got back to the pie shop, Aunt Erma was catching up on all the gossip she'd missed while she was a cat. Even thinking this statement made me wonder if I was losing my marbles a little.

'This calls for a celebration.' Lena began to dig around in her purse. She produced a bottle of champagne and handed it to me. How many bottles were in there? She reached back in and pulled out enough glasses for everyone. I filled each glass with a little champagne.

'Don't be shy, honey,' Lena said. 'It's not going to run out.' Everyone laughed. I realized there must be magic at work.

'Oh, never-ending bottle of champagne, where have you been all my life?' I asked, gazing lovingly at the green glass bottle.

'How are you handling all this magic stuff?' Aunt Erma asked me.

'I still have so many questions about how it all works.'

'It's mostly spells, but some of us have magic wands and crystal balls to help us,' Lena said.

'Is that your magic wand?' I pointed to the long purple stick that held Lena's hair in a messy bun. It sparkled in the light.

'No, dear. That's just a fashion statement,' she said.

'I'll teach you,' Aunt Erma offered.

More magic questions tickled my throat, but I swallowed to save them for another time.

Flora brought up the latest 'Ask Elodie'. I glanced over at Henry who was leaning against the wall holding his fingers to his lips with a small smile. I returned his smile. He might be safe from the rest of the town, but he would definitely be hearing from me if I didn't agree with his advice. He might prefer it when I thought he was a serial killer.

Holly burst through the door. 'You're OK!' she cried, throwing herself into my arms. 'Why didn't you tell me what you were going to do tonight? I could have helped.' She squeezed so tightly, I thought I heard a couple of bones crunch.

'Holly,' I gasped, and she released me. 'I'm sorry, I thought you might try to stop me.'

'I would have. What you did was very dangerous,' she scolded. 'But Erma, I'm so glad you're back.' She hugged her too, and then Flora, and then everyone else. 'You're not going to leave us now that Erma's back, are you?' Holly turned to me, her brow wrinkled with concern.

I froze. I hadn't thought that far ahead.

'I was hoping you'd stay here with me for at least a little while,' Aunt Erma said. 'I have so much I want to show you. So much catching up to do.'

I glanced at my mother. Instead of seeing the anger I expected in her eyes, she looked a little sad.

'I think you should stay,' my mother said.

'There's room in this town for you as well,' Aunt Erma said. 'I'd like you to stay too.'

'Maybe,' my mom conceded with a small smile.

I agreed to stay, for at least the foreseeable future. I sat back in my chair surrounded by the warmth of family, friends, and pie. A magic glow was in the air.

Epilogue

'Oh, this one smells good.' I inhaled deeply over the lemon buttermilk tart I had just pulled out of the oven.

'You've said that about every pie,' Aunt Erma laughed.

'And I've meant it,' I said. We were preparing pies for Thanksgiving dinner. We had been busy all week with holiday orders. Today the shop was closed and Aunt Erma was using the opportunity to test my newly learned magic. Some of the pies we were baking were for a Thanksgiving lunch at the nursing home and the rest were for the Thanksgiving dinner we were having here.

I surveyed the kitchen full of pies trying to figure out where to set this one down. Even with the two events, I think we had enough pies to feed three times as many people as we needed to.

'Here, there's room for that one by the blueberry blast,' Aunt Erma said, giggling as she slid a couple pies around. It was bad enough she was calling it that, but did she have to giggle every single time?

I glared at her, then smiled. While both my baking and

magical skills were definitely improving, I'd had a slight setback this morning when I combined two spices incorrectly in a blueberry pie and the pie exploded in my face and all over the kitchen. I learned quickly and did better on the second two pies, but that didn't stop Aunt Erma from calling them the blueberry blast pies.

'Some magic complements each other and creates an even stronger result, but when some magic is combined it has more explosive results,' Aunt Erma explained as I wiped blueberries out of my hair. We went over which spices did what. There was one that increased happiness, one that increased honesty, one that increased helpfulness. She told me she usually tried to direct people towards the flavor of pie that she thought they needed in their life that day. I wasn't sure I would ever have the same instincts she had, but she assured me I would.

She was also teaching me the special incantations that she said would help focus the spice's magic. On top of that, she spent a lot of time showing me how to make the perfect pie crust and how to find flavors that worked well together. I wasn't a fast learner, but she was a patient teacher. I was beginning to gain confidence in my baking and I no longer cringed every time someone took a bite of a pie I had made.

In between the lessons, we spent a lot of time drinking coffee and catching up on the last twenty years.

'Help me with this last one,' Aunt Erma said. 'It's a pear crumble pie.' I helped her pour the filling into the crust. She handed me one of the spice bottles. 'Use this one,' she instructed, 'and repeat after me.' I repeated the words she said. I could feel the rush of energy tingling down my arm as I sprinkled the spice across the top of the pie. We topped it with my favorite part, a layer of brown sugar crumble topping.

As I put the pie in the oven, I asked, 'What does that spice do?'

'I thought you could bring that pie to Henry,' she said innocently. 'It enhances the feeling of love.' A wicked smile spread across her face

I felt my face turn red. 'Henry and I don't need a pie like that,' I sniffed. 'We're doing just fine on our own.' We had gone out a few times. We were taking things slowly, and I couldn't stop smiling anytime I thought about him.

'You come home pretty early from your dates. That's all I'm saying.' I threw a pinch of flour at her, and she laughed. 'Just think about bringing him that pie,' she said.

'Fine, I'll think about it.'

She put her arm around me and we stood at the edge of the kitchen for a moment to survey our work and try to decide which pie to slice into for our post baking snack.

Keep reading for sneak peek at Christmas in
Hocus Hills in the second book of
The Magic Pie Shop series...

A Slice of Christmas Magic

Prologue

There was a cottage nestled in the snowy countryside at the bottom of a hill. From the outside it looked like it belonged in the pages of a storybook, but inside life was no happily ever after.

Dennis and Stan, a father and son, were playing chess by the fire. A woman with greying brown hair and sharp green eyes walked in. The younger man felt all the muscles in his body tense.

"Did you get it?" she asked.

"No," Stan answered quietly. Dennis stared at the board.

"What?" she asked sharply. Both men flinched. "We would be in control of all the magic in Hocus Hills by now if you two blundering buffoons didn't fail at every little task." She spoke as though all the magical residents in the town of Hocus Hills were just objects for her to possess.

"Alice set us back when she got caught. I should have never let her convince me she could control people through altered magic spices. She didn't have the skills, and I don't think her heart was in the mission. She was too distracted by the loss of her sister." Sometimes Brenda just liked to hear the sound of her own voice.

"We can try something else," Dennis offered, never taking his eyes off the chess board.

"Of course, we'll try something else," Brenda snapped. "We still have two days before Ivan gets here. We'd better have some new recruits by then. That shouldn't be hard. There's always magical people who want more than to hide out in a small town."

She paced up and down the room. Her shoes clicked sharply against the floor. Stan watched his mother pace.

"Erma — she's going to be the problem," Brenda was muttering under her breath now. "But think of how happy Ivan would be if we got her magic."

She went to the fireplace and threw in a couple of logs. Sparks flew, and heat poured out as the flames rose higher.

Chapter 1

I wiped a bead of sweat off my forehead with the back of my hand and surveyed the display case. It was packed full of pies. Only ten minutes until we opened.

Aunt Erma came out from the kitchen carrying a blueberry pie, her specialty. She wore a hat with felt antlers and jingle bells.

"What do you think? Do we have enough?" She stood next to me.

"Not if business keeps up the way it has," I said. We'd sold out every day this week. Now that Aunt Erma was back and could teach me her secret recipes with her magic spices, customers had been pouring through the door.

I went back into the kitchen to bring a load of garbage out to the dumpster. I jumped back a little when I saw a black and white spotted cat sitting just outside the back door in the alley. Just one month ago, before I knew anything about magic, Aunt Erma had been the cat in the alley. An evil woman named Alice had turned her into a cat and tried to steal the spells for Aunt Erma's magic spices. Now, Alice was in some kind of magical jail. The exact details

305

about what magic jail meant were still a little fuzzy to me and no one seemed eager to fill me in.

"Meow once if you're human," I said in a low voice. She meowed, and my eyes widened.

"Are you talking to a cat," Henry appeared from around the corner. His brown eyes twinkled, and his wavy brown hair stuck out from under his dark green stocking cap. Henry was my almost boyfriend. We had been dating for a few weeks, and I think we were nearing that point in the relationship when I could begin to use the B word.

"How do you know that this isn't a person?" I asked, greeting him with a quick kiss.

"I'm magic," he said with a smile. "And I know that's Mrs. Peterson's cat."

I leaned in for another kiss but pulled back when I saw Violet rushing towards us. Violet and I had a rocky relationship. Back when I was running the pie shop alone, she kept coming in looking for Aunt Erma and making accusations. At the time, I thought she was a health inspector. Violet's eyes were wild and her usually perfectly slicked down tight bun was a frizzy mess.

"Where's Erma?" she asked.

"She's inside," I said. "Is everything OK?"

Without a word, Violet rushed through the backdoor into the kitchen. I looked at Henry, and he shrugged. We followed her inside.

"What's wrong, Violet?" Aunt Erma had rushed over and put her hands on Violet's shoulders.

"It's happened," Violet said.

"Take a breath and tell me everything." Aunt Erma's voice remained calm, but I could see fear in her eyes.

"Dennis and Brenda. Stan. The missing spice bottle. They've finally figured out how to make the altered spices on a larger scale, and they're testing them out," Violet's words rushed out. Dennis and Brenda were Stan's parents. Stan had been the delivery man in town until a month ago when we found out he and his parents were working with Alice to try to steal Aunt Erma's magic spices.

"Oh no." Aunt Erma's arms dropped to her sides, and she took a step back to lean against the kitchen island. "What can I do?"

"We need you to help us track them down," she said. "We've been working on it since they disappeared, but they've evaded us so far. You might be able to trace the magic better since it was your magic in the first place."

"Let's go to Flora's and figure out a plan," Aunt Erma said, leading us out to the front of the shop. The pie shop was supposed to open in two minutes, and already there were a few early birds waiting outside the front door. They perked up as they saw us approaching.

"Sorry, folks. We're going to be opening a little late today." We all stepped outside amid the groans. "Come back later for your pie and a free cup of coffee," she said, locking the door behind us. I could still hear a few grumbles as the people shuffled off down the street. If only they knew the reason.

Aunt Erma had let it slip once just how dangerous it was that Stan had the bottle of spices. We had gone to Sal's bar one night to celebrate. We were celebrating a lot of things these days — our reunion, the fact that Aunt Erma wasn't a cat anymore, years of missed holidays and birthdays. Aunt Erma had introduced me to a drink called a Fairy's Foot. I was a little hesitant because the name did not sound appealing at all, but it was actually quite delicious. Like drinking a chocolate milkshake. The smooth sweet flavor hid the fact that the drink packed quite a punch, and by our second glass, Aunt Erma had completely lost her filter and was sharing information about her love life that would have made me blush if I wasn't already flushed from the drink.

"Make sure you find someone with good hands," she was saying firmly. "The hands are just as important as the…"

"No," I clapped my hands over my ears. "Tell me something else."

She giggled. "Fine." She took a deep breath. "I'm worried."

"About what?"

"The missing spice bottle. Spice number three. Three, three, bo, bee," she paused to take a sip of her drink. "The things they can do with that magic." She shook her head.

"Like what?" I asked. My experience with the spices was limited, but I didn't understand what would be so bad about them.

"The magic in them is so powerful because of the secret ingredient. That's why you have to be careful to use just a little bit in the pies and make sure you're focusing on the proper intention when you add them. I'll explain it more to you one day. Maybe when I'm sober-er." She clinked my glass with hers and began talking about highly inappropriate things again before I could ask her what the secret ingredient was.

Once we were inside Flora's, she led us back to a small door in the back of the shop. I hadn't noticed this door before. That wasn't surprising. Flora's shop was packed full of books. It had probably been behind a stack or a shelf the other times I had been in there.

We went down a dark narrow staircase to a room below. It was warm and cozy with a floor-to-ceiling bookshelf filled with old volumes. Mr. Barnes and Lena were already there. Mr. Barnes was cleaning his thick rimmed glasses on the corner of his bright blue sweater. Lena reached over and patted down a stray chunk of his white hair that stuck straight up on his head. How had they beat us there? There was a quiet anxiousness in the room.

Henry and I sat in chairs next to Lena, and Violet strode quickly to the front of the room. There was a computer with a large screen on the desk. I smiled at Lena, and she flashed a quick smile back at me. Her white hair was piled on top of her head in its usual bun, but her bright blue eyes lacked their usual twinkle. Violet stuck a thumb drive in the computer, and a black and white video started playing. It was a group of people walking along in a line down the street. They took slow even steps, and something about the sight made me shiver a little. Henry reached over and took my hand. Then suddenly everyone stopped walking. People looked around as though confused, and then the crowd dispersed.

"They must be having trouble making the effects last very long," Mr. Barnes said. The video skipped ahead, and Stan's parents popped up on the screen. Even in the grainy footage, I could recognize them. They were walking along, stopped, and looked straight into the camera.

"That's strange," Flora said, her brown eyes narrowed. "They know the camera is there. Why don't they hide themselves better? They could have erased the footage if they really wanted to."

"I thought so too," Violet said. "The only conclusion I could come to is they wanted us to find them. That can only mean one thing. They're trying to draw you out, Erma."

All of our heads turned towards Aunt Erma. Her eyebrows were pinched together with worry, but she quickly rearranged her features into a brave face.

"If they want me, they'll get me," she said with a determined edge to her voice.

Chapter 2

"I'm going with her," I'd said amongst the protests.

"Neither of you is going anywhere until we figure out if this is a trap or not," Flora pulled out her stern librarian voice that made me shrink back a little.

"I have to go," Aunt Erma said almost matching Flora's firm tone. "Someone has to stop them before they figure out how to make the effects last longer. I'm best suited to do that since it's my magic they're altering. You know how dangerous it could be if they're successful. For everyone. We need to stop them before it spreads."

Everyone was silent for a minute.

"I think she's right," Violet said.

"Susie, I'm not sure you should go, though," Lena said. "I think I should go along with you."

I bristled a little at her slightly condescending tone. I might be new to this magic thing, but I knew I could be helpful. I had taken karate for three years when I was in elementary school. There were some problems magic couldn't solve.

"We should all go," Mr. Barnes chimed in.

"That might draw too much attention," Violet said.

"Susie will come with me," Aunt Erma said firmly. "She's ready, and I know you'll all be here ready to back us up if need be." Everyone nodded. "But that won't be necessary," she added with a confident smile towards me. I noticed that when Aunt Erma talked, people tended to agree with her.

"And I'll keep an eye on you through the security cameras," Violet said, pointing at the computer screen. She had paused the image on Stan's parents, and I glared at them trying to build up my confidence. If I could keep myself from being afraid of their image, then I could definitely take them on in person, I assured myself repeatedly.

I winced as I realized Henry was gripping my hand tightly. "Hey," I said, gently. I put my other hand on top of his and began to carefully pry his fingers loose.

"Sorry," he said, softening his grip. "I hate the thought of you going, but I understand why you are. Just promise you'll be careful, and call me if you need anything."

"Of course." I kissed his hand, and he smiled at me in a way that made my heart flutter.

The crowd dispersed, and Henry squeezed me tightly before heading off to his job at the nursing home.

"Come with me." Aunt Erma grabbed my hand and led me to her car.

"Are we going now?" I asked, unable to keep the panic out of my voice.

"No," she said. "There's something I want to show you." I got in the car.

"Hold on, I'll be right back." Aunt Erma ran to the pie shop. She only seemed to have one speed, fast. A minute later she reappeared with her dog Mitzy close at her heels. Mitzy was a brown ball of fluff with expressive eyes and boundless energy. Her large brown eyes showed that she understood when you talked to her. Sometimes I found that a little unsettling.

Aunt Erma opened the back door and Mitzy hopped in. Her tail was wagging so hard I thought she might take flight.

"Mitzy loves a good car ride," Aunt Erma explained. She heard her name and somehow took it as an invitation to leap from the back seat and into my lap.

"Hi Mitzy," I said flatly. I loved Mitzy, really, but I was still getting used to this furry licking creature who lived life like she did a shot of espresso every hour.

Aunt Erma drove through Hocus Hills. The town looked like Father Christmas had thrown up on every street corner. Lights twinkled on every tree and bush and along the front of every shop. I didn't see a single door without a wreath and a very elaborate winter wonderland had been set up in the town square complete with nine reindeer, several elves, and Christmas fairies. There were banners all over town advertising the snowman building contest happening next weekend. "Erma's Pies" was one of the sponsors, and Aunt Erma had been making me practice my snowman building skills for the last two weeks.

"The middle is not round enough," she'd said about one

of my practice snowmen that I'd built in the park next to the ice rink.

"But it's getting kind of cold out here," I'd said. "Can I try again tomorrow?"

"One more time," she said. "The competition is fierce, and we need to make a good showing of it."

"But I can't even win since we're sponsoring." I could hear a little whine in my voice, and I was ever so slightly embarrassed, but being this cold made me revert to my young self.

"I know we can't win, but we have to build one in support of the competition, and we can't embarrass ourselves either," she said taking apart my snowman. It turns out that when it comes to snowman building competitions, Aunt Erma is like the worst overbearing pageant mom out there.

"Can't we just use magic?" I asked as I carefully rounded out the middle ball.

"Magic is forbidden at these competitions," she said. "At least until after the judging when everyone makes their snowmen dance," she giggled. "Lena made hers twerk last year. I didn't even know what twerking was until then."

"Yeah, Lena's pretty hip." I rubbed my hands together through the mittens before reassembling my snowman.

Aunt Erma took a step back and sized it up. "Not bad," she said with a curt nod. "Tomorrow we'll work on making the perfect facial expression."

"Great, can't wait," I said a little flatly.

We drove out of town and hit the highway.

"Where are we going?" I asked. The car was finally warm,

and I sank back into the brown velvet seats of Aunt Erma's old light blue car. Mitzy had settled down in my lap. Her previous excitement seemed to be wearing off.

"You'll see," Aunt Erma said. She turned up the volume on the radio and Christmas songs filled the car. She sang "Rudolph the Red Nosed Reindeer" at the top of her lungs. I'd learned how to sing from her — off key, but enthusiastic. Her enthusiasm was infectious and soon I was singing too. Mitzy groaned disapprovingly and moved to the back seat of the car. I would have to remember this trick whenever Mitzy was annoying. Sing loud, and she'll leave. Who would have known?

We exited the highway and turned down a narrow, wooded road. Then we turned down a narrower dirt road and finally Aunt Erma pulled over as far as she could, which wasn't far on this skinny stretch, and put the car in park.

"Is this it?" I asked, looking around expecting to see something more than trees and snow.

"Yes. Follow me." She got out of the car, and Mitzy flew over the seat to follow her. I got out and wrapped my red coat tighter around my body. I shivered against the cold air.

"Are you going to tell me what we're doing yet?" I hurried to keep up with her. She was half a foot shorter than I was and twice my age, but she walked so fast! I'd asked her how she walked so fast before. Was it magic, I had asked her.

"Not magic," she winked at me. "Yoga."

I really had to start going to more of Mr. Barnes's yoga

classes this winter. Or I was going to have to stop walking with Aunt Erma.

Mitzy was frolicking in the snow and still managed to keep up with Aunt Erma. I hopped over sticks and tried to step exactly in Aunt Erma's footprints, so the deep snow didn't go over the edge of my short boots. We didn't seem to be following any path, and I couldn't imagine a house would pop up in this deserted woods. Aunt Erma stopped so abruptly and I was hurrying so fast behind her that I bumped into her, unable to stop my momentum.

"Sorry," I said, scratching my nose which had bumped against her tall fuzzy white hat.

"We're here," she said with a satisfied nod.

"We're in the middle of the woods," I said, glancing around wondering which of us was going nutty.

"There," she pointed ahead of us.

I squinted and saw a small tree that had green and red and silver balls hanging from the branches. Even in the dead of winter, it still had all its leaves. The winding branches danced in the breeze and the baubles tinkled together.

"What is it?" I asked, hoping she wouldn't just answer with the obvious "tree."

"It's a magic tree," she said, providing an ever so slightly better explanation than I was hoping for.

"I don't understand," I said. "Why does it have ornaments on it?"

"I decorated it for Christmas," she said with a sheepish shrug of her shoulders. I nodded. That was a very Aunt

Erma thing to do. Then I wanted for more information. She carefully touched one of the leaves, and the branches began to rustle a little harder. That was strange, the wind hadn't picked up.

"You've probably heard a few murmurings around town about how powerful my spices are," she began slowly.

"I've heard a thing or two," I answered.

"I've always been pretty powerful," she said. She wasn't bragging, just stating a fact. "However, I found a way to be more powerful." She gestured to the tree with a flourish of her arm. "It came to me in a dream one night. After I saw it, I woke up, got in my car, and somehow, I just knew where to go. I ended up here. This tree contains more magic than I ever even knew existed. You can feel it."

She grabbed my hand and put it on the trunk of the tree. I felt the tingling of power course through my body.

"How does it work?" I asked. I held my hand there even after she took hers away. I was enjoying the feeling of power.

"For some of the spices, I scrape off a little of the bark, and for others, I use the leaves," she said. "It's tricky with this much power to get the intention just right. That's why I keep it simple. Some of my spices spread love. Some happiness. Some make people more helpful. I never do anything big or complicated because the more complicated the magic, the more likely it is that something will go wrong. And when magic goes wrong it can get really ugly." She shuddered a little.

"What do you mean?" I asked. I wanted specifics. I was

tired of all of this, "Things can go bad with magic" stuff. I needed answers now.

"Ok, I'll tell you a story." She thought for a minute. "A while back when an elf was running a factory. Well he was part elf, like we're part fairy," she added. "If he was full elf he would look like an elf, pointy ears, the whole bit, but there are many of us who are part something, and we can just blend in with people who are one hundred percent human."

I nodded. I began to worry that this was going to be a long-winded story, and it was cold outside. I looked around for Mitzy. She was still frolicking around the trees. Maybe it was because she was enjoying it. Maybe she was just trying to stay warm.

"His factory made clothing," Aunt Erma continued. "And soon greed got the best of him. He used magic to produce more and more clothing. He made his workers move faster and faster until they were collapsing in the factory. Then to make matters worse, the clothes started acting up."

"The clothes acted up?" I asked, incredulously.

"Yes, sweaters were opening and closing closet doors, socks were banging against the side of dressers. It was a disaster. People everywhere were panicking. There was a huge rush on exorcisms." Aunt Erma shook her head. "The magical enforcement team was busy for months un-enchanting all of the affected clothing and altering people's memories, so they thought it was all a strange dream."

"Good story. Can we go back to the car now?" I was

jumping up and down trying to keep my blood from freezing in my veins. I looked down. My feet were still there, but I could no longer feel them.

"Yes, yes, let's go back to the car," she said scooting back through the trees. Mitzy eagerly followed us.

"Why did you take me here?" I asked, a little breathless as I struggled to keep up again.

"I wanted you to know where this was. In case anything happens to me," she said, matter-of-factly.

I stopped in my tracks. She was about a hundred feet ahead of me before she realized I wasn't following anymore. She turned back. I started walking again, and she waited for me.

"Is this really that dangerous?" I asked, trying to keep the quiver out of my voice.

"We'll be fine," she said firmly. "Plus, we have a vicious guard dog on our side." Mitzy yipped in agreement. I tried to smile, but I couldn't shake the anxious feeling hanging over me.

Chapter 3

My head was spinning during the drive back to the pie shop. My thoughts began to blur as the car warmed up. Mitzy settled in my lap. The snow melted off her fur and was soaking through my pants. My eyes snapped open. "They aren't going to turn you into a cat again, are they?" I asked.

"No, they wouldn't do that again," Aunt Erma reassured me as she merged onto the highway.

"Does the Morning Pie Crew know about the magic tree?"

She shook her head. "You're the only one I've told. It's safer. The fewer people who know, the better."

"But I thought you guys shared everything." I couldn't help but feel a little proud to be in on the secret, but it scared me a little too.

"Everyone has secrets," she said. She pressed her lips together and kept her eyes fixed to the road.

I stopped prying. I stared at the road too until we got back to the shop. The crowd had gathered outside again, and people began to stir when they saw Aunt Erma's car pull up to the curb out front.

321

"Come in, everyone," she said as she shuffled between them to unlock the front door.

"Someone was looking for you." Nadine, one of our regulars, whose blonde curly hair was always gathered in a poof on top of her head said to me. As far as I could tell, her job in town was to spread gossip.

"Oh yeah? Who?" I asked following her through the door.

"I don't know. Some guy."

"Henry?" I asked even though I figured he would call me if he were looking for me.

"No, some curly haired guy I haven't seen before." She shrugged.

"I guess this mystery man will have to come back if he wants to talk to me." I went back to the kitchen and stopped in my tracks.

"Mom," I said.

"You recognize me. I'm so touched," she said, barely looking up as she sliced a peppermint cream pie. My mom's brown hair was just a shade lighter than mine. Unlike mine, it was smooth and perfectly styled on her head. Instead of her usual business suit, she wore jeans and a dark green sweater.

My mother had gone back to the city a couple weeks after Aunt Erma had become human again after being a cat. We had a wonderful week where our days were full of baking and gossiping. We were a regular holiday special. Then the bickering began, and the comments under our breath, and my mother decided she had to get back to her clients at home. I didn't blame her. It was a lot of intense family time after a long absence.

"She'll be back soon," Aunt Erma had reassured me as I had watched her car drive away with a lump in my throat. I had been enjoying the gossiping and reminiscing. It had been so long since I'd seen my mother laugh that much.

That was less than two weeks ago, and here she was again. I guess I didn't have anything to worry about.

"Erma called and asked me to come help at the pie shop while you guys went on some sort of mission." My mother began cutting the next pie more forcefully than was actually necessary.

"We have to go…," I began.

"No," my mother cut me off still keeping her eyes on the pie. "I don't want to know. I know it has to be dangerous. I could tell from Erma's tone. It's best if I just worry here instead of knowing the specifics. I'll just serve pie and worry."

Ah, my mother the martyr.

"How long are you here for?" I asked.

"I booked a room at the inn for three nights, but we'll see," she answered. My mother preferred to stay at the local inn instead of squishing into Aunt Erma's apartment with us.

Aunt Erma had already fulfilled the orders of the crowd out front. The angry grumbles had turned into happy chattering as people drank their free cups of coffee and talked about their holiday plans.

"I'm taking my cats to see Santa," someone said.

"My sister is coming to visit with her four children, and they're all staying in my one bedroom apartment," I heard someone else say.

"My husband is in a Christmas play, and he wants me to go watch all twelve performances," another voice chimed in.

I heard a familiar voice say my name. I saw him in the crowd, but it didn't register because he was a familiar face in an unfamiliar place. I was shocked and speechless for a moment.

"Josh," I finally managed to croak reaching out to hug him.

"Hey, Susie," he was warm and smelled like sawdust. He held me for a second longer after I had let go.

"What are you doing here?" I asked, taking a step back to look at him. His dark curly hair had gotten a little long. He had dark circles under his brown eyes, and his usually rosy cheeks were pale. "Is everything OK?"

"Hal has me working at a big remodel in Mavisville," he said. Mavisville was just the next town over. "It should take a couple of weeks."

"That's great. We'll definitely have to get together a few times," I said.

"I need to talk to you," he said.

At least four people in the store stopped their conversations to openly stare at us.

"Let's go outside." I grabbed the sleeve of his coat and led him towards the front door.

"Who is that?" I heard someone whisper loudly as I opened the door.

"Beats me. I'd bet an old boyfriend," someone else said.

I glared over my shoulder in the general direction of the voices. Josh and I had been coworkers back home. We had grown to be good friends, but it was never anything more than that. Josh was the one I'd call when I was having trouble with a relationship, and I would give him insights on the people he dated whether he asked for it or not. I hadn't really talked to him since I'd left — just a couple quick text messages that didn't really say much.

I wrapped my grey sweater more tightly around myself and faced him. I thought longingly of my red coat hanging on the hook at the back of the kitchen. Why had I suggested going outside? The mid-December wind was biting against my skin. Oh yeah, outside was the only place we had a shot of not being eavesdropped on. However, if anyone could lipread, we were in trouble. All of the customers in the shop were blatantly staring through the window. They might as well have their noses pressed against the glass.

I took a couple of steps back toward the flower shop next door so we were at least a little out of sight. I'm not sure there was anywhere completely out of sight in this town though.

Josh stared at the ground for a minute.

"Is everything ok?" I asked again. I wanted this to hurry up, so I could get back to the toasty warm kitchen.

"So, you live here now?" he asked looking up and down the street.

"I think so," I said with a shrug. "I haven't really figured it out long term yet. I live here for now, I guess."

"I'm glad you got to reunite with your aunt," he said. Josh had heard my sob story more than once about my long-lost Aunt Erma. Usually it was after a bad day at work or a fight with my mom and a few beers.

"Yeah, it's been nice," I said. It was silent for a minute, and I was about to tell him I had to go back inside.

"You didn't even say goodbye to me," he said suddenly meeting my eyes for the first time since we'd gone outside.

"What?"

"We were friends. Maybe more. At least I thought we were," he said the last part more to himself than to me.

I opened my mouth. Nothing but air came out.

"Was I just imagining it? I kind of thought we were on track to get together. I thought you felt it too. Hell, I've loved you since I saw you fix that hole on the side of the Morrow's house. You were fearless at the top of the ladder while the rest of us were too chicken to climb that high."

I remembered that job. I had been terrified too, but I was new at Hal's Handyman Services, and I wanted to show off in front of my new coworkers. Afterwards I'd had to excuse myself to the side of the house where I promptly threw up in the trash can. I thought back to my time with Josh. Had I missed the signs? Sure, we had been good friends. I would even consider him to be one of my best friends. I hadn't meant to drop him when I came to Hocus Hills, but finding my long-lost aunt, discovering magic is real, and trying to squash an evil plot to take over the world all takes up a lot of one's free time.

"Josh, I…" I paused for a minute. "I'm sorry I didn't say goodbye." It sounded lame when I said it. He looked at me expectantly. "And I'm sorry I haven't kept in touch better. It's been so crazy around here."

I didn't even know where to begin with his other confessions. There had been a time a few years ago when I thought about him that way. I'd even tried to flirt with him and hang out with him more than usual, but shortly after I began to have those feelings, he began dating a woman his sister set him up with. It was serious for a while, and I moved on too. I hadn't really thought about it since then.

I jumped when I felt a hand on my shoulder. I turned, and it was Lena.

"I hate to interrupt, but we have to get going," she said with a polite nod towards Josh.

"We?" I asked.

"I'm Lena," she stuck her hand out towards Josh.

"Nice to meet you, Lena. I'm Josh." He shook her hand. "I'm a friend of Susie's from back home."

She looked at me with raised eyebrows.

"So, we need to get going, huh?" I said.

"Right, yes," she said.

"Bye Josh. I'll call you later." I followed Lena inside trying to ignore the guilty feeling in the pit of my stomach when I looked over my shoulder and saw him watching me go.

The chatter inside the pie shop stopped immediately when I came through the door. No doubt they were all talking about me. I ignored them and went back to the kitchen.

"I'm coming too," Lena burst into the kitchen carrying her large yellow purse.

"Now, Lena," Aunt Erma began in a tone I knew meant she was about to try and talk her out of it.

"Don't you start with me, Erma. There's room in the car for one more. I'll drive." So that's how I ended up in the backseat of Lena's car clinging to the handle by the window with one hand and gripping the blue velvet seat with the other. Speed limits were merely a suggestion in Lena's world. I swear as we rounded the corners, the car tipped up on two wheels. When I said this out loud, Lena told me to stop being so dramatic.

"You'll thank me when we get there and get this taken care of quickly," she said, speeding up as the light in front of us changed from green to yellow.

"Here, eat this," Aunt Erma passed a small square to me, and Lena popped one into her own mouth. I inspected the square before eating it. It was white with little green flecks in it.

"What is it?" I asked.

"It will protect you," Aunt Erma answered.

"From what, a car accident?" I asked.

"The magic."

I took a tentative bite. It tasted like salt water taffy, so I put the rest in my mouth and chewed. I always expected to hear wind chimes when I ate something magical, but to this date that had not happened.

In between muttering wishes for a safe arrival, I thought about what Josh had said. Henry and I were having such a wonderful time, but Josh and I went way back. He was comfortable in a way that only someone you've known a long time can be. He was like a thick warm comforter. But then with Henry there was a spark. People always said the spark doesn't last forever — that you need more in your relationship besides electricity. But the spark sure felt good right now. Maybe it would develop into the comfortable relationship I had with Josh. Maybe it would be even better. Plus, Henry knew about magic. There was a whole part of my new life that I wasn't sure if I could share with Josh. The people of Hocus Hills are very private about their magic, and I certainly don't blame them. You never know who you can trust, and if word got out that there were magic people in the world, there would be chaos.

We squealed into a parking spot on the street at the edge of town. I still wasn't any closer to figuring out my love life, and it didn't seem like the time to ask Lena and Aunt Erma for advice.

"We should walk in so we can sneak up on what's happening. Get a feel for what we're getting into," Aunt Erma suggested.

"Everyone take note of where we parked in case we get separated," Lena pointed to the street signs on the corner. My stomach flipped. In case we get separated? That thought hadn't even crossed my mind.

The streets were deserted. It was Saturday. Most towns would have people coming and going from the shops. We peeked into the window of a bakery. A bakery on a Saturday should have people buying their bread and donuts, but it was empty.

We kept going down the street. We walked close together, and I resisted the urge to reach out and grab Aunt Erma's hand for protection.

Everywhere was deserted. It was spooky. It was like every horror movie I'd ever seen, but even more surreal because it was real life. I kept looking around expecting a tumble weed to roll down the street.

"Where is everyone?" I whispered as we neared the center of town. The layout was similar to Hocus Hills except their town square was a little smaller, and there was a duck pond near the gazebo.

Lena shrugged.

"I don't know, but it can't be good," Aunt Erma said.

I stopped in my tracks. "I hear something," I said. They both stopped, and I held my breath as we listened. There was a sound coming from the church.

"We need more yarn," we heard a deep voice yell. The church was a large white wooden building with steps leading up to a set of dark wood double doors. We crept up the steps, and Lena pushed the door open a crack. She peaked inside.

"I think we found everyone," she said pushing the door the rest of the way open.

The church was jam packed with people of all ages. It was a flurry of activity, but I couldn't figure out what they were doing. Some people were rushing around the room picking up balls of yarn and moving them from one pew to another. Several people were knitting. Knitting? I noticed a large red circle in the middle that they were all working around.

"What are they making?" Lena wondered aloud.

"A mitten," a man with an armload of knitting needles yelled as he rushed past us.

"The world's largest," one of the women who was knitting called.

"Why are they doing that?" I asked. I almost felt dizzy from the frenzy around us. This seemed like more than just a quirky small-town activity.

"It must be part of the spell," Aunt Erma said.

"But why?" I asked. It seemed like such a strange activity, and not at all in line with their ultimate goal.

"It's probably an accident," Aunt Erma said. "They're too power hungry to focus on getting the spell right. They're frenzied as they alter the spices. It's very hard to get the intention right — takes a lot of finesse. They were probably trying to hit a kitten or flit off to Britain and somehow it came out to knit a mitten. That's why you should always keep it simple." She was speaking to me now. I nodded as I looked around at the chaos. I certainly didn't ever want this to happen.

"How are we going to break the spell?" Lena asked, jumping out of the way of a frenzied boy who was chasing the armload of yarn balls he had just dropped as they rolled across the floor.

"Do we need to break it?" I asked, looking around. I mean, what they were doing was crazy, but it didn't seem to be harmful. Unless they started capturing people inside the giant mitten once they finished knitting it.

"It could be dangerous to leave them like this. They won't be able to stop until they've finished no matter how tired they are, and some of them could actually work themselves to death," Aunt Erma said. OK, that sounded bad. She was surveying the scene intently.

"I'm going to need a kitchen to get the job done," she said. "Unless," she turned to Lena, "Do you have anything?"

"I told you you'd need me," she said as she fished around in her yellow purse. She set it on the floor, and her whole head disappeared as she leaned into it. I was tempted to grab her feet, so she wouldn't fall. I didn't know what exactly was inside there. I had asked her once how the magic purse worked.

"Oh no, dear, I couldn't tell you that. Your aunt may be ready to divulge all of her secrets, but I like to keep one or two up my sleeve," she had said.

"Ah yes, here it is," her muffled voice emerged from the purse a second before she did. She triumphantly held up an Erma's Pie box.

"You keep a pie in there?" I asked.

"You never know when you'll need one," she said. "Impromptu dinner party, afternoon snack, to stop crazed knitters."

Aunt Erma took the box from Lena and opened the lid. She took a deep breath.

"The triple berry. Yes, this one should work. The unaltered spices will counteract the altered spices they used," she said. "They're not all going to eat willingly. We're going to have to coax them."

Lena did some more digging in her purse and emerged with three plates, three forks, and a knife. We divided the pie. I watched Aunt Erma approach a young man who was knitting and offer him a bite of pie. He shook his head vehemently, his sandy brown hair flopping across his face. Without missing a beat, Aunt Erma shoved a bite into his mouth. His eyes widened so much I thought they might pop out of his head. He chewed and swallowed all the while making, "Mmmm," noises. Then his face changed. His brow furrowed, and he looked around.

"What's going on?" he asked.

"Don't worry about it," Lena said. "You're just having a strange dream. Go home."

The man shrugged and shuffled off.

"Alright everyone, understand the plan?" Aunt Erma asked.

Lena and I nodded. Then we all set off shoving small bites of pie into people's mouths. Most people I encountered were easily convinced to take a bite. They were probably hungry after all this knitting. The church began to clear out as people wandered back home.

"Aren't they all going to talk and figure out they had the same strange dream?" I asked Lena as I airplaned a bite into a young girl's mouth. Lena did the same with the girl's mother. The girl dropped the yarn ball she had been winding up and followed her mother out the door.

"Most of them will have forgotten about this completely

by tomorrow. Only a few will have a distant memory of this strange dream," she said. "It won't be enough for them to put it together that it actually did happen."

"Some of them might be a little sore tomorrow from all the work," Aunt Erma said as she ran past, chasing a man with gray hair and thick glasses. The man threw a ball of yarn at Aunt Erma, and she tackled him and shoved the bite of pie into his mouth before he could stop her.

It wasn't easy, and I was bit at least six times, but we finally cleared the church of all frantic knitters. I leaned against the wall and began planning which pajamas I was going to wear, the footy pajamas with the turtle print, and what I was going to eat, pizza with three sides of pie.

"We have to get all this out of here," Aunt Erma motioned to the giant knitted circle that was apparently on its way to becoming the largest mitten in the world.

"Why?" I asked. I didn't want anything to keep me from that pizza any longer than necessary.

"It's a lot harder to convince people it was a dream when they can come to the church and find two tons of yarn and a knitted circle as large as a parachute.

After we'd cleared everything, dispersing some of it and shoving the rest of it into the back of Lena's car, we headed back to Hocus Hills.

"What are those?" As we pulled into Hocus Hills, I pointed at a light pole plastered with sheets of paper.

"I'm not sure." Lena slowed the car down. Aunt Erma finished reading first and gasped.

In big bold letters, the signs said, "Tired of hiding? It's

time to work for the Improvement for Magical People. If you're ready to step out of the shadows, stay tuned for more information from the IMPs." The flyers were plastered all over town.

"It was all a circus. They just wanted to get you out of town, so you couldn't stop them from doing this," Lena practically yelled.

Aunt Erma let her head fall to the back of the seat. "I don't know why we didn't see that before," she sighed.

A crew led by Violet was already pulling posters down.

"We were so focused on what you guys were doing, that we didn't even see this happen until it was too late," she said. "They worked fast. It was done in a matter of seconds."

Aunt Erma's brow furrowed. "Their magic is getting stronger."

"I know. The regular spells aren't working to clean it up, so we're doing it the non-magic way," Violet said.

I grabbed a bag and went to work pulling signs off the light poles and the sides of some buildings.

"Hey," Holly appeared by my side. "I heard you had some hunky curly haired stranger show up today."

"Hunky?" I asked.

"My mother's words, not mine," she said.

"How did she see him?"

"Nadine texted her a picture," she said as though the answer was obvious.

"What?!"

"I forgot you're still new to this small town living where

everyone knows your business," she said. "So, what's the story?"

"Josh is a friend from back home," I said evasively. I quickly asked her about the latest book she was writing, and she was off telling me how she wasn't sure if she should kill off one of her favorite characters or not. I was off the hook for now, but at the end of the clean-up, we made plans for a girls' night out on Friday, and I knew there would be more questions then.

Later that night I was wrapped in my very large new red knitted blanket watching television when Henry stopped by. I struggled to get out of the cocoon I had wrapped myself in.

"Did everything go OK?" he asked after greeting me with a long hug.

"I didn't realize magic was such hard work, but yes, it went fine," I said. I was too tired to give him the details, and I was pretty sure he would have heard them already from someone in town. News spreads fast. Especially the news that you wanted to keep quiet. Just yesterday I heard Mrs. Lansbury yell across the street asking Mr. Kelley about his colonoscopy.

"Anything interesting happen before you saved the world?" his tone was strange, like he was trying to stay super casual, but his voice was too high and too tight.

"Oh yeah," I said, also trying to keep my tone casual as though I was just remembering something that I'd actually been thinking about all day. "A friend of mine from back home stopped by."

"Really?" he tried to sound surprised, but his acting wasn't that good.

"Yeah, we were coworkers. He came to say hi." I shrugged in what I hoped was a casual gesture.

"That's an awful long way to come to say hi," he said.

"He's working on a job in Mavisville for a couple of weeks," I said.

Just then Aunt Erma bustled in. "Oh, I'm sorry to interrupt. Henry, how are you?"

Aunt Erma's arrival saved me from an awkward conversation. Her glance out of the corner of her eye told me she knew exactly what she was doing.

Henry left after a little more small talk. He said he had some work to finish. I was the only person in town, other than his editor, who knew that he wrote the "Ask Elodie" advice column in the newspaper. I had asked him once if all the letters were sent in from people in town. He said some of them were, but some days there weren't any letters, so he would make up letters and then answer them as Elodie. "So, you set up a problem you know you can answer?" I had teased him. Then I began to quiz him about which ones he had written. "I'm not going to ruin the magic for you by giving away all the secrets," he'd said.

I felt bad for not telling him more about Josh, but I wanted to be able to process it more myself first. I hadn't figured out how to present the facts because I hadn't figured out how I felt about the whole thing.

The truth would come out eventually though.

Acknowledgements

This book began with one page. One page over and over and over. Without Char Torkelson's unending patience and encouragement, I might still be writing that first page. Thank you!

I'm so lucky to be a part of a fabulous Monday night writing group. Thank you Marilyn, Anne, Fay, Patty, Margie, Susan, Charissa, and Ruth. I love you all, and appreciate your feedback and weekly doses of inspiration and support (and for laughing in all the right places).

I'm very grateful for all the wonderful teachers and critique partners I've had, especially Mrs. Dunbar for creating a magical world in a second grade classroom (and Molly for living in that world with me) and Mary, Maureen, and Mary for reading and commenting on chapters of this book and helping me grow as a writer.

Thank you to the Harper Impulse team for making my publishing dreams come true, and Charlotte Ledger for making this happen and being an absolutely amazing editor!

I'm blessed with wonderful cousins! A special thank you to Lisa who helped me visualize and create my dreams over cups of tea, and Sarah who listened to and believed in my dreams over glasses of wine.

Thank you to my grandma, Jean, who was one of the first people to read the book. She called me up to give me my first glowing review. I will remember every word for the rest of my life.

Thank you to my husband, Chris, for always answering my questions no matter what he was doing or how bizarre the question was. Love you!

> Me: Can I drop all of our plates on the floor so I can hear what it sounds like?
> Him: Yes.
> Me: Can I start a fire in the kitchen to see if I can put it out?
> Him: No.
> Me: Just a little one.
> Him: No!
> Me: But I'll keep the fire extinguisher...
> Him: NO!

Thank you to my brother, Daniel! When we're not competing to be Mom and Dad's favorite child, you're pretty supportive.

How do I even begin to thank my parents, Richard and Sheila? You guys believed in me from the start and kept me caffeinated enough to make it happen. I love you guys!

Order your copy of *A Slice of Christmas Magic* now!